Who Walks These Halls

Cherie Lee

This is a work of fiction. While, as in all fiction, the literary perceptions and insights are based on experience, all names, characters, places, and incidents are either products of the author's imagination or are used fictitiously. No reference to any real person is intended or inferred.

Copyright ©2007 by Cherie Lee Blanton

Design and layout by Jennifer Wehrmann
Cover Illustration by Adam Thomas

ISBN: 978-0-9792780-5-1

Published and distributed by:
High-Pitched Hum Publishing
321 15th Street North
Jacksonville Beach, FL 32250

www.highpitchedhum.net

Who Walks These Halls

Cherie Lee

OTHER TITLES
BY CHERIE LEE

A LITTLE FUR IN THE MERINGUE
NEVER REALLY HURTS THE FILLING

For my sister, Betty Williamson, who pushed and bullied me until I found a publisher. Thanks, sis, I owe you one.

And for Jean Osborn, friend extraordinaire, who insisted that I never, never, never give up.

Chapter One

It was the time of the full moon but the night loomed black, intense and brooding. Clouds massed and gathered as the storm poised, preparing to spring. Emma sat ramrod stiff on the straight-back chair at the foot of the spiral staircase, eyes scanning each dark corner. The deep-yellow orb that should have bathed the enormous Victorian home in a golden glow lay smothered behind ominous layers. The house, the creatures in the surrounding woods, even the night held its breath awaiting the violent eruption.

A soft sibilant sigh broke the silence of the starless night. Even though the atmosphere was still and flat, something parted the tall cattails growing around the edge of the small lake. Something disturbed the grasses pressing their delicate stems flat into the heavy soil. Something slowly dragged itself from the watery depths, a trail of slime following its passage. Now the creatures of the night no longer watched and waited for the storm. Eyes distended, hearts pumping, they scurried frantically for the safety of their burrow. Without a backward glance, they darted into the farthest corner freezing into a protective ball of fur.

Emma had been sitting for hours, waiting, not for the storm that threatened the exterior of her home, but for whatever it was threatening the interior. She thought she might be frightened, but as time passed and nothing occurred, Emma realized she was more nervous than afraid, concerned the strange events of the past few weeks might be figments of her imagination, that at age eighty, she was growing senile. Emma wished she had asked Jessie, housekeeper/cook, to fix her a sandwich and thermos of coffee, but did not want the other woman to know what she had planned. Emma was already aggravated by the snide remarks the bossy old fool made about her mental faculties. She would be damned if she was going to give her yet another reason to think she had lost her mind.

Just because Jessie was five years younger, she thought she was twice as sharp. When actually, it was Emma who was forever retrieving bottles of cleanser and dust rags from rooms where Jessie had forgotten and left them. But, Emma ruefully admitted, Jessie was not complaining about things going bump in the night. She slumped, dejected. Concerned about her mental stability, Emma slowly caressed the barrel of the antique shotgun on her lap, deriving comfort from the familiar feel.

The grandfather clock began striking midnight–the witching hour. At that instant, the heavy draperies hanging at the tall windows in the large entrance hall began to sway. A blast of cold air hit Emma solidly in the face. She dropped the gun, throwing up her hands to protect herself from the invisible chill. The clatter of the weapon hitting the marble tile didn't drown out the laughter. It came from all directions, growing louder and more eerie, causing the crystals on an ornate chandelier to tinkle and chime from the shrill vibrations.

The first time she heard something, it was soft, almost melodious, but tonight, tonight she clapped her hands to the sides of her head trying to shut out the abrasive noise which was worse than a shrieking car alarm. If the hellish racket didn't stop soon, she was going to scream. Emma opened her mouth. The noise ceased.

Drawing a trembling breath, Emma bent to retrieve the fallen gun, eyes darting fearfully around the empty hall. As her fingers closed over the stock, the weapon gave a violent jerk, flew from her grasp, skidded across the floor and slammed against the opposite wall. A child's mischievous laughter rang through the air, but whether boy or girl, she couldn't decide. It stopped as abruptly as it began. Now, Emma would have welcomed the unholy sound, for the chilling quiet seemed twice as menacing.

Emma started to rise, to retrieve the gun, then thought, how foolish. Whatever had entered her home would not be intimidated. Whatever this was, it would only mock her if she sought protection from such a useless weapon. She decided to remain seated, watching and waiting, perhaps gaining a clue as to what was happening and why. A slight tremor shook her gaunt frame. Emma could not help herself. She wished she had used some common sense and asked someone to watch with her.

Nothing moved. Each passing minute measured by the antique clock's ticking seemed endless. Emma shifted on the chair. The hard cane bottom pressing against her bony posterior was as sharp and uncomfortable as she had hoped, making it virtually impossible for her to relax her vigilance. That, coupled with her acute hunger and thirst, a sure sign of nervousness in Emma, had her ready to tell whatever lurked in the hall to go straight to hell. A location, she decided, it was probably intimate with. Suddenly, out of the silent depths of the house came a faint melody, soft and sweet. A child's voice hummed some nursery rhyme. It had been years since Emma had heard the tune. Back to the days of her childhood she delved. Long forgotten words came stealing from her past, their grisly promise making her shudder.

Three blind mice.
Three blind mice.
See how they run.
See how they run.
They all ran after the farmer's wife.
She cut off their tails with a carving knife.

What in God's good name, she wondered, was the presence of

a child doing in her entrance hall? She had been mistress of this house for thirty years, and never, never in that time had Emma experienced anything like what was taking place. And never, never in the twenty-four years of her marriage, had she heard her husband even hint that Shadow Lake, his ancestral home, was haunted.

Haunted. There was no longer any getting around it. Either Emma had gone stark raving mad or something ugly had taken up housekeeping with her. No matter how hard she might try, after tonight, she could no longer dismiss these disturbances as odd noises made by the wind buffeting an old house. After tonight, Emma was going to have to ignore all that common sense she was so proud of and admit something weird was happening. Something, or somebody, was trying to frighten her, to scare her away from the home she had grown to love.

The singing ceased. Emma heaved a sigh of relief. The repetitive tune was beginning to grate on her nerves as bad as the laughter. She wished the damn thing would do something besides make noises. She wished it would show itself. Then afraid it might read her mind, afraid of what she might see if it should materialize, her courage quickly faded.

As if in answer to her thoughts, a bolt of lightning blazed from the sky, flooding the interior. Desperately, her eyes searched each corner, expecting any second to see some horrible apparition rise from the shadows and descend with evil intent. But try as she might, Emma saw nothing in the dim glow but familiar surroundings, now totally alien, taken over by some unknown and malevolent presence. Slowly, she expelled her breath. With trembling fingers she wiped the beaded sweat from her forehead. Immediately the laughter assaulted her ears, but this time, adding to the hellish din, were the doors. One by one they shut, opened, slammed. Every door in the three-story house. Over, and over, and over and over. The eerie laughter sailed above the incessant banging of the heavy paneled doors until the house reverberated. The entire structure shook from top to bottom as thunder roared across the sky, Nature adding her voice to the voice already loose in the halls.

Emma shook violently. The loud noises, the fear of an unknown being, the storm and lightning raging were all too much for someone her age. She closed her eyes and prayed, not knowing what else to do. A terrible shriek rent the air! Her eyes opened on an unforgettable sight.

Cleo, her female Siamese, belly swollen with kits, was midway up the stairs. Fur standing high on her back. Tail raised and fluffed. Ears flattened. Eyes huge and dilated. Teeth barred in a grimace, she slowly backed down and away from some invisible threat. The cat's initial cry of fury turned into a series of guttural snarls, then into a mouthing of fear and despair.

No longer afraid of the consequences to herself, Emma rose, determined to do battle against the force threatening her beloved pet. She was too late. A streak of white and chocolate launched itself across the marble floor, leaping the stairs three at a time, charging the air with a scream of rage so fierce it drowned out the storm's mad crescendo. In awe she watched Anthony, Cleo's mate, defy whatever monstrous thing had invaded his territory.

Chapter Two

Hours after Anthony had chased away the devilish spirit, Emma still couldn't sleep. Cleo was curled into the tight ball which perfectly fit the contours of her mistress' stomach, but Anthony ignored the familiar comfort of Emma's warm backside. Instead, like his ancestors who had guarded sacred temples in exotic lands, he assumed a watchful position at the foot of her bed–ears alert, eyes wary, tail twitching, body poised and ready for attack. Somehow, this attitude of Anthony's bothered Emma as much as the mysterious laughter. Nervously, she tried to imagine what manner of creature had intimidated her gutsy Siamese, what terrible danger it presented, and what in God's good name it was doing at Shadow Lake.

She tossed and turned. Cleo glared, crossed her eyes and rumbled deep in her throat. Emma forced herself to stop moving, trying not to further annoy the irritable mother-to-be. This also seemed to quiet her own whirling thoughts. As her breathing deepened and heartbeat slowed, Emma willed herself several months back in time, determined to trace the odd events leading to this evening's eerie disturbance.

***

"Jessie. Damn it, Jessie. Was that the mailman?"

"I 'spects it could'a been."

The answer drifted from the back parlor up the winding staircase to the landing where Emma stood tapping her foot.

"Well then, where's the mail?"

"I 'spicions in the box, if you even gots any."

"Of course I got some, you aggravating woman. Otherwise, the postman wouldn't have driven up the drive."

"I 'spects not."

"Jessie, are you watching those damn soaps?"

Silence greeted Emma.

"Jessie."

"I hears you."

An enormous black lady waddled slowly from the depths of the house, totally unconcerned about the other's obvious impatience.

"Jest cause you don't care 'bout what happens to Miss Ellen and Dr. John, don't mean other folks don't. I swear, if I was to get all het up like some people, I 'spects my blood pressure would shoot sky high and I'd be dead 'fore mornin'." She glared at Emma who was still tapping her foot. "I also 'spects I see somebody that gonna have that happens to them, if they don't simmers down."

Jessie opened the front door, passed over the threshold, and returned moments later, a stack of mail in her hand.

"Don't know what's so all fire 'portant 'bout a bunch of bills you'd be makin' an ole woman miss the only pleasure she gets outta life." She pouted. "Well, Miss Fidgety Britches, here it are."

She thrust the mail in Emma's direction. "Ain't you gonna come get it? You havin' sech a mighty fit I thought you'd done snatched it outta my hands by now."

"If I snatch anything, it's gonna be the hair off your head. Now, quit acting the fool and bring me my mail."

"I 'spects I'll jest meets you halfway. You know I don't like climbin' them windly steps any more than I has to."

"I know you're incorrigible."

"That don't bother me none, 'cause I don't know what that

funny word means, but I do know the meanin' of some fancy ones. I could, if I had half a mind, do some name callin' of my own 'bout skinny ole' white women too bossy for their own good."

Emma stomped down the stairs snatching her mail from the outstretched hand. "I don't know why I put up with you."

"You ain't got no choice. I be the only one 'live who'd put up with you."

Each glared daggers, repeating the endless sparring that neither ever tired of.

Jessie had worked at Shadow Lake for years. Her family before her. Emma, who'd married Richard Thatcher late in life, had immediately developed a bonding friendship with the cook. Despite the constant verbal battle, there existed a tremendous wealth of love and affection between them.

"Look, Jessie, it's not just bills." Emma's plain face glowed. "There's a letter from Carol."

"What she say?"

"I haven't opened it. I'm almost afraid to. Do you think she's really going to come? Lord, how I pray she gets custody of Lucy."

"Won't it be a heap of fun havin' a young'un here? Hurry up and see what it say. Lawd, ole' age be makin' you slow."

Deciding to exact revenge for the black woman's snide remarks, Emma stuck the mail under her arm. With head in air, she swept past Jessie into the library.

"I'll read it later when I have time. Right now, I need to pay these bills. Why don't you bring me some coffee and a piece of that pound cake I smelled baking."

"You not gonna read that letter?" Jessie was incredulous.

"I'll save it to enjoy with my coffee."

"Ha. You not foolin' me. You jest bein' ornery cause I called you ole' and skinny." The dark eyes flashed. "But how you stays that size, as much sugar as you stuff in your mouth, be a mystery to me."

Emma stared with emphasis at the cook's more than ample

bosom. "It's certainly no mystery how much goes into yours. The evidence is displayed right out in front for everyone to see."

Bested at last, Jessie turned and stalked down the hall. Emma smiled, savoring her minor victory, but scowled a moment later when the cook's disembodied voice floated from the kitchen.

"I bet them skinny ole' bones jest plum stuffed full with that 'close trail' them doctors always talkin' 'bout."

A crash resounded through the house. That time Emma had known the hand that slammed the door.

Delighted at having thoroughly annoyed Jessie, she crossed to a gleaming mahogany antique desk. Walking behind the handsome piece, Emma opened a pair of heavy velvet drapes, exposing the richly paneled room to a flood of bright sunshine. Whatever the season, she never tired of the scene that greeted her, but thought spring her favorite.

The window overlooked a brick terrace situated at the back of the house. White wicker chairs and tables were scattered about the flagstone floor, while huge clay pots of bright red geraniums and smaller ones stuffed full of pink and white petunias added color to the already colorful landscape. Scarcely a dozen yards away, a small lake shone like a many-faceted jewel. It was filled with water lilies. Their long green stems tangled like Medusa's snakes between the huge flat leaves and creamy white blossoms floating over the surface. Massed around the water's edge were dozens of purple, pink, and deep-red azaleas. The blooms so enormous, the colors so vibrant, they appeared artificial. At the back of the lake stood the regal pines, tall and straight. The wind made a soft melody as it blew the heavy yellow pollen from the newly-formed pine cones across the water, covering the surface with a shimmering golden fairy dust. Standing sentinel, an iridescent blue heron posed. One thin leg was pulled tight against his body, the other immersed in the shallows, his eyes alert for the faintest telltale ripple made by some unsuspecting minnow.

Emma sighed happily, her heart lightened by a sight that always filled her with wonder. A sight so complete, so sane, so beautiful, she instinctively knew only God could have created such perfection. She wondered anew how heaven could possibly be any more desirable than Shadow Lake, located on the outskirts of Fernandina Beach, Florida.

Her satisfied contemplation of the view was broken by Jessie clumping loudly into the room bearing aloft an enormous tray. Amused, Emma watched the cook place her burden on a mahogany table in front of the ornately carved fireplace dominating the center of the room. Pulling two wingback chairs close to the table, Jessie promptly deposited her ample girth in one.

"I decides I join you."

"I noticed."

Emma walked to the opposite chair, sat, and politely poured the coffee. Still playing hostess, she passed the cream and sugar pursing her lips in distress as she noted the more than generous amount Jessie added to her cup, before she sliced a larger than life portion of cake for both.

"Ummm, I is one good cooker." Jessie lustily smacked her lips. Without asking permission, she sliced another wedge.

"For once, I won't argue. In fact, if it weren't for that redeeming feature, I wouldn't put up with such a fat sassy person eating me out of house and home."

"I has the 'quaintance of someone who runs me a close race." She stared hard at the fast disappearing cake on Emma's plate.

"I assumed you'd be having coffee in the kitchen with Ellen and John," Emma teased, knowing full well the only reason Jessie had joined her was curiosity about Carol's letter.

"Won't hurt me none missin' jest one day. Anyway, them folks gettin' plum silly."

"Silly." Emma burst out laughing. "The damn characters in those soaps are ridiculous. I've been telling you that for years."

"You been tellin' me a heap a things fer years, but that don't mean I pay them no mind."

"So, what's sillier than usual?"

"If that ain't jest like you. Always makin' fun of me fer watchin', then always wantin' me to tell you what they be doin'."

"I do not."

"You does too. Anyways, it is plum silly. They tryin' to prove Miss Ellen been molested by her pa when she were a little girl."

"It does happen, and probably more than we realize."

"Not to nice folk." Jessie was outraged. "One time I heerd my maw tellin' that 'bout some family, but they was pure dee white trash, not folks that knowed better."

"Believe me, it happens in the best of families," Emma said, pouring another cup of coffee before slipping off her shoes and tucking her feet beneath her.

Anyone sitting as close to Emma as Jessie, would know they were speaking to an older woman, but from a distance the four-score had deceived more than one. The lean figure Jessie poked such fun at was the ultimate rage in fashion, and many a younger woman envied Emma's thin suppleness. She moved with an easy grace, probably from years spent astride a horse or working in the garden she loved. Unless one looked close, the fine line of wrinkles around her eyes and mouth went unnoticed, lost in a face constantly animated and in motion. The blue eyes sparkled. The mobile mouth curved upward in a wide smile, or when sparring with Jessie, turned down in a frown. Her carrot colored hair might be a secret only her hair dresser shared, but it still sprang thick and curly around the elfin features that had so attracted her husband. She favored tailored shirts and slacks, having sense enough to realize they looked good on her spare frame and since not many women her age wore them well, they were practically her only conceit.

She had been an old maid when Richard proposed, and marriage had not changed habits already established. She was independent, bossy, quick to anger, but as quick to love, and loyal to a fault. She had never gotten over the fact a handsome, wealthy widower chose her over the bevy of southern beauties throwing themselves at his feet, not realizing her aloofness was what had piqued his interest. Emma had fallen head over heels the moment they were introduced. Never dreaming he would look at her twice, she barely acknowledged his presence, tongue-tied at his nearness, and almost fainting when he began their courtship.

The years of marriage were a fairy tale. Not only had he been the man of many women's dreams, but as if that weren't enough, he had brought her to Amelia, an island lying off the coast of northeast Florida, famous for being the only United States location to have flown under eight different flags.

Emma became quickly fascinated with its bizarre history, beginning with the band of French Huguenots who arrived in 1562, seeking escape from religious persecution. They had fled to the island, which had been home for more than 4,000 years, to the tall, handsome Timucuan Indians.

Within three years the Spanish arrived, slaughtered the French, and set about converting the Timucuan to Christianity. A hundred years later, the Indians were almost extinct, wiped out from being exposed to European diseases.

Emma mourned the loss of the original inhabitants and raged at the callousness of man's inhumanity to one another. She thought it a shame they had not survived to share their heritage and love of the island, and was certain the white man could have learned much and profited from their knowledge.

The Spanish settlement fared no better than the French. In 1702, James Oglethorpe, later chosen Governor of Georgia, claimed the charming spot. He christened it "Amelia" after his king, George II's, daughter.

Not until the close of the American Revolution did Spain regain the island. It was then Britain returned Florida to the Spanish, who founded the town "Fernandina" in honor of their King, Ferdinand VII.

Then the little island really began to buzz, becoming a huge hive of illegal activity. Human cargo and contraband–even piracy– was rampant, as the Spaniards encouraged the border town to run wild.

Emma was amazed at how similiar all this was to the swashbuckling Errol Flynn movies she had been such a fan of in her youth. She avidly absorbed every fact she could uncover, particularly those concerning pirates and the mysterious legends of their buried treasure.

In 1812, a group, "Patriots of Amelia Island" desperate to be rid of the lawless, overthrew the Spanish and raised their own banner. Almost immediately, the American government ousted them, returning the island, once more, to Spain.

A Scotsman and his band of mercenaries arrived next. They ran out the Spanish, hoisted their flag, and in no time, were removed by a bunch of renegades aided by the pirate Luis Aury. This time, the Mexican Rebel Standard flew, encouraging Amelia to become an even bigger haven for outlaws.

Emma recalled how amused Richard was that his bride was so enthralled with her new home and its history. He would politely and patiently listen as she excitedly related some new fact she had discovered, a fact to which he had been privy for years. However, he was determined not to squelch her enthusiasm. Emma's zest for life and knowledge was one of the major things that had attracted him to this rather skinny but enchanting lady.

In silence, he allowed her to continue his education. In 1821, she breathlessly informed him, Spain ceded Florida to the United States. Fort Clinch was built, and the Americans remained in control until the Civil War. At that time the Confederate Army proudly flew their flag, the Southern Cross. However, a mere year later, it was lowered by the Union army. The Southerners, few in number, were quickly overrun by the sheer mass of Federal troops. The Fort was taken without a fight, and Old Glory had flown ever since.

Emma had fallen almost as much in love with the island as she had with her husband. What wasn't to love? It was a paradise and she reveled in the sunshine and ocean. Life was like nothing she had ever imagined. She could not believe God had blessed her so completely.

When her husband died of a heart attack six years ago, Emma thought the world would end. She turned down all invitations, moped about the house, mourned her loss and held a gigantic pity party. But gradually, Jessie's constant badgering and her own cheerful nature asserted themselves. Putting her grief behind, she reentered the world of the living with as much gusto as she had shown at birth, her cries heard before the doctor could free her from her mother's womb.

"You ever gonna read that letter? 'Cause if you not, I might jest as well go sees what Miss Ellen say 'bout her pa."

Taking pity on the friend who had denied herself the favorite entertainment of the day, Emma reached in her back pocket.

"I really should pay these bills–"

"Them bills ain't goin' no where, but I is, if you don't tell me is we gonna have company or not."

Tearing open the envelope, Emma unfolded a single sheet of stationery scanning the brief missive.

"Well?"

"They'll be here in six weeks."

"The young'un?"

"Yes," Emma almost shouted. "The court awarded Lucy to her mother. They're both looking forward to living with us."

"Praise the Lord. I can't hardly waits." Jessie's dark face split into an enormous grin. "Won't we jest has us some fun?"

Emma frowned. "Are you certain about this? It's going to mean a lot of extra work. It'll be more mouths to feed and more to clean up after."

"If you don't minds, I probably gonna ask Ruby, my sister's gal, to help."

"Billy Bob's sister?"

She nodded.

"He's certainly been a blessing. I don't know what we'd do without him."

"Ruby's a good gal, too. She do whatever we need doin'."

"I'm sure she will."

"That man Miss Carol married must be pure-dee tacky. 'Magine tryin' to take 'way her little Lucy, and him the one runnin' 'round while Miss Carol out makin' the livin'."

"It's not that unusual in this day and age."

"Why he want her, anyways? I think a chile be crampin' his style."

"He's engaged to marry some wealthy woman. I believe Lucy was part of his charm. Evidently, the woman can't have children and fell in love with Lucy while she was seeing Ron."

"You mean he took that babe with him when he were steppin' out on Miss Carol?"

"It appears so."

"If that don't beat all." She shook her head in amazement. "Poor little girl. I wonders if that little miss like sugar cookies?"

"Jessie, nobody in the world would turn up their nose at your sugar cookies."

"They is good, ain't they? I might jest has to go make a batch right now and gets back in practice."

"I need to get busy too, now that I know for certain they're coming. I've been thinking about having M & M contractors redo the nursery."

"You mean the one in the south wing Mr. Richard kept locked up?"

She nodded. "That seems so foolish. I didn't mention it while he was alive. Heaven knows, we had plenty of room, but I think it would make a lovely apartment for Carol and Lucy. If nothing else, it'd give them some privacy from two old broads."

"Speaks for yourself, thank you."

"Do you think it's a good idea?"

"Seems like to me. I never knowed why it weren't used anyway."

"Funny, I thought you did. Richard told me it was where he, his wife and daughter had their rooms. I just assumed the memories were so painful he locked the doors when they died and never wanted to reopen them."

"Poor man."

"They were extremely young when they married. It must have been a real love match." Emma was startled by the pang of jealousy which pierced her heart.

"I warn't livin' here. I'd done left with my own man and never did 'spect to be back," Jessie confessed. "My ma, she warn me he were no good, but I didn't listen. When I got pregnant and couldn't bring home no more pay, he hit me so hard I lost my baby. My little girl." A tear trickled down each plump cheek. "I guess that's why I'se so all fired anxious to get my hands on Miss Carol's chile."

"You never told me that."

"I don't like thinkin' 'bout it. It still hurt, Miss Emma. After all these years, it still hurt bad."

"Bless your loving heart. You stop thinking about it right now. You just start thinking about all the fun we're going to have getting the house ready for our new family."

"I is. But how did Mr. Richard's family die? Did they sicken, or what?"

"I don't know. Richard hated discussing it and I hated prying. Didn't your mother tell you?"

"My poor ma done dead by the time I come back to Shadow Lake. Mr. Richard jest moved me in her cabin and say if I be as good a cook and housekeeper as she were, I had me a job."

"And so you were." Emma rose, giving her a hard hug. "And furthermore, I'm damn glad."

"Fer a skinny ole white woman that cusses, you ain't too bad neither." Jessie's eyes sparkled.

"It will be fun having someone young around."

"Sure nuff. Won't that little girl jest love playin' in this big yard, ridin' them horses, swimmin' in the lake . . . ."

The hair on the neck of both women prickled and stood up straight as they grabbed each other for comfort and support.

"What in God's name was that?"

"Lawd, Miss Emma, I don't knows. I never heerd sech a awful

sound." Her eyes rolled wildly.

It pierced the air again, long and mournful, wailing and plaintive as a voice calling from the grave.

Emma removed herself from Jessie's vice-like grip and crossed to the window.

"It's Rascal."

"No, ma'am. My dog ain't never made no sound like that."

She ran to Emma's side. Together they watched, amazed, as Jessie's mongrel shepherd threw back his head and cry after desperate cry poured from his tortured throat.

Chapter Three

"I've found them."

"Well, praise the Lord. I done turned this house upside down, till I'se plum wore out. Where?" Jessie was climbing the stairs, huffing and puffing as she pulled herself up by the railing. "Lord, I sure is feelin' my years."

"I *spects*, as you're so fond of saying, it's the pounds, not the years, that you're feeling."

Jessie chose to ignore the insult.

"Where were they?"

"I remembered a metal box on the top shelf in Richard's closet. I climbed on a chair, and sure enough," she dangled a set of keys in the other's face before adding, "there they were."

"It's a wonder you is, woman your age climbin' on chairs. Ain't you got no sense?"

"Sense enough to find what you couldn't," Emma retorted, tired of forever being reminded of her advancing years.

"Whew." Jessie reached the landing where Emma waited. "Now that you most broke your neck to find 'em, ain't you gonna use'em?"

"I was waiting on you. I thought you'd want to be here when I opened up the wing."

"I is curious."

"Face it, Jessie, you're nosy as hell. If I'd gone in those rooms without you, I'd never heard the last of it."

"I dunno. It sort'a gives me the creeps."

"What, for heaven's sake?"

"Goin' in those rooms after all this time. What if they ain't supposed to be opened? What if Mr. Richard had him a good reason for shuttin' them up?"

"He did have a good reason, you goose. He was grief stricken. He didn't want to be reminded of the family he'd lost."

"Lots of people loses their families but they don't lock up their rooms."

"Most people's homes aren't large enough to give them a choice."

"Maybe."

By now they were at the end of the hall facing the door opening into the south wing.

"Well," Emma announced, "here we are."

"So, if you ain't got the willies, how come you jest standin' with the keys in your hand and a stupid look spread all over your face?"

Emma thrust one of the keys in the lock, twisting hard. Both caught their breath at the faint click. With beating heart and dry mouth, Emma slowly turned the handle.

"See." She heaved a sigh of relief. "I don't know what you expected. You acted like you thought Richard had murdered them and left the bodies in here to rot."

"Good Lawd. Don't be sayin' sech things." Jessie's eyes rolled as she clutched her companion's arm.

"Phew. Speaking of rot. It really smells. The first thing we need to do is air it out."

"Un huh."

Jessie was staring into each corner, still uneasy in this suite of rooms that hadn't felt a person's step for years.

They were standing in the center of a short hallway. Two rooms opened off either side, at the end of which, a gorgeous stained-glass window faced the door they had entered.

"Shall we check out the master suite?"

"All rights with me."

But Jessie waited for Emma to step across the threshold and walk well inside the room before she followed.

"This is lovely. Won't Carol be pleased?"

Emma pulled open the drapes hanging in tatters at the windows, exposing a large room decorated in shades of pink. Although faded, it still retained its original charm and elegance. The furniture was French Provincial, a trifle feminine for a master bedroom Emma felt, but perfect for her niece. Carol would adore the kidney-shaped dressing table and the hand-painted roses spilling across the headboard of the bed.

"I don't see Mr. Richard sleepin' here in all this fluffs."

"They were young. He probably let her decorate the room to suit herself. He couldn't have cared less. He certainly never objected to anything I did to the house."

"You never fancied it up none."

"No, but then I'm not a very fancy person. Looks like his first wife was. Maybe that's why he chose such a 'plain Jane' second time around. He didn't want anyone that might remind him of Lettice," she ended in a wistful way.

"That her name? I never knowed anyone named after that particular vegetable."

"It is unusual, isn't it?" She was opening drawers and closet doors. "I was afraid he might have left everything like it was when she died, but thankfully someone's cleaned out the personal items. I'm glad. I didn't want to go through her clothing or private mementoes."

"I think these rooms laid out jest like yours."

Jessie was poking her head into two adjoining doorways. One was a bathroom. The other a sitting room. A magnificent marble fireplace, floor to ceiling bookcases, and a pair of French doors opening onto a small balcony overlooking the lake caused Emma to gasp in delight.

"Actually, the view of the lake is prettier than mine."

"Change then," Jessie suggested. "Give Miss Carol your wing, and you takes this one."

"Heavens, no. Richard and I spent over twenty years in that room and that mahogany four-poster bed. I wouldn't trade it for the world. He told me that bedroom had belonged to his parents. They offered Richard and his bride this one so they could have their privacy. The same as we're doing for Carol and Lucy. I believe their child had the small bedroom across the hall."

"What were her name?"

"That's odd. I don't believe Richard ever said. I'm quite sure he was the one who told me Lettice was his wife, but maybe not, maybe it was his sister, Maureen."

"We ain't seed her in a long time."

"She's been in Europe. I'm hoping she'll come when we get Carol settled. Remind me to write and invite her."

"She probably won't. She hardly ever do. I don't much think she like this place."

"Don't be ridiculous. The woman grew up here. This was her home."

"I jest sayin' what I thinks."

"And not the first time, either." Emma frowned. "I never felt she was unhappy when she visited. Do you think she resents Richard leaving the house to me?"

"If she minded, you'd knowed it. No, I tellin' you she don't like it here, period." Jessie was adamant. "Course, that don't bother me none, cause you talk 'bout bossy ole women,' that Miss Maureen done take first prize."

"She's not that bad. She's never married and had to learn to compromise. She's used to getting her way."

"Don't matter what the reason, she still one bossy lady."

"I suppose," Emma agreed. "Anyway, we're spending all our time talking and getting nowhere. Let's check the other rooms. I need to see what has to be done before I call M & M."

This time Jessie led the way across the hall, her nervousness forgotten.

"I wonder what color be Miss Lucy's favorite? You should asks and then do the room . . ." Her speech halted. She looked at her friend in concern. "What's wrong, Miss Emma? You feeling sick?"

Emma was standing inside the threshold of what had been the child's bedroom, a stricken expression on her face.

"Miss Emma? Answer me, Miss Emma."

Emma shook her head as if to clear it, before raising a hand to her forehead and rubbing her brow.

"What's the matter with you? You lookin' plum strange. I say, you answer me. You hear me now?"

Emma's eyes, which had been clouded and unfocused, cleared. She appeared startled by the other's distress.

"Lord, Jessie, why are you carrying on so?"

"Oh." Her companion clutched her heart before sinking into an overstuffed chair which creaked in an alarming manner. "You jest 'bout scared the pants off me."

"That would take some doing." Emma snickered, unable to imagine what had frightened her old friend.

"I 'fraid, when I saw your face, you'd had a spell of some kind."

"Why on earth would you think such a thing? I did have a little chill when I entered the room, but what's that old saying, 'must have been someone walking over my grave.'"

"Lawd, Miss Emma. You shuts your mouth."

"Stop that. You're letting your imagination get the better of you. I'm fine."

"Well, I ain't. I got to sit here a minute and catch my breath. You perch on that pretty little bed in the corner and let me keep my eye on you."

"Old fool."

"Jest sit down and shut up."

Disgusted, Emma flopped onto an exquisitely carved antique bed pushed against the outer wall. She immediately shot bolt upright. A look of absolute horror flooded her features.

"Now whats? You scarin' this ole' woman plum bad."

"Jessie." Emma's breath came in gasps. "Did you feel that?"

"How could I? I'se sittin' clean over here."

"It was awful."

"What?"

"I don't know." Emma frowned, perplexed. "I can't seem to remember what it was."

"We done 'nuff explorin' for one day," Jessie informed her. Rising, she took Emma by the arm and firmly propelled her through the door. "We is gonna get us some cake and coffee, then take us a little nap."

"You think I'm old and crazy, don't you?"

"I don't think nothin', 'cept I'se tired and needs to put my feet up a bit."

"You're a terrible liar."

"Don't you be callin' me names. I ain't 'bout to take no flap from you. Never has, and don't aim to start now. You jest get that skinny ole' butt outta this door and down them steps quick like I says."

Jessie pushed Emma, protesting, before her.

"You can stop all this fussing. There's not a damn thing the matter with me."

But Emma's mind reeled. What in the name of hell had happened when she stepped across the threshold of that room, and even more to the point, what in the name of hell had happened when she sat on that bed?

Chapter Four

"I'm having the furniture refinished and upholstered. Everything else is aged past the point of no return. Of course, you'll probably need to check for termites, water leaks and other structural problems," Emma informed the young contractor standing opposite her in the larger of the two bedrooms.

"After this length of time, it wouldn't be a bad idea. Particularly important is the wiring. When something goes unused, like this has, it wears out in a hurry. In addition, today's women use hair dryers and such, and will need newer outlets."

"I hadn't thought about wiring. I'm glad you mentioned it. And another thing, should we replace those old fixtures in the bathrooms?"

"Tell you the truth, Mrs. Thatcher. People are absolutely crazy about those claw-foot tubs. They're even selling reproductions for new houses."

"You're saying they're so out-of-date, they're in?" She smiled at the handsome young man facing her.

"Something like that. Anyway, yours are in perfect condition. Seems a shame removing them."

"Then, the only difficulty left is the lack of storage space. You know women. We need a place for our creams and lotions."

"That's no problem. We'll simply enclose the original sinks with built-in cabinets and extend the vanity tops."

"That should do the trick. You're sure it will be attractive?"

"When I finish with these rooms, you'll be wanting to trade places. Your niece will be tickled pink."

"Speaking of pink, what do you think about using the original colors? I don't believe we could improve on that pale ivory woodwork or those soft shades of rose."

"Me either, especially if you're going to use the deep-rose silk for the draperies and that wallpaper you picked out that's sprigged in rose buds."

"You like the samples I showed you?"

"They're perfect. We'll carry those colors throughout your niece's side of the wing. In fact, I'd like to see you upholster the chairs in silk stripes using those same shades. I'll paint the walls of the sitting room a soft mauve that will blend perfectly with the rose."

"Heavens, Mr. Mason. I knew you were an excellent carpenter, but I'd no idea you possessed such an artistic talent."

"Customers kept asking my advice until I decided to take a course in interior decorating. Turned out I really enjoyed it."

"Well then, what's your suggestion for the child's half of the wing?"

"Yellow. White and yellow can't be beat. It's bright, perky and kids love it."

"I think you're right. I remember adoring yellow when I was young. It made me feel cheerful. Matter of fact, it still does. Mr. Mason, you've been a world of help. Now, if you can get in and out in six weeks, we're in business."

"I've just finished the Hedgepath house. I don't have another project planned for at least a month. I'll throw my whole crew in and we'll be out in no time. In fact, if you don't mind, I'll get started this afternoon. My sister Gertie's boy isn't too bright, but he works well on simple jobs like stripping paper and cleaning."

"That suits me to a tee."

"You don't mind someone like him around, do you?"

"Heavens, no. I'm sure he's no problem or you wouldn't

employ him."

"He's rather slow is all, but some people object to somebody like that in their home."

"Not me. He'll be more than welcome if he'll clean up this mess."

She wrinkled her nose in distaste at the dirty remnants of drapes, dust and cobwebs surrounding them. Emma had waited in the master bedroom while the contractor looked through the rest of the wing. She wasn't sure why she hadn't followed him, but still felt uncomfortable after her previous experience.

"Mr. Helms will pick up the chairs and love-seat tomorrow. He's re-covering them and making the drapes. He promised he'd have everything finished before Carol arrived."

"I don't enjoy gossip, but Mr. Helms has been known to break more than one promise."

"Not after signing a contract if they aren't done in the specified time, I get them for free."

He burst out laughing. "Does that mean I'm about to be handed something similar?"

"It's in the library along with Jessie's coconut cake. I remember how fond of it you were when you repaired the porch last year."

"You really know how to hold a man's feet to the fire." He chuckled. "However, for a slice of Jessie's cake I'd do most anything."

He failed to notice the tiny shudder of relief Emma gave as they stepped out of the south wing and began descending the stairs.

"I'll bring Gertie's boy and another man out after lunch. They can begin cleaning while I check the wiring."

"I'm back."

As promised, the contractor returned after lunch, calling out to let the two women know he'd returned.

Emma stepped out of the library where she had been working a crossword puzzle, only sneaking an occasional peek at the answers.

"That didn't take long. You must have gobbled lunch."

"Didn't eat any," he admitted. "Ate so dang much of that cake I was stuffed to the gills."

"Remind me and I'll have Jessie send some home with you."

"I won't forget. Now, let me call Stanley and Raymond. They need to get started if I plan to make something out of this job besides dessert."

Reopening the front door, he leaned out, motioning to two young men. They slowly climbed from his truck.

"They don't seem too anxious."

"They don't mind the work. It's just that Raymond's real shy and I've already explained about Stanley."

They entered, eyes downcast, faces averted.

"Raymond, I'd like you to meet Mrs. Thatcher. She's the lady this beautiful house belongs too. She'll expect you and Stanley to do a bang–up cleaning job."

"Yes, sir. Me, and Stanley, we'll do just what the lady wants."

"Thank you, Raymond. I'm delighted to meet you, and Stanley. I'm sure you'll please me."

The men nodded. Suddenly, Stanley's face lit up. An enormous grin spread across the vacuous features.

"Lo-look, Uncle Ti-Tim. This lad-lady's got a pus-pussy cat."

"She certainly does." He looked where Stanley pointed.

Cleo, closely followed by Anthony, emerged from the library. At once they began giving the strangers a thorough inspection.

"Stanley loves animals. They seem to have a special affinity for one another. I've never seen one that didn't take up with him."

As if to corroborate this statement, both cats ran to the side of the child-like man, twining themselves around and between his legs.

"The-they love me." The dull features glowed. "An-and I love them." He sank to his knees caressing each. The cats were delighted, arching their backs and purring loudly. "Lo-look, Uncle Tim. This one is real fa-fat." He giggled.

In an aside to Emma, Tim Mason whispered, "You can see he's only a child, even if he stands well over six feet. This has about killed his mother."

"I know it's hard on her and her husband."

They were speaking in undertones, but they needn't have. Stanley was totally engrossed in the cats, not paying the slightest attention to them.

"You might mention this." Emma's sympathy went out to the family of this challenged young man. She tried to think of some comfort for the uncle to pass on. "At least today when raising children is so difficult, with all the alcohol and drugs available, she'll be spared that agony. I think it would be a far worse thing having a child born whole and sound, then having to stand by helpless while he destroyed his own health and sanity."

"You know, I believe you're right. I never thought of it like that, but there can be lot worse problems than Stanley has. I'll tell Gertie what you said. I know she'll appreciate it."

"Oh, sh-she is re-really fat." Stanley was stroking Cleo's stomach.

"She's going to have babies."

"Right now?" He jumped to his feet clapping his hands.

"Soon."

"Tha-that one too?"

"No, that's Anthony, the father."

"I ju-just love kitties. I do-don't have one." His face fell.

"Perhaps, Stanley, if you check with your mother, you could have one of Cleo's kittens."

"On-one of these? Oh, Un-uncle Tim. Cou-could I?" He was so excited, he wiggled like a puppy.

"You mean that, Mrs. Thatcher?" The contractor was shocked. "I know these aren't strays but pedigreed animals."

"Of course, I mean it. Stanley can have the pick of the litter."

The low brow wrinkled, almost disappearing into the coarse shaggy hair growing profusely around his face. "I do-don't un-understand."

"After they're born and old enough to leave their mother, you can be first to chose a baby."

"Fo-for my own?"

"Your very own."

"Th-thank you. Is-isn't she a nice la-lady, Uncle Tim?'

"Very nice."

"I-I'll clean ex-extra good for her." He puffed out his chest. "I-I'll clean be-better than any-anybody ever cleaned."

"Well, don't let Jessie hear you say that." Emma laughed.

"Whe-when do we start?"

"Right this minute," Tim said. "I'll take them up. Will you be in the library if I need to ask about anything?"

"Probably."

"We'll leave you then and get busy."

She stood at the base of the stairs and watched the young contractor lead them up and into the south wing, the cats trailing worshipfully behind their new friend.

***

Tim left. He had gone into town to order supplies from a list he'd made, and now, it was growing dusk.

Emma finished her puzzle, took a short nap, had a visit with Jessie and was returning to the library when she heard the cry.

"You hollerin' at me, Miss Emma?" Jessie stuck her head in the doorway.

"No. I think it was one of the men. Maybe they need something."

"Well, I be happy to let you go see. I done climbed them steps twice today."

"I'm surprised they're still working."

A loud crash shook the house followed by a blood curdling shriek.

"Whew. Did you hear that?"

"I'd have to be deaf not to."

She ran from the room, Jessie puffing along behind. In seconds they reached the south wing. Emma stopped so suddenly Jessie collided into her.

Bag after bag of refuse had been filled and stacked neatly in the hallway. Stanley, having removed a poker from the sitting room fireplace, was systematically breaking open each bag. The filthy contents were strewn everywhere, dust rising in such dense clouds it almost obscured Emma's vision.

"Stanley. What's the meaning of this?"

The boy slowly swung his head around. Gobs of spittle hung off his chin. Claw marks had opened up one cheek.

"Where's Raymond?" she asked so terrified she could barely get the words out.

Hearing a faint whimper, she turned and ran into the master bedroom. He was on the floor, face ashen, blood running from his forehead. As she bent over him, Jessie cried out. Whirling around, Emma was able to duck the blow Stanley aimed at her. Frantically, she fled to the opposite side of the room and ran behind the bed.

"Stanley. For God's sake, son, can't you hear me?"

His eyes were glazed. His breathing ragged. A high keening issued from his throat. Saliva bubbled out his mouth. The poker whizzed through the air again and again as Stanley brought it down on the bed, desperately trying to reach across and strike Emma.

Jessie screamed. At the sound Stanley turned. He shuffled awkwardly toward her, a maniacal look on his face, guttural grunts pouring from him. Raymond summoned up what little strength he had left and lunging forward, caught hold of Stanley's ankle. When the crazed boy realized what had happened, he raised the poker above the head of the injured youth lying helplessly on the floor. The two women screamed in unison. For a moment the sound seemed to pierce Stanley's consciousness. As he hesitated, the contractor flew into the room tackling his nephew. While Stanley lay stunned, he yanked the weapon from the boy's grasp throwing it to Emma.

"For heaven's sake, use it if you have too!"

Stanley began struggling, and Jessie, with great presence of mind, promptly sat atop him. She knocked the breath from him but almost immediately he recovered and began pushing her off. Doubling up his fist, his uncle struck him. Stanley blinked a second, then letting out a bull-like roar spilled Jessie to the floor, fingers outstretched for the older man's throat. Suddenly, he slumped to the floor. Emma stood trembling, tears streaming down her cheeks. She let the poker fall from her grasp.

"What have I done to that child?"

"The only damn thing you could have."

Tim whipped the belt from his pants. Turning the limp form over, he bound Stanley's hands behind his back. Then, he felt for the pulse at the base of his neck.

"He's fine. You've only knocked him out. Now will somebody tell me what the hell's going on?"

"First, I think we better get Jessie off the floor and send her to call an ambulance. Raymond looks terrible and we'll need someone competent to deal with Stanley."

Together, she and the contractor pulled the stout woman to her feet.

"I never thought I'd be thankful the Good Lord made me big as a watermelon, but I sure 'nuff were grateful today."

"Oh, Jessie." Emma was crying and laughing, close to hysterics. "I'm going to thank Him too, and I'll never, ever say another word about how much you eat."

"What started this?" The contractor was frantic. "Raymond, do you have any idea?"

"No, sir. It was plum crazy. I never saw Stanley act like this." The boy's eyes rested on his companion, an expression of horror mirrored in them. "We'd done finished cleaning the stuff from this side of the hall and except for Stanley stopping to play with the cats, we hadn't had no trouble. Then, we crossed over and began on the other side. I saw Stanley was looking funny and he kept mumbling. I asked him what he was saying but he just ignored me, so I stopped paying him any mind. Pretty soon he started humming. It was getting on my nerves. I mean, he kept singing the same tune over and over, getting louder and louder all the time."

"What was it?" Emma sank to the bed keeping a watchful eye on the limp form.

"I don't know. Sounded like something I 'member from when I was a kid. Anyway, he left the room and came back carrying one of the cats. I think it was the daddy."

"Anthony? I'm surprised they weren't already in there. I thought they wouldn't let Stanley out of sight."

"They didn't at first, but when we crossed the hall they stayed in here on this bed. I guess they were napping. He must'a made that one mad cause it scratched his face all to hell."

"That's hard to believe." Emma was astonished. "He's never clawed anyone before."

"And I've never seen Stanley aggressive before. None of this makes sense."

"It might not make sense but it sure as heck happened."

"I'm not doubting your word, son. When I got here and heard all that racket, I thought a war was going on. No, I don't doubt you."

"When he brought that cat in, it went as crazy as Stanley," the boy continued, "I mean, it screamed something fierce, scratched his face, jumped outta his arms and streaked back across the hall. Stanley followed and the next thing I knowed, he was breaking open those bags we'd stacked. I tried to get him to stop but he chased me in here and popped me a good one."

"Lord, Mrs. Thatcher." Sweat was pouring down the builder's face. "I don't know what to say. Here I'd just finished telling you what a nice, harmless boy my sister has, and then this happened. I can't tell you how sorry I am."

"Un-uncle Tim." Stanley's eyes slowly opened. "My he-head hurts." Tears rolled down his cheeks. "My he-head hurts re-real bad, Un-uncle Tim."

"Stanley." Emma dropped to her knees. "Why were you trying to hit me?"

"I-I never. I ne-never tried to hi-hit an-anybody. Never!" He was so upset he was shouting. "My-my hands won't move. Un-uncle Tim. I ca-can't move my hands."

"Hush, Stanley. Hush now." Emma took the hem of her shirt and gently wiped the blood the cat's claws had drawn. "Jessie's calling a doctor. He's going to fix your head and the cheek Anthony scratched."

"Why'd he do-do that? I tho-thought he li-liked me." He seemed totally bewildered, completely unaware of the previous state he had been in.

"I'm sure he does." She sought to comfort him, heart breaking at the thought of how this would add to his mother's burden.

"Who-who is that ba-bad person, Mrs. Thatcher?"

She was startled. "What bad person, Stanley?"

"Ca-can I still ha-have a kitty?"

Her eyes met those of his uncle's, unable to mask the pain he was experiencing.

"Certainly. Just as soon as you get well, and as soon as they're old enough to leave their mother."

"Oh, th-thank you." He smiled sweetly, then drifted off to sleep.

Chapter Five

A week passed. In that time Tim Mason had finished cleaning the south wing. Now his crews were busy building vanities, stripping wallpaper, caulking and repairing cracks in the ceiling and woodwork. The sound of their hammers made a cheerful rat-a-tat. Emma felt relieved each morning they trooped up the stairs to commence their noisy labor. These were sounds she welcomed. It was the ones at night she found disturbing.

She had been unafraid her entire life, but since the incident with Stanley, her nerves were on edge. She lay sleepless in bed listening to noises never before noticed. She realized old houses had creaks and groans but these seemed different, especially those coming from the newly-opened wing. She could have sworn someone was pacing the floors. Twice a child giggled. Sometimes, heavy sighs were heard. Long drawn out gasps of pleasure drifted down the hall to her room, reminding her of the first years of her marriage when the lovemaking was so intense.

Once she even left her bed, going to stand before the apartment entrance. Straining her eyes and ears, she was afraid to enter, afraid of what she might find if she became too bold. She had seen nothing. Nothing but dust motes floating in the light cast by the moon. Common sense told her there had always been noises, house noises coming from those rooms, but since they had been closed she had failed to notice them. Now though, she made certain the door leading to the wing was shut each evening when the workmen left.

Emma refused to mention her uneasiness to Jessie who would only use it as another sign of her advancing age. Determined to prove that was not a factor, Emma spent the next few afternoons gardening, working outside from early morning until late afternoon. Jessie fumed and fussed at her, constantly threatening she would overdo and become ill.

On this particular day, and with that thought in mind, Jessie dragged Emma indoors for lunch, afterwards insisting she rest. To keep peace, Emma agreed. Curling up on the wicker chaise in her room, she sorted through the mail, delighted to discover a letter from Carol hidden between the catalogues and advertisements:

> *Dear Aunt Emma,*
> *Lucy's so excited about coming to live with you, especially after you wrote Cleo's kittens would arrive shortly. I really don't know how to thank you. You're so kind, loving and generous with your home and yourself. Remember the year I spent with you and Uncle Richard while Mom and Dad traveled around the world? I never had such fun. I often think of those days and know Lucy will love Shadow Lake as much as I did and do.*

Emma paused, putting the letter aside for the moment, her thoughts returning to that time when the young girl had been left in her charge. She had been so worried Carol would be miserable living with someone with no experience with teenagers, but she need not have been.

A sophomore in high school, Carol had fallen in love with the small town, immediately making dozens of friends, particularly those in the Randsome family. She and Grace Randsome soon became inseparable and the house rang with their laughter. As much as they'd dreaded the commitment forced upon them by

Emma's sister, she and Richard found themselves equally dreading the day the girl's parents would return taking her with them. In no time, they grew accustomed to weekend bunking parties, all night giggling, cookie crumbs scattered over the floor, and the telephone ringing constantly. When they had begun to take all that in stride, Carol fell in love.

Phillip was what most young girls dreamed about. Tall, handsome, with emerald green eyes, hair a deep copper, lips full and sexy, plus, a senior and captain of the football team. His old Ford coupe soon became a permanent fixture in the Thatcher drive. The sight of Carol, blond ponytail flying as she ran in and out of the house, was a constant delight.

Those days, when Carol lived with them, were some of the happiest Emma had ever known. She sighed with regret for what was past before returning to the letter.

I've one more week before I can leave my job. One more should give me time to pack and store my furniture. I don't know who is more excited, Lucy or me. I can't wait to see Grace and catch up on everybody. We've always kept in touch and she's already playing cupid. Grace swears Phillip never married because he was waiting for me. I seriously doubt it, but it is a marvelous ego boast for someone who's been made to feel like a frump.

Tell Jessie I want a Milky Way Chocolate Cake with Fudge Icing the minute I walk through the door. Thanks again for being the most wonderful aunt a girl could have. I don't know what Lucy and I would do without you. I couldn't bear to stay in the same town as that two-timer I married, and with the meager child support I received, don't know how I'd manage financially. Aren't you just an angel for taking us in? It will be so much fun. I was always so glad Mom and

Dad sent me to stay with you. They were such free spirits. I miss them dreadfully but am thankful they went together.

A tear trickled down Emma's cheek. She hated to give way to grief, but Carol's generous thanks, her mention of her parents who died in a plane crash, and the remark about losing loved ones, was too much for Emma who never went a day without longing for Richard. She removed her glasses, wiped off the salty water smeared on the lens, replaced them and with a determined shrug finished the letter.

Again, I am unbelievably happy to be returning to Shadow Lake. I often recall the times all of us would jump in somebody's car after school and head to Main Beach. I never could decide which I liked best, splashing in the waves or hunting for shark teeth. Remember when I found one that was four inches long? What a mouth that guy must have had. Lucy is dying to find some of her own, and I can scarcely wait to take her hunting. She has had me describe the island so many times I'm getting a tongue burn.

And remember when I almost dug up the entire yard? You and Uncle Richard never said a word. Of course, I was positive I was going to discover pirates' booty. All those legends about Luis Aury. The stories of Spanish coins, and the man who found $18,000.00 in his yard. I really did have visions of striking it rich. Gosh, I better get my shovel out and go for it again. I sure could use it now. What was the tale? Something about the treasure being marked by a tree with a chain hanging from it? Isn't it supposed to be somewhere on the river side of Amelia, and supposed to be the largest amount of loot ever buried by a pirate? Wow. I just

might arrive with my shovel in tow. Only kidding. I
promise to leave all the petunias in the ground this
time. Just being with you and Jessie will be treasure
enough, and as I said, Lucy is beside herself with
excitement.

Speaking of which, enclosed is a short note from the
little devil. She's sealed it so I feel sure she's going to beg
for a kitten. I think she's extremely smart for a ten-
year-old but don't let her know I told you. She's
already learned to play her father and me against one
another. No matter, I'll soon have her away from him
and things will settle down to normal.

> *All my love,*
> *Carol*

Emma folded Carol's letter carefully, laid a gentle kiss on the three sheets of scented stationery, and picked up the letter from the child in happy anticipation.

Dear Auntie Emma,
Mama said Cleo was going to have kittens. Can I
have one? Don't tell Mama I asked. She said you
were <u>real</u>, <u>real</u> nice, and I <u>really</u>, <u>really</u> want a kitty. I
never had one. We live in an apartment and can't
have pets. Mama said there was a big yard and a
lake. Are there fish in the lake? I have a friend who
goes fishing with her father. She says it's fun. Maybe I
can go and catch my kitty a fish to eat. Please tell
Cleo not to have them till I get there.

> *Hugs and kisses,*
> *Lucy*

The letter from the child dispelled her black mood. Emma was smiling as she removed her glasses, placing them, along with the folded letters, on the table next to her. She gave a contented sigh, then settled down for a nap. Closing her eyes she began planning a dinner party for when Carol arrived. She would invite Grace and her husband. She was long overdue repaying them for a lovely evening in December. Of course, she'd have Phillip . . .

What in the world? She could swear something was scratching on the window pane but she was on the second floor. That would be impossible. Impossible or not, something was out there, either trying desperately to get inside, or to capture her attention.

Lord. She wished she hadn't slept so hard. Her eyes were like lead. She thought they would never open; in fact, was not sure they had, not sure if she was actually awake or still dreaming. Dreaming something was at her window. That she was rising in a trance-like state and crossing the floor.

This could not be real. This had to be a dream. Her common sense sought to assert itself, to assure her the nightmare vision swimming behind the panes of glass existed only in her imagination, but even if that were the case, it was still horrible.

Her heart raced. Her breath came in gasps as she frantically fought to regain consciousness and escape the clutches of the nightmare she was in. The evil apparition leering at her seemed to be pulling her closer. She could not tear her eyes from the hands, tiny, bony skeleton fingers, nails like talons curved and clawing, scraping down the glass. She wanted to scream but couldn't force the sound past her frozen lips. Any minute she knew the glass would shatter. The bony hands would close around her throat. Whatever was out there would be inside. She thought her heart might stop, her fear was so great.

"Miss Emma. Lord, Miss Emma, wakes up." Jessie was shaking her. "What's the matter, Miss Emma? You looks like you seed a ghost."

Thank God. It was a dream.

Emma released the breath she had been holding. "Oh, Jessie,

I've never been so glad to see anyone in my life."

"What in this world? I heerd this screamin' and I thought, what now? I tell you the truth. My ole' heart can't take much more of this runnin' up these stairs." She sank onto Emma's bed. "Don't be tellin' me you was jest havin' a bad dream and I 'most had a stroke getting here."

"That must have been what it was, but Jessie, I could have sworn it was real—that I was awake. It was terrible." She covered her face with her hands.

"Well, no wonder after what happen when that poor boy went so crazy. I been havin' bad dreams most ever night. I jest don't hardly sleeps any more at all."

"Really?" The news lightened Emma's damp spirits. She had been afraid she was the only one disturbed. "I suppose it was pretty traumatic for two silly women living all alone."

"Don't know what that word means, but I know it were sure hard on this ole' black lady's nerves."

"Bless you, Jessie. You always make me feel better. I'm sorry I frightened you, but you can't imagine how real that dream seemed."

"What were it 'bout?"

"I thought something was trying to get in the window."

"On this floor?"

"I told you it was a dream." Emma was embarrassed.

"Which window you talkin' about?"

"That one." Emma pointed. Her finger froze. "Jessie, look."

Jessie crossed to where Emma was staring.

"I don't see nothin' 'cept fer some funny streaks. 'Pears to me like some of them slugs been crawlin' on the panes. I'll get Billy Bob to wash 'em off tomorrow."

"I never saw slu-slugs do that." Emma's teeth chattered. "It wa-wasn't a dream, Jessie. So-something was trying to get in."

"You talkin' plum silly. I tell you those marks be from slugs. I sees them all the time on the walkways."

"You're su-sure?"

Jessie frowned. "That must'a been one bad dream. You still ain't over it."

"I'm acting the fool. I don't know what's the matter with me. I think you're right. I'm becoming senile." Emma's voice wavered.

"That's jest not so."

Jessie couldn't believe her ears. Hearing Emma declare that she might be losing her mental faculties upset the old cook no end.

"You jest needs to relax some. When Miss Carol and the baby get here, you'll feel better."

"I hope." Emma couldn't tear her eyes from the slimy marks on the window. "Oh, God. I hope so."

"They be here 'fore too much longer. You jest see if that don't perk you up."

"I almost forgot." She gave a shaky laugh. "I got a letter from Carol. She's requested one of your four-layer chocolate cakes."

Emma sought to put things back into perspective, desperate to return to normal, dismiss the strange dream and peculiar tracings on the glass.

"I'll has one baked the very day she get here." Jessie's face split into a wide grin. "She do love that chocolate."

"Lucy wrote too. I'll read you their letters."

She put on her glasses and reached for them, still loathe to look away from the tainted window. There was only one sheet of stationery on the table.

"That's odd. I know I put them down together."

"This what you lookin' for?"

"How on earth did it get there?" A chill crawled over her body. "Who wadded it up? How did it get so wet?"

"I 'spects the cats got hold of it. That Anthony can spot a loose ball of paper anywhere."

"But it wasn't in a ball. It was folded like this one from Carol."

"Then he probably ball it up hisself. You know how he love to chew on stuff. That's how it got wet, him mouthin' it 'round and 'round."

"Then where are the tooth marks?"

"I ain't got no idea but you quit trying to make somethin' spooky outta it. You jest read me what that little girl say.

Chapter Six

"Mr. Mason, would you please step into the library?"

"On one condition." He ducked his head. "That's if you'll stop being so formal. Please, call me Tim."

"I'd like that. Heaven knows we've gone through enough to be on a first name basis. Mine is Emma."

"How about if I call you, Miss Emma?" He followed her into the paneled room.

"If it's going to be more comfortable for you. I realize there's a vast difference in our age."

"Surely not." But his eyes twinkled even as he protested. "My mama taught me it was polite to say ma'am or sir, and she insisted I always put Miss, Mrs., or Mr. before a name."

"She taught you well."

Emma gazed thoughtfully at the young contractor who appeared to be in his late thirties. He was not much taller than her five-foot-nine, but a life spent doing carpenter work, much of it outdoors, had given him a muscular frame and a healthy year-round tan. His eyes were a startling shade of blue, and when he removed the cap he habitually wore, a profusion of black curls tumbled from beneath. He had a boyishly engaging smile which he used often, his teeth flashing white against his swarthy complexion. Emma thought him extremely sexy and knew from the concern he had shown over his nephew he was a caring person. The reputation his firm enjoyed told her he was honest, dependable, and took great pride in his work. She felt sure he would do exactly what he promised her. She sighed contented, pleased with her choice.

"Thank you. Now was there something you wanted to ask? Is anything wrong with what we're doing?"

"My gracious, no. I'm more than pleased. To tell the truth, now that the cabinets are built, the crews papering and painting, I'm so excited I can hardly wait for Carol to see the results."

"Excuse me. I don't mean to be nosy, but is this the same girl who visited several years ago?"

"It certainly is. She and her daughter are coming."

His face fell. "Oh. She's married."

"Not anymore. That's why she's coming. She's just gone through a messy divorce."

"That's too bad." But his face didn't mirror his concern.

Emma chuckled. "I can tell you're all torn up."

He had the grace to look sheepish. "I guess I'm not too upset. I remember when she was here before. I was five years older, or I'd have asked her out. I thought that blond pony tail and those baby-blue eyes were the prettiest sight I'd ever seen. However, she quickly took up with Phillip Randsome and I figured I'd lost my chance."

"Aren't you married?"

"Never had the time. Dad was sick for years. I was the only boy, but I had a bevy of older sisters. Someone had to take over the family business and make sure they were fed."

"Speaking of family, that's why I wanted to talk to you. How's Stanley?"

"About the same. The doctors are mystified. He doesn't have a violent nature. They can't understand why he went berserk."

"Tim." She dropped her eyes, afraid of what she might see on his face when she posed her question. "Do you think houses can be haunted?"

"Daddy did."

"Really?" Her heart leaped. Maybe she wasn't crazy.

"Yes'm. He told me when he was a little fella, he and his dad were doing some work on an old barn. He said every time they walked in a certain stall they'd about freeze to death. They finally mentioned it to the farmer and he laughed. Said the old man that owned the place before him had shot his wife and lover in that stall, then killed himself. The farmer said it was always cold. Said he never put any animals in that particular stall because they'd go plum crazy. He only used it for storage."

"Tim, do you think something like that could account for the way Stanley acted?"

"You mean, like the animals? Stanley being so simple he would have a reaction to a haunted room?"

She nodded.

"Well, I don't know. That's awfully far-fetched. Why do you ask?"

"That wing's been sealed for years. Richard told me he'd shared those rooms with his first wife and I assumed he'd locked them because he didn't want dredging up old memories." She paused, embarrassed. "But what if the truth was, he didn't want me frightened?"

"You mean, of a ghost?"

"Lord, Tim, your guess is as good as mine. I just know ever since I unlocked that wing I've been uncomfortable."

"Maybe you're feeling guilty for opening it against Mr. Richard's wishes."

"No." She shook her head hard. "It's not guilt I'm feeling, but dammit, it's something."

"Has anything strange happened?"

"Like things that go bump in the night?" She sighed. "Not exactly. Nothing I can actually lay a finger on, though I have heard odd noises."

"That's common in old houses, particularly when we've been working in them disturbing the studs."

"I know, but . . ." she paused. "I feel a cold chill when I step in the child's room, and that was where Stanley began his episode. Have you noticed anything?"

"Just the opposite. In fact, that particular room gives me a warm cozy feeling. I figure it's the yellow paint. That, and the fact the sun pours through those windows so much of the day."

"I had this horrible dream."

"No wonder, after what my nephew put you through. I've been having nightmares myself."

"Then, there's Stanley and his problem." She plowed on, determined to make him realize something was not right about that wing, and in particular, that room. "Raymond said he was fine until they moved across the hall."

"I tell you, Miss Emma. I've about decided it was the cat. I think when it scratched Stanley, the boy went a little crazy. He's never had an animal do anything but love on him. I think when Anthony clawed him, it hurt so much, he lashed out in pain and got confused."

"But what about that strange remark?"

"Which one?"

"When he asked who the bad person was?"

"You don't think he meant the cat was acting bad?"

"Honestly, Tim, I'm not sure about anything, but no, I believe he meant an actual person."

"Gee, Miss Emma, I never heard any talk about this house being haunted, and my family's lived on this island for generations. Has anything else happened?"

"No, except I'm uneasy and I've never been before."

"Was there anything strange about the way Mr. Richard's family died?"

"Not that I know of. However, I'm going to get in touch with his sister and see what I can find out."

"I think you're wrong about this house, but if it were haunted, it wouldn't be the first on Amelia."

"Don't you start spouting some Chamber of Commerce nonsense."

"Well, Miss Emma, I know they can sound pretty far-fetched, but the truth of the matter is, more than one person has seen strange things, and they've been fairly well-documented for years."

"Have you ever?"

"No, thank goodness, but I know people who have."

"Who for instance?"

"Well, you know the Captain's House in Old Town?"

"The one where they filmed the *Pippi Longstocking* movie?"

"There's a ghost there."

"Now really, Tim." She playfully wagged a finger at him.

"I wouldn't put you on, Miss Emma. I'm afraid I'd never get another piece of that cake if I did."

"Darn tootin'. All right. I'm convinced you're being truthful, or as truthful as a ghost story will allow."

"A few years back, one of the men on my crew lived in the part of Fernandina called Old Town. He swore he saw the ghostly form of a woman in the tower window of that house. She was spanking a child. It scared him so bad he never took that way home again."

"I think I've heard that story before," she admitted, "but I dismissed it as just that—a story."

"I don't think so. Ed was really shook up. He left Fernandina not long after."

"Any others? I mean that one's been around for quite awhile. Ed could have let his imagination get the best of him." She giggled. "Or, he could have stopped in at the Palace Saloon on the way home. I understand there are lots of spirits there."

"Well, I almost hate to tell you. I mean, I don't want to get you any more upset than you already are."

"You better not worry about how upset I'll be and spit out whatever it is you know, otherwise, it'll be more than cake you don't get." She looked meaningfully at the checkbook on her desk.

"You know the Addison House? The Bed & Breakfast on Ash Street?"

She nodded.

"Well, a couple from England bought it. They had some work done before they opened it to the public, and since then, they've had a non-paying guest."

"Tim."

"It's true, Miss Emma. I didn't want to tell you because of the similarity. I mean two old houses being renovated, and suddenly they start having mysterious occurrences."

"Oh, Tim, this is unbelievable. What exactly is happening at the Addison House? How do you know about it?

"Their contractor had coffee with me not long ago. Said it was the strangest thing. They'd even called him back to see if there could be a logical reason for the disturbances."

"And there wasn't?"

He shook his head. "Nothing he could find. I mean, it isn't horrible. It's just that they have this problem with Room One and sometimes Room Five. The doors open and close, and the beds are messed up like someone's been sleeping in them."

"And no one has?"

"No. It's particularly bad when the rooms aren't rented. Even worse if they shut the drapes. Their manager's so frustrated she spent hours in Room One waiting to see if she could see something."

"Did she?"

"No. However, while she was in there, the shower started running for no earthly reason."

"What did she do?"

"I couldn't tell you. But if it had been me, these feet would have sprouted wings."

"That's creepy." She shuddered.

"The contractor figured they'd probably disturbed some entity that had been around for a long time. He told me he'd seen this happen more than once in these old homes, and nothing surprised him any more."

"Had there been a murder, or anything traumatic in its past

that would warrant the presence of someone from the other side?"

"The only thing anyone knew of, was that the house had been used as a hospital during the yellow fever plague in the late 1800's. Naturally, a number of people died there."

"Could that be the answer? Could we have disturbed some poor unhappy soul?" Emma wrung her hands.

"No, ma'am. I don't believe so."

"I do realize there are ghost stories flitting all around Amelia Island, and in fact, several of the B.& B.'s have them, but I honestly never gave them much credence. I figured they were tales put out for the tourist's entertainment."

"I don't think all are. I know the Museum has a Ghost tour beginning in that spooky cemetery behind St. Peter's Episcopal Church. I can't think the Museum would do that if they didn't have some basis. I know St. Augustine offers an even more detailed tour than ours. My understanding is, it's so involved you take it on the train ride. A friend of mine said it was lots of fun and quite interesting."

"Yes. I've been told that. You know, I always intended taking the tour here in town," she admitted, "but was too embarrassed."

She squirmed in her chair, ill at ease with the subject.

"However, I have toured St. Peter's, and Tim, if you haven't gone inside you've missed a treat. I've traveled to Israel and viewed the Chagall stained glass windows and they, at least to my way of thinking, aren't one bit more beautiful than the windows in that church. The colors blow me away. I could sit for hours and soak up the atmosphere. And the organ and carvings are exquisite. Oh, Tim, as a builder, you must."

"Believe me, Miss Emma, I've been. In fact, whenever I have company that's one of the first places I take them."

"I suppose," she said, "'there is more on heaven and earth than we mortals realize.' And, I guess there wouldn't be ghost stories and tales of witches, and such, if there weren't some basis for them. Nor, would people be so intrigued if they didn't believe in the supernatural." Emma looked ready to cry. "Oh, Tim, am I losing my mind? Am I some old woman starting signs of dementia?"

"He was growing more uneasy and concerned by the minute. "Don't be ridiculous. I know you're not crazy, but I don't believe the house is haunted either."

"Then I have to be losing my mind. You must think that and are too polite to tell me."

"I said I don't think there's a ghost. I believe Stanley upset you far more than you realize. I feel terrible I brought so much grief on you."

"You didn't. Please don't blame yourself."

"Miss Emma, if I thought for a second something was wrong in those rooms, I'd turn the key in the lock myself."

"What if it's too late? What if we've already released whatever it was held captive?" her voice wavered.

"Come on, Miss Emma. It isn't like you letting your imagination take the upper hand."

"You do think I'm being a silly old woman."

"I didn't say that. Don't you be putting words in my mouth." He laughed. "Now, I'd better get upstairs and check on that crew or I will be doing this job for nothing but cake." He smiled that boyish grin. "Feel better now that we've talked?"

"I'm not sure. You've tried to convince me the wing isn't haunted. At the same time, you've given me evidence such things are possible."

"Not here," he firmly assured her.

"Tell your men to leave the door open when they go home."

Her heart stopped a beat at her boldness. She wondered if she were a fool. As soon as he was out of sight, she rose and began pacing the room. At last, she paused before a straight-back cane chair so uncomfortable no one could endure sitting in it for long. She pursed her lips thoughtfully, then satisfied with her choice left the room. Walking briskly down the hall, she stopped before a small cabinet. Unlocking the door, she reached inside removing an old shotgun, and checked to see if it was loaded. Satisfied that it was, she replaced it in the cabinet and returned to the library. She lay down on one of the long sofas, determined to nap, feeling certain she would need some rest before the night was over. The night that would leave her no longer in doubt. The night that would prove whether or not Shadow Lake was haunted.

Chapter Seven

Emma was almost relieved. She now knew for a fact there was something in this house besides herself and the cats. However, Anthony's furious assault had seemed to work a magic. The hellish intruder had left as abruptly as it had come. For a solid week, the only noises coming from the south wing had been those made by the carpenters.

The house quickly settled into its comfortable, familiar routine and Emma could scarcely wait for Lucy and Carol's arrival, but seemed, much to her amusement, no more anxious than the young contractor. He daily stopped by on some outlandish pretense, always staying for some of Jessie's delicious delicacies and any news of Carol that might be forthcoming. This morning his excuse was bathroom drains. He had barely finished his coffee and rich cinnamon cake before Emma hurried him from the library and up the circular staircase. She had thought of a way to get more shelving in the narrow closets and wanted his opinion. She was talking and gesturing a mile a minute when Jessie's scream caused her heart to stop.

It was back! Emma whirled, terrified, when the front door flew open and Carol burst into the foyer.

"I sees you pullin' in the drive." Jessie tore out of the library where she had been dusting. "I sees you first so I gets first hug."

Emma's knees buckled. Her relief so overwhelmed her, she

sank weakly to the steps.

"Miss Emma, are you all right?" Tim's hands reached for her, but his eyes never left those of the woman standing below.

"I'm fine, no thanks to that damn fool screeching like a banshee." She glared at Jessie. "I'd think at your age, you'd have more sense than to go around screaming like some teeny bopper at a rock concert."

Hands on hips, the glare was returned. "I 'spects I so much nearer a teeny bopper than you, I hasn't forgot how to scream when I see somethin' I been waitin' a long time fer."

"Isn't this the most wonderful homecoming imaginable?" Carol was ecstatic. "Lucy, it's like it was only yesterday. These two were at each other's throats the day I left, and here they're still going strong. Oh Lord, I do love you both."

She hugged the old cook hard. "You first, Jessie, because you sounded the alarm and because I know there's a fat chocolate cake in the pantry with my name on it."

"You right 'bout that, darling." Jessie returned the hug, adding a resounding smack on the lips. "Mmmmm, you even tastes good." Abruptly, she released Carol. "Now, you lets me get at that young'un." She clasped Lucy in an enveloping embrace.

"Let her go, Jessie. You'll suffocate the child stuffing her face between those two big mountains. The poor thing can't get her breath."

"And don't you jest wishes you had somethin' to suff'cates somebody with. Lord, Miss Carol, you best hurry up and give that skinny old white woman a hug 'fore she jest grumps us pure to death. She be so jealous cause I sees you first, and cause I got sech a fine figure, and she shaped like a broomstick."

"Mama," Lucy's voice came muffled from Jessie's more than ample bosom, "you didn't say they were funny. This is better than television."

Tim could contain himself no longer. He sank to the step beside Emma, and howled.

"O-oh, I-I'm sorry, but Lucy's right. This is better than TV. I wouldn't have missed it for the world."

"Who's that?" The child had managed to extricate herself from Jessie's clutches.

"That's the man what fixes the most beautiful rooms in the world fer you and your sweet ma. They jest plum lovely."

"Thank you, Jessie." Emma was furious. "Thank you for spoiling my wonderful surprise. Well, I guess since big mouth's spilled the beans, we might as well go straight there. Tim, would you help with the luggage?"

"Tim?" Carol's brow wrinkled. "You seem so familiar." Her eyes widened. "Now I remember. You were that dreamy older boy all the girls were crazy about. You used to build houses with your father. We'd walk by so we could peek at you with your shirt off."

"Really?" His chest visibly expanded. "I never knew that."

"We were furious because you never asked any of us out. We thought you were dark, mysterious and utterly unattainable."

He smiled ruefully. "And I thought I was too old."

She shot him a roguish glance from beneath long lashes. "Now you know better."

"Now we all know better," Emma snapped rising from the stairs. "Tim, do you feel too old to carry in the bags?"

"No, ma'am," he answered, embarrassed.

Carol extended her hand. "Here's the trunk key. If you don't mind starting by yourself, I'll be out to help as soon as I give this skinny ole white woman some love."

***

Emma lay watching Anthony's ballet. He leaped and pirouetted gracefully after the dust motes floating in the brilliant early morning sunlight. Normally Cleo would have frolicked alongside, but now was so monstrously swollen, she was more than content lying quietly pressed against her mistress, lazily viewing her mate's antics through half-crossed eyes.

Emma stretched, sighing happily. It was amazing the difference her guests had made in such a short period of time. She had not felt so alive since Richard's death. Even Jessie seemed to have shed ten years. She supposed, without realizing, they had withdrawn into a comfortable but dull cocoon. One which Carol and her daughter had quickly stripped, freeing Emma like a beautiful butterfly into a bright and exciting new world. She could not remember how long it had been since she had wakened anxious for what the new day might bring, but she felt rejuvenated and was grateful.

It really was great fun having Carol around. She had immediately become the main object of the town's two most eligible bachelors. Emma was overjoyed as she watched the young woman's self-esteem and confidence grow daily. Carol had been so hurt and degraded after the ugly divorce and custody suit, however, no one could help becoming inflated from all the lavish attention she was receiving, or the intense sexual sparring generated between two competing stallions. In less than two days, she had been offered a job as receptionist for Phillip Ransome's law firm, and bookkeeper to M & M Construction, but much to Emma's amusement had opted for a secretarial position with Dr. Wendell Rallings, Grace's husband. In fact, Carol's love-life, plus the entertaining tales she carried from the doctor's office, had to Emma's amazement, almost weaned Jessie from her soaps.

"Even that incests," she informed Emma, "can't hold a candle next to the sure 'nuff real stuff'in."

The cook unmercifully pumped Carol for the day's gossip, or for almost embarrassing particulars of her social life. In good-natured fashion, Carol revealed all. She had no secrets, realizing the dullest of her day's adventures, particularly the ones she slightly embellished for Jessie's entertainment, gave the ladies a vicarious thrill. It was the very least she could do to repay their love and hospitality.

Of course, they were both foolish over Lucy. She was all anyone could ask of a young child. Intelligent, anxious to please, pretty as a pot of petunias and so delighted with her new room she could hardly be pried from it. In fact, that was the only reservation Emma had about the child. Her intense desire for privacy seemed to be worsening daily.

Emma had invited children over and Lucy entertained them graciously, but it was soon apparent she was relieved when they left so she could return to her room and dolls. That too, puzzled Emma. The day of Lucy's arrival she had brought her baby dolls out for her aunt's scrutiny, naming and giving the history of each. Since then, no one had seen them. Like Lucy, they stayed closeted away. Emma also couldn't help but notice none of the guests were invited to the lovely room Lucy had exclaimed so happily over the first day.

Emma kept recalling the disturbing events and odd sensations she had experienced there, as well as the violent reaction of Stanley. She felt herself growing more and more uneasy. She would like to speak with Carol, but was loathe to worry her, particularly when she seemed so happy for the first time in months. Surely the child's mother would sense if something was amiss. After all, what did Emma actually know about Lucy? Perhaps she had always been a private, shy child. Certainly the divorce and the ugliness over which parent got custody would go far toward making her become withdrawn.

Emma admitted she had a tendency to let her imagination run berserk. Richard had constantly scolded her about that. There, just remembering her husband's admonitions calmed her. She resolved to allay her stupid fears by making an effort to entice Lucy out on some fun excursion. This decided, she tossed off her covers, kissed a disgruntled cat between its wandering eyes and was reaching for the robe lying across a chair when there came a slight tap at her door.

"Yes?" Emma called out.

"May I speak with you, Miss Emma?" Ruby, Jessie's niece, peeped around the door.

"Of course." Emma was always delighted to see the young

woman. Jessie was so proud of her. The way she looked, dressed and 'de jest lovely ways' she spoke the English language. Especially the fact she was making top grades attending the town's community college. Emma was proud too, and more than a little fond of Ruby. She had watched her grow from a toddler into a beautiful young lady.

"I've been wanting to tell you how much I appreciate you helping us. Jessie never could have managed this upstairs cleaning and all the extra laundry."

"I don't mind." Ruby smiled. "I love working here. The house is so beautiful. I enjoy cleaning and touching all your pretty things, and the extra money does come in handy."

"Well, thank you, darling. You're too sweet for words, like always. Now, are you wanting to get started cleaning in here? I'm warning you. Cleo refuses to get out of bed."

"Oh, I'll get her out when I need too." She giggled. "I swear the poor thing looks like a whale."

"It's pitiful, isn't it? I can't believe she's gone so long without giving birth." Emma fondly stroked her pet's distorted stomach, kept in perpetual motion from the kittens wiggling deep in their mother's snug nest.

"She'll have them soon or burst," Ruby declared flatly. "Poor ole mommy. I'll let her sleep a tiny bit longer. I'm really not ready for your room yet." Suddenly, Ruby blurted, "I'm having some trouble with the little girl."

"Lucy?"

The maid nodded. "She won't let me clean her room. I don't want you thinking I'm not doing my job."

"Believe me, Ruby, I'd never think that. Lord, I've watched you practically scrub the paint off the walls."

"Well, it sure needs something done in there. I don't rightly know what to do."

"What happened?"

"She wasn't ugly or anything like that." Ruby hastened to assure her. "She just gently pushed me from the room, and politely closed the door in my face."

"Well, I call that ugly." Emma was aghast. "Not only ugly but downright rude."

"I don't want to get her in trouble. She's probably not used to having someone messing with her things. She seems like a sweet child, Miss Emma, sort of shy like I was at that age. I thought maybe you could explain to her what my job is so she'd understand better. Tell her I'll put everything back the way I found it."

"I've half a mind to make the snippy little miss clean her own room."

"Don't do that, Miss Emma. She's too young to do a thorough job and it needs a good turning out."

"How could it? Lucy hasn't been here anytime. Everything in there's brand new, except the furniture, and it's been refinished and newly upholstered."

"I don't know but something in there needs a good airing out. It smells in that room." Ruby wrinkled her nose in distaste. "I mean, it really smells bad."

Chapter Eight

Emma fastened her blouse with trembling fingers after promising Ruby she would talk to Lucy. The maid's disturbing disclosure had frightened Emma. Without a doubt she knew she was deceiving herself. Whatever fiendish thing Anthony had assaulted was not gone. Instead, like any clever antagonist, it had found a new and more subtle way to infiltrate her home. It was all her fault. She knew she had unleashed some malevolent force almost as soon as the door to the south wing had been opened.

Damn Richard. He should have told her the house was haunted. Why not warn her about what lurked inside the empty rooms? It must have something to do with his first wife and child. But what happened to his family that they sought to return? Did he feel so responsible he couldn't bring himself to tell her they walked the halls of those rooms? And, *who* was it that was walking so destructively? The child, or Lettice, his wife? And even more important, why had Emma ignored his wishes and not kept the door locked on that particular Pandora's box? Silly, foolish old woman wanting to please and surprise her niece. Well, she would surprise her for damn sure. Wait till some night Carol woke and realized there was something in the room with her. She shuddered at that monstrous thought. Then, she resolutely straightened her shoulders, finished dressing and with heart thumping, marched like the warrior she was, down the long hall to Lucy's room. The door was closed but Emma heard voices. Assuming the child's mother was inside, she turned to leave. The opposite door opened and Carol stepped out.

"Well, good morning, Glory. Aren't you up bright and early?"

"No, not really."

Emma didn't know what to do. She did not want Carol around when she confronted Lucy, but was puzzled by the sounds coming from the room and was determined to get an answer.

"I thought I'd see if your daughter wanted to go shopping." Emma couldn't believe the quick lie that sprang from her lips.

"I don't know about Lucy, but I know somebody else that would love to." Carol made a face. "That's the worst thing about working. Bosses have this unreasonable hang-up about their employees being at the office." She brightened. "Hey, I could meet you guys for lunch."

"That would be nice." Emma took a deep breath, then plunged. "Carol, am I imagining voices in my twilight years, or is there someone else in Lucy's room?"

The younger woman pressed her ear to the child's door. Turning back to Emma, she smiled. "Nope. It's just Lucy. She's been doing that a lot lately."

"Doing what, dear?"

"Talking to herself. It's probably a result of the divorce. I asked Wendell and he said children react in different ways."

"But Carol, that's not Lucy's voice."

"I know. The first time I heard her it threw me for a loop. However, my talented daughter showed me how she could change her voice for each of her dolls. It was real eerie. Who knows, maybe she's going to be an actress."

"She didn't talk for them before you moved here?"

"Oh, sure." Carol shrugged. "She talked with them all the time. It was just that no matter who was supposed to be speaking, it always sounded like Lucy. Anyway, Doc said it was harmless. That children do lots of strange things to compensate after a divorce."

"I suppose." Emma was growing more apprehensive the longer Carol spoke.

"I bet she'll jump at the chance to go shopping, though." Carol raised her arm and knocked.

"Who is it?"

"Your mother, silly. Whom did you think?"

"Just a moment."

Emma stared in amazement. "Do you always knock on your daughter's door?"

"Just lately," Carol admitted. "She's suddenly become a privacy freak. Has a fit if I barge in unannounced, which is totally ridiculous since we shared a room in that cramped apartment. However, some wonderful relative spoiled her with a beautiful room of her own and she guards it like a dragon. See what you did, you old sweetie pie?"

"Yes," Emma responded weakly. "I'm afraid I do."

The door opened and Lucy stood framed. It was difficult to imagine something so small, so lovely, so fragile could pose a threat, but looking past the blonde curls, the perfect features, looking deep into the china-blue eyes, Emma thought she caught a glimpse of hell.

***

Emma was delighted when Lucy accepted her invitation. After that earlier brief second when she felt something foreign, almost evil, Emma could see no difference between Lucy and any other young child. She'd grabbed the older woman by the hand, almost dragging her out to the car, then sat bubbling over with excitement.

The more she giggled and squirmed, the more confused Emma became. She began to be horrified she had ever thought anything was wrong or failed to understand what had made her feel there was. She hoped she was not becoming like some of her friends, so obsessive over their homes they conjured up dozens of ridiculous reasons for keeping guests at bay. Was it possible that deep in the recess of her subconscious she had imagined this? After all, the sequence of events was too bizarre to be believable and for years, Jessie had told her she was getting dotty. Damn it, if Emma wasn't beginning to believe her, especially since she seemed to be the only one aware something was amiss. Talk about letting your imagination run riot. Other than Stanley going berserk, which could be the start of seizures; and Ruby telling about Lucy barring her from her room, other than that, nothing had taken place that anyone besides Emma had witnessed. The strange noises, that terrible night in the foyer, the horrifying dream, the sensation of something alien lurking in Lucy's eyes, only Emma had experienced these. She drew in a deep, quavering breath. What if the real reason no one had mentioned these disturbances was that there weren't any? What if she were growing senile and beginning some form of dementia? She tightened her grip on the steering wheel and audibly groaned. "Oh, dear God, not that."

"What's the matter, Auntie Em?" Lucy reached across gently patting one of the clenched fists. "You know. I just love calling you that. It's like being Dorothy in the *Wizard of Oz.*"

Emma turned, forcing herself to look deep into the depths of the little girl's eyes. There was nothing mirrored there but concern.

"I'm fine, my precious." Emma fought back a wave of nausea. "I'm having a hard time deciding where to take such a pretty young lady shopping."

"I really, *really* like the shoe stores most." She sighed wistfully. "Especially the ones that have tennis shoes with lights."

Like magic, Emma's black mood vanished. If she was going crazy, so be it. That was entirely out of her control and by damn, she would at least enjoy the time she had left.

"You're putting me on." She giggled.

"No, I'm not." Lucy was adamant. "They really do. If I had a pair I'd show you, but Mama says we don't have money to spend on fads and foolishness." Her face fell.

"Well, thank heavens, Auntie Em does. Besides, Auntie Em also knows the exact location of three wonderful shoe stores. Surely one of them carries such marvelous slippers."

The child launched herself, throwing her arms around Emma's neck, hugging her so violently, she had trouble keeping the car on the road.

"Watch it," Emma cried happy. *This was fun.* "Wait till we're parked, otherwise we're liable to end up in the hospital with no shoes at all."

At once, Lucy quieted, sitting prim and proper the rest of the journey, unable to keep a huge grin off her face.

***

It took a moment for their eyes to adjust from the sunlight to the darker interior of the restaurant where they'd arranged to meet Carol. When they did, Emma was pleased her niece had already arrived. Tim Mason was with her.

"Look, Mama. Look at my feet." Lucy danced across the floor, the tennis shoes winking brightly, attracting the smiling attention of other diners.

"Aren't they beautiful?"

"I think colorful would be a mite more appropriate," Emma commented dryly. "It's certainly nice to see you, Tim. I'm delighted you could join us."

He rose, pulling out her chair. "Well, I never could resist the pleasure of three beautiful ladies."

"Spoken like a true southern gentleman. You'll have to keep an eye on this one, Carol. He can charm the . . ." She abruptly stopped, remembering the child's presence.

"Charm what, Auntie Em?"

Tim's lips twitched. "The spots right off a leopard. Wasn't that what you were going to say?"

"I told you he was a smooth talker," Emma warned again. "Probably has a tongue like satin."

"Promise?" Carol giggled, locking eyes with Tim.

"Carol." Her aunt gasped, before laughing. "La, I've listened to enough of Jessie's soaps to know times have changed, but this new generation will never cease to shock me."

Lucy had been following the exchange. Failing to make much sense of it, she'd grown impatient.

"Mama, you didn't answer. Don't you love my new shoes?"

"I surely do, darling. Though I'm afraid your aunt is spoiling you."

"Wait till you see what else I got. Show her, Auntie Em."

Looking sheepish, the other woman opened a huge sack and begin displaying various articles of clothing.

"Emma Thatcher." Her niece fixed her with a stern and reproving stare. "I didn't intend for you to dress my child. It's more than enough letting us live with you. I don't know how I can ever repay you," she ended crestfallen.

"You can't, because there's nothing to repay. I'm having a ball. I haven't had this much fun shopping in years, and I've certainly never purchased anything even remotely as exotic as shoes that light up. Wouldn't Richard have loved this?" For a moment her face fell.

"I love you, Auntie Em. I only wish everyone could have a special someone like you in their life." The younger woman covered the older one's hand with hers. "Just please, don't let us take advantage of your time, love, or checkbook."

"Don't worry." She brushed away the tears that were forming. "I only do what I want to do. If you don't believe me, ask Jessie."

"I'll drink to that." Tim hooted, holding his water glass aloft. "In fact, I bet we could ask almost anything of Jessie and get a ready answer."

On that statement, the waitress arrived and the luncheon continued in a lighter vein.

Chapter Nine

Emma intended speaking to Lucy about cleaning her room on the ride home. However, as soon as they piled their purchases in the trunk, the child climbed in the back seat, curled into a tight ball and fell asleep. Emma was surprised, thinking her a little old for naps, but decided the day's excitement had done her in. Truth be known, a short snooze would not go amiss with Emma either. With that in mind, she drove home as fast as the speed limit allowed.

She had scarcely pulled into the garage before Jessie burst out the back door, arms wind-milling in the air, shrieking at full volume.

"Good Lord, Miss Emma, I been waitin' and waitin' fer you. Gets yourself in here right now."

Emma's heart plummeted. She had tried laying her fears to rest but admitted she had been pretending, enjoying the simple outing for all it was worth. Deep inside she knew she was not going crazy. Knew something strange was taking place in her beloved home. Knew she had been putting off the moment when she would have to confront whatever had moved in, or if not moved in, then awakened from some hellish slumber. One cry from Jessie and her peace was shattered.

"What's the matter?" Emma's heart beat so hard her chest ached. "For God's sake, Jessie. What is it?"

"You won't believe. Jest you get in here like I says." She turned and ran back into the house.

Emma ran too, forgetting all about Lucy in the back seat. "Where are you, dammit?"

"In here."

Emma entered the empty kitchen screaming in frustration. "How the hell am I supposed to find you when you've gone off and left me?"

"You needs your skinny ole legs to move faster," came the disembodied voice. "I'se in the libraries."

Emma was shaking like a leaf.

What had happened to get Jessie in such a state?

"In here I says."

Emma came to an abrupt halt, then promptly burst into tears.

"What's the matter with you? I thought you'd be plum outta your mind."

"I am, you ole fool. But what do you mean scaring me half to death?" Emma was sobbing loudly, madder at Jessie than she could ever remember. "You almost gave me a heart attack."

"I think you must be needin' some vit'mins," Jessie said. "Lately, you been acting like a bitin' sow. Maybe you need a good dose of castor oil like my mammy used to give us kids when we got them moody spells."

Jessie was right. She had over-reacted. Of course, Jessie seemed oblivious to the cloud hovering over Shadow Lake, so she would not be sharing Emma's fears. She felt terrible for yelling at her like she had. Naturally, Jessie was excited, and naturally, she could hardly wait to show Emma. She was flooded with guilt.

"I'm acting like a hysterical idiot, Jessie. I sincerely apologize." She gulped hard, trying to stop the flow of tears. "But please, please, don't make me take castor oil."

Jessie's arms opened wide. Emma fell into them, comforted by the love and soft warmth of Jessie's massive breasts.

"I know somethin' worryin' you. I 'spects when you feel like the time be right you gonna tell your ole' friend all 'bout it."

Emma nodded.

"Sometime it do a person a heap of good to get stuff off their chest."

Emma snickered.

"Now what?"

"You must be carrying a really heavy load, cause I don't see where you've ever gotten any off of yours."

Like two children they hugged, giggling. At last, Emma composed herself, blew her nose, stepped back and demanded, "How many?"

"Last count, I got fives. Don't that jest beat all? That silly Cleo crawlin' in the Master's desk drawer to have them babies when we has a nice soft bed all fixed in your room."

"I don't care where she picked. I'm just so relieved she's finally delivered. I thought for a while the poor thing might explode." Emma crossed to Richard's desk. A bottom drawer had been left ajar. Cleo's silky head popped out.

"There are six now. How long ago did you last check?"

"'Bout an hour. I 'spects that's it then. Ain't they jest 'bout the prettiest little babes you ever seed?" Jessie crossed to Emma, bent by her side and gently touched one tiny ball of fur. "How come they all white? They don't look like their ma or pa."

"The darker markings will show up when they're older. Oh, Jessie, they are so beautiful."

"What's beautiful?"

"Lucy. I forgot all about you. I'm sorry."

Emma rose, beckoning her over. "Look what we have."

The child's eyes grew round. "Oh, Cleo. You've had your babies." She reached out, then snatched back her hand. A thin trickle of blood appeared on the surface. "She bit me."

"Cleo." Emma was aghast.

"Don't worry none, Miss Emma. It jest be she a new mama. Besides, this her first litter. That's not a bite anyways, only a little scratch. You come with me and I fixes you up. You too big a gal for that to bother you none. I 'spects Cleo be glad to let you see her babies in a few days. Right now she jest actin' like a good mama and protectin' them."

Jessie took Lucy's uninjured hand leading her from the room. Emma watched, and a terrible sense of foreboding engulfed her. Jessie was more right than she knew. Cleo was protecting her young, but in the dear good Lord's name, what was she protecting them from?

***

The new arrivals were the main topic of conversation throughout dinner. It was not until dessert that Carol asked her aunt if she would mind if she left Lucy with her while took in a movie with Tim. Emma was relieved since she still had not talked to the child. This would give her that opportunity.

The doorbell chimed before they left the table. Lucy jumped up to answer it. She quickly reappeared with Tim. Before anyone realized what was happening, she pushed him into her vacant chair and crawled onto his lap.

Carol's eyebrows rose. "I think I'm getting competition, the little minx," she whispered to Emma, though her eyes were troubled.

At once Lucy began telling about the birth of the kittens. Suddenly, she lifted her scratched hand to his lips begging, "Won't you please, please kiss it. That will make it all better."

Tim planted an embarrassed peck on the proffered band-aid. "Now, it's fixed."

"Oh, yes," Lucy gushed, throwing her arms around his neck, pressing tightly against him. "That felt sooo good."

Before she could stop herself, Emma cried, "Get down, Lucy. Tim doesn't want you crawling all over him. You'll crease his pants."

"Yes, Lucy." Her mother was frowning, sensing something strange. "It isn't polite to climb on grown ups. You're too big for that now."

"Am I, Tim?" Coyly, Lucy ducked her head peering from under lowered lashes.

Good grief. The child was coming on to him. She was acting like some simpering tramp.

Emma could not believe what she was seeing.

"I said get down, Lucy." Carol was aghast.

"If you say so, but I'll bet Tim doesn't mind." Lucy slid slowly, almost seductively, off his lap.

"Mr. Tim to you, and you'd better not forget it. Now you march straight to your room. I'll speak with you later."

She threw her mother a look of pure hate, turned on her heels and stomped up the stairs.

"I'm sorry, Tim." Carol's face was ashen. "I can't imagine what got into her."

"Probably seen too much television. I don't know what's going to happen if they don't get the networks to clean up the tube."

"I hope that's all it was. I never saw her act that way before. Are you sure you don't mind if I leave, Aunt Emma? I don't want you saddled with a problem child."

"She'll be no problem," Emma assured her. "At least, none I can't handle. You enjoy yourselves. Lucy just needs the attention of a man. I'm sure she misses her daddy making over her."

"I guess, but . . ." Carol looked perplexed.

"But what, dear?"

"But she seemed so different."

"She's fine, Carol. You're making a big deal out of nothing. Miss Emma can handle Lucy. Hell, Miss Emma could handle the devil himself." Tim chuckled.

Emma's heart skipped a beat.

Oh, please, Tim. Please don't tempt fate.

She smiled, then waved them out the door before doing something she had never done before. Crossing to the crystal whiskey decanter sitting on the huge mahogany sideboard, she poured a shot into a cut-glass tumbler and drank it down neat.

"You 'bout ready for that talk?" Jessie had silently slipped into the room and been observing her.

"Jessie, I think I may be going mad."

"Not yet, but somethin' 'bout to drive you there. I never seed you act like this."

"We'll talk, Jessie. I promise. But first, I have to tuck Lucy in for the night."

Chapter Ten

Emma was not surprised to find Lucy's door closed, but was startled by the volume and intensity of the voices coming from within. Emma thought the child must be reenacting the angry scene with her mother. She tried distinguishing what was being said but the solid oak door muffled the words. Her eavesdropping a failure, she gave up, knocked and nervously waited.

"Oh, it's you." Lucy stood with one hand on the frame, the other on the door barring Emma's entrance.

"Yes, dear. I wanted to check and see if you needed anything. We were so late arriving home today, and with the excitement over Cleo's kittens, I decided you probably hadn't had time to put away your new clothes. I thought I might help."

"Has Mama left?"

"She and Tim went to the movies."

"I bet he would have asked me if she hadn't acted so ugly."

"Lucy." Emma gently pushed against the door forcing the child to back up so she could enter. "Your mother and Tim had already made arrangements. I'm sure there will be times when you're included on some of your mother's dates, but not tonight, and not always. You'll have to get used to that. I know you've been spending lots of time with her, but mothers have a life of their own. You mustn't get angry if you're left out on occasion."

"I'm not." Lucy pouted, tossing her curls. "I don't care what *she* does. She shouldn't have yelled at me like she did. Tim liked me sitting on his lap."

"You'd better stop calling him Tim, dear. Your mother's already warned you."

"She's just jealous."

"Lucy, that's not true. Your mother is teaching you manners. You're a child and Tim is an adult. It's not respectful to address him by his first name."

"He doesn't care."

"How do you know? Did you ask him?"

She ducked her head. "No."

"Well, he might have minded but was too polite to say so. That's what manners are about."

"I think they're dumb."

"The older I get, the more I agree, but like most things, they are a fact of life."

Emma walked over to the bed heaped high with the day's purchases. "If you'll hand me your new clothes, I'll help put them away."

Dutifully, Lucy began emptying the bags. She handed the apparel to Emma who hung it in the closet, all the while furtively sniffing the air for any peculiar odor, and stealing glances into every corner to see if anything seemed amiss.

But nothing did. To Emma, it looked like a young girl's room straight out of some decorating magazine. The walls were painted a bright yellow. Around the top of the ten-foot ceilings ran a wide, white papered border of daisies entwined with pale-blue ribbons. The same pattern was repeated in the quilted spread covering the antique bed with a perky white organdy dust ruffle peeking from beneath the edge.

The one large window was curtained in the same crisp organdy and a huge overstuffed chair in the daisy print was piled high with stuffed animals. A large rag rug in every color of the rainbow spread itself gaily over the floor, almost obscuring the varnished hardwood planks. A chest of drawers and matching night stand were the only other pieces of furniture. Everything but the bed, chest and stand were newly purchased. Emma had been absolutely thrilled with the way it turned out, and in fact, still was. It was such a bright, cheery room. She was unable to imagine anything dark and sinister emanating from it. She wondered again if she was becoming an imaginative old fool.

"That's all." Lucy gathered the sacks rolling them into a big ball, vainly attempting to stuff them in her waste basket.

"I don't think they'll fit."

She shrugged, letting them spill out onto the floor.

"Would you mind if I sat and visited a spell?" Emma asked.

"I guess not."

She crossed the room intending to sit beside Lucy on the bed, but the child leaped to her feet. Taking Emma's hand, Lucy pushed her into the already overcrowded chair.

"You sit here. My babies love company."

Emma felt she'd been slyly out-maneuvered, but nevertheless wedged herself among the many dolls.

"You're not like your babies, are you Lucy? You don't like company."

"Sometimes I do." She had returned to the bed.

"Ruby told me she came to visit and clean your room, but you pushed her out the door."

"I don't know her. Why would she want to talk to me?"

"Well, you enjoy chatting with Jessie."

"Yes, but she gives me cookies and makes me laugh."

"Ruby can't bring you treats but she's very nice and fun to be around. Besides, I pay her to keep the upstairs clean. It upsets her if she's not allowed to do her job."

"I can clean my room."

"Ruby does this to help pay her way through college. You wouldn't want to take away her income, would you?"

Lucy said nothing.

"I'm sure you're proud of your room and want it to stay fresh and pretty."

"I love my room. Oh, Auntie Em, I love it here. I don't ever, ever want to leave. I won't have to, will I?"

She jumped off the bed throwing herself against Emma's legs.

"Certainly not until you're ready, darling." Emma was taken aback by the child's intensity. "However, I suspect your mama will want her own home someday."

"Why?"

"Lucy, your mother is young and pretty. She'll be wanting to find you a new daddy. Mr. Tim and Mr. Phillip are already hopping around like frogs after flies."

"So who cares. She can leave, but I can stay. Please." She lifted her face to Emma. A look of anguish passed over her features. "I *love* Shadow Lake."

"I know you do, darling. I felt the same way when Mr. Richard brought me here as his bride. I didn't ever want to leave, but you'll have to go with your mother when she makes that decision."

"No."

"Sweetheart, you'll always be welcome."

"It's not the same. This is my very own room. It belongs to me. This is *my* very own home. I'll never, ever leave."

Emma did not know what to think. She was amazed anyone this young could become so obsessed with a house. She wondered if, this too, was common in children of divorced parents.

"Let's talk about it some other time. Your mother has no intention of leaving anytime soon."

"Auntie Em." She reached for the older woman's hand and gently began stroking it. "You don't have any children of your own, do you?"

"Carol is the closest to a child I'll ever have." She smiled at Lucy. "So, I suppose that makes you my almost granddaughter."

"Does that mean you're going to give Shadow Lake to my mama when you die?"

"I don't have anyone else."

"What about me?"

Suddenly, Emma was uneasy. The soft stroking no longer comforted. Now it felt sly and sinister.

"You're only a little girl, darling. Your mother would be the person you'd inherit the house from, if she didn't sell it."

"Why would she?"

Emma flinched. The small hand was squeezing hers painfully.

"Well, there could be any number of reasons. Sometimes people need extra money, or they want to live in another location. I truly hope your mama will choose to stay here, but I can't promise what someone else will do, or what the future might bring."

"I'd *never*, ever sell Shadow Lake." She rose haunted eyes to Emma. "What if Mama dies? Would you leave Shadow Lake to me then?"

"Lucy. What a terrible thing to say. I don't even like thinking about it. Now, you quit worrying about this nonsense. You're staying right here in this room for a long time yet. I don't like listening to such foolish talk. You get on your pajamas and go to bed. All you need to fret your pretty head about is what to name Cleo's kitten when you pick one out."

The child threw her arms around Emma's neck hugging her hard.

"I get one for my very own?"

"I promised, remember?"

"Yes, you did." She stepped back looking thoughtfully at her aunt. "Do you always keep your promises?"

"I try."

"You are nice. I'll be such a good almost-granddaughter, you'll want me to have Shadow Lake, just like you want me to have one of Cleo's babies.

Emma said goodnight and slowly left the room. With heavy heart she walked down the stairs into the library where she knew Jessie would be waiting.

"You want some of this here tea I brewed up, or you wants 'nother shot of the strong stuff?"

"I'd prefer whiskey, but I think I'd better stick to tea."

"You 'bout ready for that talk?"

Jessie poured. As quickly as the liquid flowed into the cups, the words spilled from Emma into the listening ears of her old friend. She began from the first inkling of anything strange, clear through the conversation she had just finished with Lucy. When she ended, she was trembling. The horrified expression on Jessie's face did nothing to calm her.

"Jessie?"

Emma was becoming alarmed. She had never seen her like this. Jessie had not opened her mouth throughout the long recital, not even taken a sip of tea.

"Jessie, are you all right?"

Still without a word, the cook rose and walked to the sideboard, returning with the decanter and two glasses. Still without a word, she removed the cups, saucers and teapot, then with great dignity, poured two shots of whiskey. She tossed hers down, refilled the glass and sank heavily into the chair across from Emma.

"Good Lord. We done got us a haunted house."

"My word, but it felt good telling you."

"Why you wait so long? I thought us done too old to keep secrets."

"It wasn't a secret." Jessie's remark made Emma ashamed she had not confided sooner. "I just didn't want you thinking I'd lost my mind like you're always saying."

"That's nothin' but silly teasin' to get you all riled up. You know I don't really think any sech thing. You a sharp ole woman for your age. Jest 'bout as sharp as me," Jessie ended graciously.

"Then you do believe me?"

"Well, I heerd Rascal too, 'member? And I ain't said nothin', but I been thinkin' it kind of strange he don't come up here with me no more. He jest sort'a hangs round my little place. And I sure 'nuff saw that boy havin' that crazy fit, and Ruby already done tole me 'bout Lucy and how funny she were actin'."

"And you saw the marks on the window. The wadded up letter."

Jessie nodded, eyes round as saucers. "Who you think spookin' this place? And Lawd, why after all these years would some ghost be hauntin' us now?"

"I think I know why they've come." Emma leaned close to Jessie whispering. Both casting furtive glances over their shoulders. "I think it began when I decided to open the south wing. I believe that's the real reason Richard kept it locked."

"You think he know the house were haunted?"

Emma nodded.

"But he used that wing with his wife and little chile."

Again, Emma nodded.

Jessie's eyes grew even larger, if possible. "Then that must mean it be either he wife and chile comin' back or," her voice fell to a whisper, "or both of them doin' the visits. Lawd, Miss Emma. What on earth happen to turn them into haunts?"

"I don't know, but I sure as hell plan to find out."

"How you gonna do that?"

"I'm about to pay his sister a visit. I haven't seen Maureen in too long anyway."

"She sure don't come here much."

Emma's face darkened. "Maybe we've discovered why."

"You gonna tell Miss Carol?"

"Not yet. Not till after I've talked with Maureen. Carol seems unaware of anything strange. Actually, it hasn't made itself felt as strong as it did that night in the hall. I don't want to get it stirred up again."

Jessie shuddered at the mention of that dreadful evening. "When is you goin'?"

"I can't leave until after the weekend. We've got that dinner party planned for Carol, remember? I'll call Maureen and see if she's free around the first of next week."

"You gonna tell her what's happening?"

"Yes, but I want to see her face when I do. Well you be able to manage while I'm gone?" Emma frowned. "I'm scared to leave Carol and Lucy alone with it."

"I gets Ruby to come. We sleeps in your room. I make Billy Bob stay at my place, close by."

"That's a wonderful plan. I promise I won't be gone more than one night."

"You best not. I don't know how good I gonna be, spendin' nights with ghosties."

"I feel so relieved, so much better now that you know."

"I wishes I could say the same."

With those profound words, Jessie poured each another drink. They sat sipping quietly, the hairs on their necks prickling as if they felt the unseen presence of a third party lurking in the shadows.

Chapter Eleven

"You look like hell."

"Takes one to know one," Jessie retorted pulling out a chair, sinking wearily onto the soft cushion. "I didn't sleep none last night. I don't know how you been keepin' this all to you self without sure 'nuff losin' your mind."

Emma carefully removed the coffee pot from Jessie's clenched fist and proceeded to pour each a cup. "I probably haven't any left to lose."

Emma had risen at dawn thinking she would fix a treat for her old friend, but Jessie, like Emma, was already awake. By the time she made it to the kitchen, bacon, eggs and grits were emitting taste-tempting odors, and a basket of fluffy biscuits, butter and homemade jam was laid out in the cheery breakfast nook.

This was a favorite room of both. A maple table and chairs nestled comfortably in the curve of a bay window which matched the same enchanting lake-side view as that glimpsed from the library. Adding extra warmth to the soft cream walls and hunter-green trimmed woodwork was the sunlight, which more often than not, shone through the many faceted panes. Emma had vetoed curtains, not wanting to shut out a single inch of the picturesque lake, but had made up for lack of pattern in the quaint colorful needlepoint pillows thrown carelessly onto a maple bench.

An enormous hutch was filled with her collection of ceramic soup tureens in every imaginable shape, size and color. A small sideboard stood opposite, over which hung a primitive oil depicting a scene from the past. A cotton field–the worker's sacks slung across their backs as children and dogs frolicked around their feet as they walked the snowy white rows of cotton. Here too, huge rag rugs in multicolored stripes crisscrossed the wide planked floors, and if not forewarned, the kalediscope of riotous colors was apt to take away one's breath.

It was almost impossible to be depressed sitting amid such cheerful surroundings. Normally, both women's spirits rose each morning they drank their coffee there, but not today. Today both hearts were heavy, confused, and even worse and more alarming, frightened.

"Well, you sure nuff won't has no minds, and I won't neither if us don't get to the bottom of this. I'se thought and thoughts, Miss Emma. I jest can't figure out why Mr. Richard's family be comin' back to haunt us. What you reckon happened to them folks?"

"I have no earthly idea." Emma rubbed her forehead where a dull ache had started. "Richard never mentioned his family but once, right before we married, when he told me he was a widower. He then informed me he kept one wing of his home closed off. The wing he'd lived in with his first wife and child. He said they were both deceased." She shook her head sorrowfully. "Damn, Jessie, I assumed it was because the sight of those rooms brought him so much pain. I was so in love I'd have believed anything, or done anything, and never questioned it."

"I know, little darling." Jessie reached over to pat the trembling hand. "You had no reason to 'spect anything else. Mr. Richard were a good man. I worked fer him all those years and I never 'spected nothing were wrong in this house. I been cleanin' it from top to bottom, all but that wing." She shivered slightly before continuing, "and no boogie man ever jumped out before this. You don't need to be thinkin' you should'a knowed any different."

"But ghosts, Jessie. Do you realize we're sitting here drinking coffee and discussing ghosts? Hell, I don't even believe in them."

Jessie's breath quickened and her eyes darted to each corner of the room.

"So all right," Emma admitted ruefully. "I used to not believe in them."

"I gots a story to tell you." Jessie took another fearful glance over her shoulder. "This be somethin' happened a long time ago to my Gran'na." Her hands were shaking slightly. "I never knew to believe it or nots, but my mama swore it were true."

"What story, Jessie? I thought I knew all your stories."

"I thought this one were jest silliness so I never tole you. Anyway, my Gran'na cleaned houses like me and my ma, and she got hired to do one of them old, old houses downtown. She needed the work in the worstest way, so were real happy, but from the first day she went there, she say the place act funny. The front door kept comin' open and she kept hearin' somebody walkin' up the stairs, but no one be there when she go look. Finally, she say somethin' to the people who owned the house and they just sort'a laughed. They told her if she stay long 'nuff she see and hear more than that. They tell her things get moved from one side to the next during the night, but to jest pay it no mind."

"You're not putting me on? That story has been around for years. I believe it's about one of the Bed & Breakfasts. In fact, several of them are supposed to be haunted. Frankly, I figured it was a tall tale."

"I don't know 'bout no tall tales. I jest be tellin' you what happened to my gran'na." She poured each another cup of coffee. "Anyway, gran'na didn't want to stay but she need the money bad. She figured what could doors do, anyway? Then, 'bout after two weeks, she were in the kitchen sweepin' the floor. She look up and see this woman all dressed in black. Gran'na started to ask her what she want, when the woman jest walk plum through the wall. Gran'na lit outta there right then. She didn't even go back for her money, bad as she need it."

"Well, I guess there are things that go bump in the night. I feel confident your grandmother wouldn't have made that story up."

"What make ghosts, Miss Emma? I mean, what would make them come to Shadow Lake?"

"How the devil should I know? What little I've read or heard, a spirit returns to the place where it can't find rest."

"Why can't it find rest?"

"Jessie, I don't have a clue. I suppose if it's been in an accident, murdered, or something that cut its life off sooner than normal, then it can't accept the fact it's dead. It keeps returning until something guides it to the other side where it finds peace."

"What we needs us then is a guide."

"I'm only repeating what I saw on television. There was a program on seances and that's how this woman medium explained it."

"Did that medium lady say ghosts would hurts the peoples live in their houses?" Jessie's eyes widened. "'Pears to me like Mr. Richard's family ain't being any to 'spitable."

"You might know I'd switch channels and miss the rest of the show," she answered in disgust. "Jessie, that's what has me so concerned. This ghost, or entity, or whatever it is, seems evil. I feel that in my own spirit. It's not some poor lost soul wanting to find rest. It's a malevolent, wicked creature. I think it wants to inflict pain, and I cannot for the life of me imagine Richard married to someone like that."

"I wishes we knowed more about that woman and her honey chile."

"What child?" Carol bounced into the room. "Ummm, that smells wonderful."

"I'd just mentioned Richard's family. We were wondering about his child."

"Lisbeth? I think she was around Lucy's age when she died."

Emma and Jessie stared open-mouthed as she heaped her plate high.

"Uncle Richard told me all about her." She continued serving herself, oblivious to the undercurrents. "He said she was his precious darling and he was devastated by her death."

"How did she die?" Emma could scarcely get the words past her throat.

"You know, he never said." Carol's forehead puckered as she tried to recall. "Isn't that strange? I remember him telling me how much she loved Shadow Lake, but I don't believe he ever told me how she died. I suppose I hated to ask. I could tell discussing it distressed him."

"When was this, Carol? I mean, when did you and Richard have this talk?"

"Oh, years ago. I think that time I stayed for the winter. I asked him about the south wing being locked. That brought the subject up."

"And?" Jessie could keep quiet no longer.

"And he said it was where he lived with his first wife and daughter. That he didn't want to go there again because it made him sad."

"So, you don't know how they died?"

"No, but surely you do." She stopped buttering a biscuit to look at Emma. "Didn't he tell you what happened?"

"No."

"That's odd. You never asked?"

"Like you, I didn't want to bring back painful memories."

"Oh, these are so good. I'm gonna weigh a ton if I keep this up." Carol picked the last biscuit from the basket. "How was Lucy by the way? Did she give you any trouble?"

"No, darling. She was perfect once you left. I went to her room and we had a lovely time hanging up her new clothes and chatting. Children always enjoy acting tacky in front of their parents."

"Tacky isn't how I'd describe it." Carol poured more coffee. "If Tim hadn't been here, I swear I'd have flipped her bottom up and applied a good one."

"And how often did someone apply a 'good one' to you?" Her aunt grinned knowingly.

"Maybe once," she admitted shamefully, "but Aunt Emma, I don't know what to think. I mean if she'd been a few years older, I'd have sworn she was coming on to him."

"Miz Carol."

"You were in the kitchen, Jessie. You didn't see the way she rubbed against him." Her hands shook so hard her fork fell to the floor. "She was acting like a cat in heat."

"Carol, stop that. Lucy's a child. She's simply wanting a man's attention now that her father is unavailable. You'll have to guide and show her the proper way to get it."

"I'm over-reacting. Is that what you're implying?"

"You and Lucy. You've both been through a tremendous ordeal. It's going to take time to get your feelings and emotions back on a normal keel."

"Little girls get really bad flirty, and don't you think they don't know what they doin'. They know men like cuddles and lovin'. It's up to the mama to teach them how to use all that 'natural no how' in the right way. That's why these little girls have their papas wrapped so tight 'round their thumbs."

"But Lucy seemed so—so sensual."

"She came on a little too strong, that's all. You'll have to explain she's gotten too old to be crawling onto men's laps, hugging and kissing them."

"Yes." Carol grimly attacked her breakfast. "Yes, I most certainly will."

"Darling, I've been thinking of visiting Maureen. Would you mind?"

"Heavens, no. I don't want you making any change in your lifestyle because we're here. I think you should go see her, especially if I don't have to go with you. What an old battle ax."

"Carol. Maureen is not any such a thing. You and Jessie are wrong. She's always been lovely to me, although she can be a mite hard to take if she doesn't get her way."

"You gots that right." Jessie rose and lifted the egg platter. "I best scramble some more of these 'fore little miss gets here. She do like my eggs."

"Everyone loves everything you cook. In fact, I'm not positive that's not Tim's main attraction."

"Forget it, Carol." Emma smiled in spite of her fears and nagging headache. "Tim likes food, but believe me, the largest and most important appetite a man carries is below his belt, not the one above in his stomach."

"Aunt Emma."

"Now that is the good Lord's trufe." Jessie's laugh could be heard all the way from the kitchen. "That's the pure dee gospel trufe."

Carol glanced at her watch. "Speaking of little girls, I'd better check on mine. I'll run upstairs and get her moving. She's late. I will be too if I don't get going."

"I'll take care of her, dear."

"Thanks, Aunt Emma, but I want to tell her good-bye and give her a kiss even if I am peeved." She pushed away from the table. "When are you going to Maureen's?"

"I don't know. I haven't called her yet."

"Well, you're a sweetie to check on her." Carol giggled. "I still say she's a royal pain in the butt."

"Shall I pass along the message?" Emma's eyes twinkled.

"Don't you dare. Now, gimme a kiss. I've got to hurry."

Emma smiled as she watched her niece rush through the door, heels clattering noisily as she flew up the stairs.

Suddenly, a shrill scream split the air. The sickly noise of a body thumping and bumping down each step reached Emma's ears, leaving an ominous silence afterwards.

"Good Lord. What that noise?" Jessie pushed through the swinging door leading from the kitchen.

"Carol," Emma whispered, so shaken she couldn't rise from her chair. "Jessie. I think Carol's fallen down the stairs."

"Oh my Lawd."

At last, Emma moved. Together they dashed down the long hall to the front foyer. The sight of Carol's still form sprawled at the base of the stairs, blood flowing freely from her head, brought them up short.

"Carol." Emma sank weakly to her knees beside the prostate form. "Oh, my darling. Jessie. Quick, call 911. Jessie?"

Not hearing the other move, Emma looked up, afraid of what she might see, frightened that Carol's fall might have been too much for the old woman's heart. What she saw was even more chilling than what she imagined. Jessie was standing, wide-eyed, face ashen, staring at Lucy at the top of the stairs.

"Jessie."

Abruptly, Jessie shook herself hard. "I'se gonna call, Miss Emma. I be right back."

"Lucy, what happened?"

Slowly the child descended, a huge doll clutched tightly in her arms. "Mama was coming up the stairs as I was going down. I had my doll in front of me and didn't see her. I guess we bumped."

"How could you not hear her, Lucy? Those shoes she's wearing make a terrible clatter."

"Well, I didn't." She continued to the bottom of the stairs, where she paused to gaze dispassionately at her mother. "Poor, Mama. Is she dead, Auntie Em?"

"I hope to hell not."

Emma had been frantically feeling for Carol's pulse. She finally detected a faint beat.

"Run get the throw off the sofa in the library, Lucy."

"Why?"

"I need to wrap your mother in something warm."

"Why?"

"For shock, child. Now move!"

"I think someone's at the front door."

"Lucy, for God's sake."

"I'll see who it is." She swung about and with short ladylike steps minced to the door. "Oh, it's *Mr.* Tim." Her upper lip curled scornfully.

Thank you Lord, Emma prayed silently.

"Let him in, Lucy, then go get the damn throw like I told you."

Chapter Twelve

"Pull behind the house, Tim. I think I caught a glimpse of Lucy through the trees. They must be at Jessie's."

He no more than rounded the curve of the back drive before the cook appeared. She was running as fast as she was able. Her breath puffing in tiny spurts out of plump cheeks, her apron flapping in the breeze, both arms stretched out to Emma.

"What happened? How's my precious baby? Where is she? Did you goes off and leaves her all alone? Is she gonna be all right?"

"Stop it, Jessie." Emma was out of the car before the engine died. "If you don't calm down and get control of yourself I'll be making another trip to the hospital, and heaven knows, I haven't the strength." She hugged her friend hard. "Shush now. Carol's going to be fine. She has a broken collarbone and wrist, a head split open, luckily in the hair line, and a slight concussion. However, nothing's wrong that stitches, a cast and time won't heal."

"Oh thank you, sweet Jesus." Jessie burst into tears. "I knowed my baby were dead when I seed her lyin' so still and white, all that blood pourin' outta her head." She pulled back looking Emma straight in the eye. "You ain't jest tellin' poor ole Jessie stories to make her feel good."

"I wouldn't dare. She's going to be all right. Honest." With that pronouncement, Emma broke, sobbing as loud, if not louder than the other.

"Hey, stop that. You two keep on that way and the whole yard will be flooded. Come here." Tim tried embracing both. "Whew, I've heard of 'hugging and chalking' but this is ridiculous."

Jessie started giggling. Even Emma smiled.

"Mr. Tim, you sure was a sight fer sore eyes. I don't knows what you was doing here so early in the mornin', but the blessed Lord must'a sent you."

"Miss Emma told me I could bring Stanley to see the kittens. He was waiting in the car."

"Poor child, he won't ever come back. He'll forever associate Shadow Lake with an ambulance and someone getting hit over the head."

"Naw, he's okay. I dropped him off at his mother's as I followed the ambulance in. He couldn't wait to tell her about the hurt lady and the big white car with the flashing light."

"How's my mama?"

Emma turned. Lucy stood, tears streaming down her cheeks.

"How's my mama, Auntie Em? Oh, I hurt her so bad." She began crying in earnest, great racking sobs shaking the small frame. "I almost made my mama die."

Jessie scooped her up. "Hush, chile, you mama fine." Her eyes locked with Emma's over the little girl's head. "Lucy been so upset. *'Bout an hour,*" she emphasized the words, "after we been to my house, Lucy started shakin' and gettin' all nervous over her mama's fall."

"She didn't fall. I pushed her."

"Lucy." Emma's face turned grey.

"I did. She reached for me and I think I sort of shoved her." The child's sobs ceased, her brow creased in concentration. "I mean, I think I did," she whispered.

"Don't be a silly goose." Tim plucked her from Jessie. "You didn't push your mama down those stairs. You ran into each other at the top. Your mama lost her balance and fell."

"Really?"

"Really. Now, I've got to check on a crew at the Langley house, but after that, I promised Stanley lunch to make up for not seeing the kittens. Would you like to come?"

"Oh, could I?"

"If Tim's sure you won't be too much trouble." Emma could scarcely keep the relief she felt from showing in her voice. She was dying to talk to Jessie but didn't know what to do about Lucy. This would solve everything.

"I'll be a little lady."

"I'm sure you will, sweetheart." Emma carefully watched Tim fasten the seat belt across the lap of the young girl detecting nothing strange or sensual in her behavior.

"Have a good time. Tell Stanley he can pick out his pet in a few days. That's probably better anyway. By then, they'll be almost ready to take home."

Lucy waved until they were out of sight. At once, Emma turned on Jessie. "What happened? What did you see? When I looked up from Carol you were white as a ghost."

"Don't even says that word."

"Well, what was wrong? I was screaming at you to call 911, and you weren't even listening."

"I weren't hearin'," Jessie informed her, "coz I were lookin' at that chile. Emma, there were something standin' by that baby's side." Her eyes grew enormous. "That weren't only Lucy at the top of those steps."

"What do you mean?"

She shook her head trying to remember. "Something else were there. Something dark and wavery likes."

"You saw the ghost?"

"I saw something," Jessie snapped. "An whatever it were, it were taller than Lucy. Not by much. Jest a mite."

"A child? You saw a ghost child?"

"Lawd, I don't know. I jest knows I saw a ghost something."

"You're sure it wasn't a reflection?"

"I tell you what, you bossy ole' woman, I don't rightly knows what I saw, but it weren't no damn 'flection. 'Flections don't have eyes that send shivers clean through a person's bones."

"It had eyes?"

"Now, what I jest say?"

"What else?"

"What else, what?"

"What else did it have? Did it have on clothes? What color was its hair? Who did it look like?"

"Lord, if you don't beat all. You think I gonna jest march my fat butt up them stairs, steppin' right 'cross the body of Miss Carol, and pretty as you please, pat that ghostie on the shoulder and says, 'Why hello, Miss Ghostie, let me takes a *real* close gander at you. Let me see jest *who* it is you be 'mindin' me of.'" Jessie snorted loudly in disgust.

"You said, miss. That must mean it's a female."

"How you figure that? I don't even know why I say miss."

"It was an unconscious slip." Emma put on her best detecting face. "Without consciously realizing it, you were subconsciously aware the apparition was female."

"Un-huh. You can jest sub-un-and whatever consciously all you wants. I don't know nothin' but that whatever that thing was, it most near caused this black woman to pee in her panties."

"I wish I'd seen it."

"Oh no, you don't. And as soon as you and that ambulance gone, I grabbed Lucy and we scooted right over here. I weren't stayin' in there with that ghosties and Lucy acting so strange. She were 'bout as spooky as the goblin."

"She's not now."

"No, but it took least an hour of bein' away from the house 'fore she even act like a little girl, and 'fore she show any signs of frettin' over her ma."

"I noticed that."

"What?"

"How unconcerned she seemed. She acted as if she didn't care whether Carol was hurt or dead, and honestly, I had the feeling she'd prefer her dead."

"Miss Emma."

"It's true. She seemed almost disappointed when I said she was alive, and certainly never showed the least bit of remorse over the accident."

"What's we to do?"

"Well, we certainly won't be having a dinner party this weekend, so I'm going to try and run down Maureen. Surely she'll be able to throw some light on this."

"Lawd. I hopes so."

"Me too." Emma took a deep breath. "I guess we'd better clean up. Carol bled all over the floor."

"And it still there. I didn't worry 'bout no cleanin' when you left. I jest took my feet outta there as fast as they carry me."

"I have to pack Carol a bag. Phillip was with a client at the hospital. He had a fit when he saw who the ambulance was unloading, and a bigger one when he saw Tim race up behind it. Anyway, to make him feel part of the program, I told him to come out later for some of her things."

"Those are two nice young men. I don't know how she ever gonna chose."

"Me either." Emma smiled wistfully. "I certainly can't offer any sage advice. I never had such an entertaining problem."

Jessie simpered. "Well, I 'spects I might jest be able to give her a little 'vice. You knows, I always has me a fine string of fishes on my line." She strutted all the way to the back door of the house where she paused. Turning to Emma, she graciously offered, "You can go first."

"Thanks a bunch, Delilah." Taking a deep breath, Emma slowly turned the knob on the door.

"See anything funny?" Jessie's head peered around the other.

"Your black cowardly puss." Emma marched down the hall to the front foyer leaving Jessie to follow.

The only thing that seemed amiss was the pool of drying

blood at the foot of the stairs, but when the women approached it, both cried aloud and clutched one another tight.

Through and around, holding them spellbound, was the blood. Bright red smudges smeared over the white marble floor in a pattern of bare footprints. Footprints like those left by some youngster cavorting in a mud puddle.

When her heart slowed enough she could speak, Emma asked, "Could Lucy have done this?"

Jessie shook her head. "Lucy never been outta my sight since you left and never once had her shoes off. I told you I seed a ghostie chile."

"What in God's good name happened to Richard's daughter to make her into something as unholy as this?"

At once the doors started. Slamming and banging till the house reverberated with the noise.

All at once Emma screamed, "Shut up you damn little bothersome brat! Shut up this instant!"

The silence was so intense they could hear each other's heart pound.

"I has a feelin' we a bit too ole' fer these kinda' goin' ons. I believe we gonna have to get us some hep."

"What kind of help?" Emma's eyes darted from one corner to the other, alert for what the next second might bring.

"They a woman I heerd tell 'bouts. I knows people that uses her. She a white witch. She be better at this stuff than we is."

"A witch? Really, Jessie."

"I 'spects a witch be jest what we needs," Jessie was whispering. "Goblins and witches don't much like one 'nother."

"How do you know?"

"I heered tell."

"Well, I'm not interested in having some witch spouting mumbo jumbo in my house. Seems to me we've already got enough of the devil's own."

"I say she were a *white* witch."

Emma's chin jutted out defiantly. She spoke loud and clear so that who, or whatever, was there, might hear and know war had been declared.

"I'm not afraid of whoever this is, and I can handle doors banging and bloody footprints without anybody's help but yours, Jessie."

"Mine?" Jessie's eyes rolled to the back of her head. "Why you need me if you so all fired unafeerd and," she added darkly, "I might 'vise you remember. It do pushes people down the steps."

Emma chose to ignore the sinister reminder. "Let's get busy and clean up this mess before Phillip arrives and starts asking questions. After he leaves, we'll call Ruby and Billy Bob. Ruby can stay at your house with Lucy. You, Billy Bob and myself are going to get rid of whatever is haunting Shadow Lake."

"How you gwine do that?"

"We're going to perform an exorcism."

"A whatism?"

"Never you mind. You wash off the floor while I pack Carol's bag. Then, we'll call the others. When they get here, you fill them in on what's been happening. I have to go to town."

"Why you got to go there?"

"To get some information from the library and buy whatever I might need."

She gingerly skirted the pool of blood. Holding tight to the rail, Emma slowly climbed the stairs.

Jessie watched till she reached the top safely before leaving for her cleaning supplies, all the while muttering aloud.

"There ain't nothin' worse than a bossy ole white woman that's crazy as a loon and stubborn as a mule, but one thing, and that's having to work fer one."

Chapter Thirteen

"I not sure this be too good a' idea," Billy Bob stated flatly.

Emma ignored him, ticking off the list of items she had placed on the large serving tray he held.

"You sure you know what you're doin', Miss Emma? I ain't never had no truck with ghosts before." He glanced over his shoulder. The tray shook like jelly.

"They're not going to bother you half as much as I am, if you don't hold that tray steady and end up spilling something," Emma threatened. "Anyway, you don't have to worry. I've got everything we need to defuse that ghost. I intend to send it back where it belongs in nothing flat."

"Does you now?" Jessie was peering around the kitchen door, anxiously watching for any signs of strange activity.

"I got a book at the library."

"Well, ain't that somethin'? Don't that jest gives you the relief, Billy Bob? Knowin' Miss Emma read a book?"

"No, ma'am. I read a heap of books, but I ain't never read one on how to get rid of spooks. I don't 'spects I wants to, neither."

"Quit being such 'fraidy cats." Emma's lips curled in disgust. "I'm telling you, I've got the situation well in hand. I did my research thoroughly. I even went to see Father Lester at St. Michaels Catholic Church. Now there's a landmark with some history. I'd think they would have spirits floating all over.

Anyway, he gave me holy water, communion wafers and the cross from around his neck the Pope had personally blessed."

"I'd feel a heap better if he'd given the neck and body that went with it," Jessie grumbled. "How come he didn't offer to come heself?"

"It's too involved. A priest can't perform an exorcism without permission from his higher up, who has to get permission from his higher up, and so on, and so on. We'd be dead by the time help arrived from that quarter."

"That state of sit'ation is just what I 'feerd of," Jessie complained.

"Don't be so damn silly." Emma pulled two more items from a paper sack. "Here's a cross for you and one for Billy Bob."

"Where the garlic?" The young man grabbed the cross, holding on to it like it was his lifeline. "I thinks I read where ghosts don't much like garlic."

"That's vampires."

"Mercy, sweet Jesus. Don't even mentions them." Jessie's eyes rolled backwards. "We see us some toothy Drac'la, this ole' lady drops dead, cross or no crosses."

The tray made a steady rattle.

"Stop it, Jessie. You know there isn't any such thing as a vampire."

"Yes, ma'am, that I does. Jest like you know there ain't any sech thing as ghosts."

Bested, Emma remained silent.

"You reckon we could use us Anthony? You say he done run that spook off 'fore," Billie Bob asked through chattering teeth.

"It might not hurt. Has anybody seen him?"

"He probably over at Jessie's. I jest meander over that way and see," he hastily offered.

"No. The cat was here earlier. He'll turn up once we get started."

"Him and what else? Is we really gonna do this?"

"You're damn right. Actually, Jessie," Emma's eyes sparkled

with the gleam of battle as she announced, "I'm looking forward to it."

"Oh, dear Lord, save us." She threw her apron over her face, but quickly removed it to follow the two who were quietly tip-toeing down the hall to the foyer.

"Now. Set the tray on that chest, Billie Bob." Emma directed him to a huge Bombay standing against one wall.

"What all that stuff fer anyways?" Jessie eyed the tray and its contents skeptically. "I don't see how they gonna help."

"Well, they certainly will. First, we have crosses to ward off evil."

"Please and thanks you, dear Lord," Billy Bob whispered, holding his against his chest with both hands.

"The flashlights are in case the dratted thing manages to knock out the lights."

"Whoa. I don't like the sound of that. You knows I don't cotton kindly to walkin' 'round in the dark."

"That's why we have flashlights, Jessie. Don't worry. I've thought of everything," Emma bragged.

"Excuse me, if I ain't so sure 'bout that." Jessie sniffed.

"We have a Bible."

"Why?"

"To read certain passages guaranteed to send this demon straight back to the hell it came from."

"What else?"

"Holy water."

"What that do, Miss Emma?"

"I'm not positive, Billy Bob."

"Ha. That's 'bout what I figured."

"Enough, Jessie. I'm talking to your nephew. The book I read mentioned something about holy water being good if the spirit tried touching you . . ."

"Touchin' you. Lawd. Lawd, gets these feets plum outta this door." But despite her cry, Jessie's feet stayed rooted to the floor.

". . . because sometimes you can throw it on them, rendering them helpless."

"How you gonna throw it on somethin' you can't sees?" Billy Bob's eyes were growing larger the longer Emma sought to reassure him.

"They might manifest."

"They what you says? They man-i-whats?"

"Manifest, Jessie. They might materialize. Let themselves be seen. If they do, then we've got holy water to throw on them."

"Miss Emma, that don't make me feel any too good. I 'spects I don't want to see this here ghost, and 'sides that, I think I gots a belly ache." His face was drained of color. He did appear to be in pain.

"That settles it. I'll do the damn thing alone. It's not like it would be the first time I met it head-on and alone. And then, if you'll recall, I managed fine and wasn't even properly prepared."

"I don't think you so properly prepared now, neither," Jessie spit out, "but, I guesses I stay. Crazy ole' white woman like you gonna need a able-bodied person to get you outta the trouble you bound to get into."

"Thanks for your vote of confidence, Jessie."

"I doin' this 'gainst my better judgment," Billy Bob announced, "but, I won't go off and leaves you two ladies alone. 'Sides, if I did, my ma and Ruby would eat me 'live quicker than that ghostie ever thought of."

"So, arm yourselves, soldiers. Make sure you've got your cross, flashlight and holy water handy. I'll take the Bible and wafers."

"What they fer?"

"The wafers were in a cabinet next to the holy water. I think Father Lester simply threw them in for good measure."

"You probably figure if you stick one in the ghostie's mouth, he jest up and explode like that Jaws in the movie."

"That's a pretty good idea."

"Yeah, and I wants to be there watchin' when you talks it into swallowin'."

"Her, Jessie. Remember, this is Richard's daughter, Lisbeth."

The laughter came from every room. Billy Bob and Jessie grabbed Emma. The three clutched each other while the sound changed and grew. At first it was the merry peal of a child, but soon grew louder and more raucous. In seconds, it became deafening. A shrill shriek, so painful, they released each other, putting their hands over their ears, desperate to shut out at least a portion of the ear-splitting racket. It went on and on. The prisms on the hall chandelier shook and reverberated when suddenly, one by one, each of the crystal goblets on the dining room sideboard exploded.

"Damn you to hell." Emma was furious. "Those belonged to my mother. Now you've really pissed me off."

The laughter stopped. A cold chill settled over the hall. Jessie's teeth began chattering but Emma clamped her jaws tight, determined not to give it the satisfaction of knowing how cold and frightened she was.

"I has been lookin' and lookin' but I don't see nothin' handy to throw that water on," Billy Bob's voice wavered. His fingers gripped his cross so hard they had turned white.

"Shhh. I don't either."

"Dear, sweet Jesus," Jessie moaned. "I prays we don't."

They stood for at least ten minutes. Nothing else happened.

"You want me to go clean up them goblets? I think the ghost done had his fun and left."

"She's here. I feel her."

"Where, Miss Emma?" Billy Bob jumped a foot.

"Not physically. I mean, I sense her presence. She's toying with us."

"Well, she better quit, cos I 'bout ready to leave. This ole' heart done took all the toyin' it can stand."

They heard the footsteps then, loud and distinct coming from the south wing.

"What now?"

"She's teasing us, Jessie. She's trying to lure us into her territory."

"Then I 'spects I jest stays down here in our territory, thank you," Billy Bob firmly announced.

"We're going up. If she wants a fight, she's getting one."

"I don't 'member this bein' put to no votes, does you Billy Bob?"

He was too scared to voice an opinion. He meekly followed Emma up the stairs without a word, terrified of being left alone. Jessie, grumbling, brought up the rear.

"You'd best hold hard to the rail. You knows what that ghost already done once," she warned.

The door to the wing was closed. As they approached, it slowly opened. Another icy wind enveloped them.

Emma spoke loudly, wanting whatever lurked in the apartment to hear. "Isn't this too childish? I guess next time we'll have to wear jackets since our visitor's determined to give us such a cold reception."

"Ain't plannin' on no next time," Billy Bob whispered to Jessie. "I think this time likely be my last."

"Well, here we are," Emma chirruped brightly. "So, what else have you got in mind?"

The door behind them banged shut. Immediately, all the lights were extinguished.

"Lawdy."

"You have your flashlight, Jessie. You don't need to panic. Turn it on."

Three streams of light pierced the darkened hallway.

"I don't see nothin'. So I 'spects it time we be goin'."

"Not yet, Billy Bob. Let's take a quick look around."

She entered Carol's bedroom, Jessie close by her side. They flicked the switch by the door, but as expected, nothing happened. Next, they shone their lights around the room but it failed to reveal anything amiss.

"What that Lisbeth gettin' up too?"

"Your guess is as good as mine."

"By the way, where you think Billy Bob is?"

Emma whirled around. "I thought he was behind you."

"Un huh. I thought he by you, but the truth is, he ain't nowheres."

"Billy Bob." Emma ran from the room. "Where the hell are you?"

The corridor was dark, empty and ominously silent. The door to the hall was still closed and now, so was the door to Lucy's room.

"Whew, I don't like this."

"Me either," Emma admitted, crossing the hall and reaching for the knob. "Damn!" She jerked back her hand.

"What happened? Why you holler?"

"The knob. It's hot enough to fry an egg. It burned the hell out of my hand."

"Sweet Jesus. You think that ghost be doin' that to Billy Bob? You reckon he in there gettin' roasted?"

"We have to find out." Emma pounded on the door. "Billy Bob, are you in there? Say something, damn it. Billy Bob." She banged on the door time and time again, frantically calling his name, but no one answered. Exhausted, she stepped back and began weeping. "Oh Jessie, what have I done? I'm such a prideful old fool. What have I let that young man in for?"

Jessie, as frightened as her friend, tried to comfort her. "Shhhh. He be all right. He a big boy, and 'sides, he got the cross and holy water."

"Right. And now the ghost has all three." She wept louder.

"Hush." Jessie put her finger to her lips. "Be quiet and listen. I thinks I hear something."

Emma stopped crying. Creeping to the door, she placed an ear against it. After listening a moment, she moved aside to make room for Jessie.

The cook's eyes widened in horror.

"Lord, Emma, that sound like . . ."

"I know. And Jessie, I swear I've heard those same kind of noises coming from here before."

"If they be what we thinks they be, I not so sure Billy Bob in any hurry to leaves."

"This is terrible. I'd rather the ghost were cooking him."

"He might not agrees."

"We've got to rescue him. We can't let some demonic spirit seduce the boy. Hell, for all I know, he could lose his soul in the process."

"I thoughts you said you read a book?"

"It didn't mention sex."

"What's we to do?"

Jessie was frantic at the thought of her nephew being damned for eternity. As if reading her mind, the ghost began taunting them. Seeming to realize they had heard and recognized the sound of lovemaking, the sighs and passionate whimpers increased in volume.

In a flash, Emma unstopped the vial of holy water quickly pouring it over the door handle, at the same time grasping and turning the knob. She and Jessie almost fell over each other in their haste to enter, but both stopped abruptly at the sight of the young man laying on the bed. His eyes were closed. A look of ecstasy flooded his features.

"Billy Bob." Emma ran to his side. "Wake up."

He lay silent.

"You get you black butt outta that bed this minute, you hear me, boy!" Jessie reached down shaking him like a rag. "You better open your eyes and move 'fore I slap you plum silly."

"Aunt Jessie?" He sat bolt upright. "What you doin' here?"

"Saving your worthless soul and you better be damn glad I is." She unceremoniously hauled him off the bed and onto his feet. "We gettin' outta here, now."

"But Jess . . .," Emma began.

"I say now. I'se had all this huntin' and hauntin' I wants and all I tends to have. You jest has to lock heads with this ghost 'nother time cause your soldiers has done deserted."

She pushed Emma and Billy Bob before her. The door to the

south wing swung open as they approached. Jessie marched them through, down the stairs and out the front door. As soon as they stepped outside every light in the house blazed.

"Damn her." Emma stalked up the porch steps but Jessie grabbed her from behind holding tight.

"Nots tonight, I say. You done spokes with Miss Maureen. She glad you comin' fer a visit and you gonna do jest that. Miss Carol safe in the hospital and there ain't no worry 'bout her. You leaves tomorrow and takes Lucy with you. She be outta harm's way there. Me and Ruby sleep at my house and clean up all them broken glasses when the sun out bright and shiny. You go see what Miss Maureen know 'bout this here mess. Then we come up with us a new and better plan."

"You're exactly right. That is the smart thing to do." Emma patted her friend on the shoulder. "You've really thought this out."

"I ain't dumb as some folks think." Jessie lifted her nose, sniffing audibly, then cast a stern eye on the young man at her side. "Billy Bob, jest what the hell was happenin' to you?"

In shame he ducked his head. "I can't says. It were too personal."

"Was that thing trying to make love to you?" Emma couldn't keep her mouth shut.

"Miss Emma." He backed away, unable to meet either's eyes. "If you ladies done with me, I best be gettin' home." He ran across the lawn to where he had parked his truck.

"You leaves in the mornin' and you grill Miss Maureen. Ruby and me find out jest what happened to Billy Bob. We'll compare us notes like they do on those TV po-leece shows. I bet when we get all the facts, we can do us a bang up job of gettin' that spook outta our pretty house."

Feeling she had gained the upper hand, Jessie took Emma's arm marching her to her house and to Ruby, who was anxiously awaiting news of the exorcism.

Chapter Fourteen

"If you aren't a sight for sore eyes." The tall thin woman, with iron grey hair and aquiline nose, as patrician in appearance as a Roman aristocrat, pulled Emma into a warm embrace. "You never change. My Richard might not have married a beauty second time round, but he did pick quality. A woman who ages as gracefully as wine."

"Someone just like his sister," Emma replied, not certain if being compared to a vat of old liquor was a compliment or not.

"You bet your sweet ass." Maureen laughed loudly.

She loved shocking people, early on realizing pithy remarks coming from such a dignified looking lady were apt to raise a few brows. However Emma, long accustomed to her juicier epithets, and in fact, not above using a few herself, was unfazed.

"Sugar, what happened to your hand?"

Emma thrust the bulky bandage behind her. "I'll explain later. First meet Lucy, my niece's daughter. She's been so excited about coming, especially after learning your neighbor had a pony, that she's wiggled all over the car like a puppy looking for a paper. I thought we'd never get here," she whispered in an aside.

Maureen took a hard look at her sister-in-law realizing in that first quick glance she had missed something. There were new lines etched around Emma's eyes and a droop to her shoulders never before there.

"You look a mite peaked, honey." Maureen frowned. "The drive must have been hard. You sit and relax while I walk Lucy next door and introduce her. I'll sashay right back. We'll put up our feet, let down our hair, have a couple of stiff snorts and swap the dirt."

"Sounds heavenly, if it's all right with Lucy."

"Oh, yes, Auntie Em." She grinned in delight, having decided the other woman not near the formidable figure she had first appeared. "I'd love to meet everyone, especially the pony."

"Now, isn't she just too precious? I swear, Richard would have eaten her alive." Maureen beamed.

It never ceased to amaze Emma how the handsome woman could be so intimidating to adults, yet immediately charm children and animals.

"We'll get your bags inside and you can unpack when you feel like it. Willard!"

Lucy jumped a foot, startled by the enormous bellow issuing from the swan-like throat with the very lady-like pearl choker encircling it.

"Willard. Where the hell are you?"

The child made a Herculean effort to keep from laughing aloud at the ludicrous figure that minced into the room. He was extremely short and so round he looked like the Philsbury Dough Boy. Enormous dimples and an oversized apron dwarfed him, doing nothing to dispel the illusion.

"I was in the kitchen preparing a teeny bit of something special for you to enjoy with your little snort."

With a flourish, he continued into the room waving his hands wide, displaying fingers literally covered in rings of all shapes and sizes. Lucy, fascinated, watched in awe as the bejeweled hands encircled Emma, pouting lips bestowing a moist kiss on each cheek.

Laughing, Emma returned the hug and kisses. "Every time I visit you're threatening to leave, yet here you are, still looking after this irascible woman."

"And so I am." He beamed.

"She must pay you a fortune."

"You'd better believe it, doll."

"What's irascible?"

Willard, still embracing Emma, whispered in her ear, "Bitch." Then turned to the child, patted her on the head, and lisped angelically, "Feisty, sweetie. Miss Maureen can be sooo feisty."

Maureen had taken in the entire show, had heard his whispered aside, had known in fact, she was supposed to. It was a game, very like the one played by Emma and Jessie. Neither would have it otherwise.

"You bet I pay him plenty. Take a gander at that diamond pinkie ring he's sportin' and you'll know I'm being bled dry," she grumbled fondly. "Don't know what I need with some old fool of a houseboy, anyway."

"*Butler*, darling. I do wish you weren't so doddery you forgot what my position was. See why I have to stay?" He cast his eyes contritely toward the floor as Maureen cast hers to the ceiling. "Poor dear." He sighed as if the weight of the world lay on him. "She needs me."

"Yeah, yeah." Maureen chose to shrug off the daily argument. "Bring in Emma's bags, whatever you are this week." She took Lucy's hand. "The old fool does switch jobs, you know. Week before last he was cook." She paused frowning. "I could have sworn it was houseboy this week."

"She knows damn well I'm the butler." He puffed up till Lucy thought he'd burst like a balloon filled with too much air. "And Miss Emma, I will be more than delighted to carry in the luggage of such a lovely and gracious lady. One of the kind I'm totally unaccustomed too."

"Bullshit." Maureen clapped her hand over her mouth.

"Don't worry." Emma thought of the unwelcome visitor waiting for her at home. "Lucy's probably heard worse."

"I'll take her next door." A much subdued Maureen pushed the child toward a pair of French doors. "They're expecting her.

As soon as I get back we'll have that drink and see what Willard's concocted. I do hope he's not experimenting with some new recipe."

He rolled his eyes, before mincing out the front door.

"Oh hell, I can tell he is," she announced flatly, "and if that's not bad enough, since I've insulted him, he'll pout all evening."

"Stop worrying." Emma couldn't care less what he served. She wanted to get the conversation rolling and see what Maureen knew about Richard's first family. "We'll praise it to high heaven regardless. He'll soon be back in good spirits."

"That might be easier said than done," Maureen warned. "You should have tasted what he served the bridge club. I was so embarrassed I could have died."

It only took a few minutes to unpack. Emma wasn't planning more than an overnight stay. By the time her hostess returned, she was comfortably settled in one of the fat overstuffed chairs flanking the living room fireplace.

The house had always delighted her. It was a hodgepodge of whatever appealed to Maureen, all jumbled together, many of them, items collected from the exotic lands she had traveled through. An exquisite Dresden ballerina, the lace skirt sheer as a cobweb, soft pastels glowing like muted jewels, stood on the mantel in sharp contrast to a pair of massive antique candelabra soaring half-way up the vaulted ceiling. Having once graced the altar of some Catholic church, they fascinated Emma with their symbolism-brass carved wheat sheaves, clusters of grapes, lilies of translucent white china, and seven candles representing God's number for perfection. Emma almost coveted them, along with any number of other unique accessories Maureen had scattered among the large chintz furniture she favored, delighting the eye no matter which direction one faced.

Thomasville, Georgia, where Maureen lived, was located close to the Florida border leading to Tallahassee. It was a visitor's delight with the shops, restaurants and B.& B.'s so charming, that like Amelia Island, it was constantly being featured in *Southern*

Living magazine as one of the most captivating spots in the south. Emma earnestly wished she was here to enjoy the town and her hostess' hospitality. She dreaded the thought of trying to pick Maureen's brain for what could perhaps be unhappy, and possibly frightening, memories.

"Good. I see you've started without me." Maureen stepped through the French doors. "Ha, but I spy mine waiting. Good for Willard, the butler!" She roared loudly, at the same time sinking into the opposite chair, raising her glass in a silent salute and drinking deeply. "Now, to what do I owe this visit and what the hell did you do to your hand?"

"Yes, sweetie, what is wrong?" Willard swished into the room balancing a platter piled high with nachos. He placed them on the round coffee table between the women, poured himself a drink from the sideboard, pulled up a chair, sinking into it after breaking off a large section of chips and popping them into his mouth. "Yummy. And you better not say otherwise, Miss Feisty Maureen."

"You know better. I adore these." She leaned across the table handing a napkin to Emma. "You'd better grab some while they're still available."

"As long as you don't nosh too long. I'm dying to discover why this sudden desire to share our company." His mouth was so full she could hardly understand him. "Not that we weren't thrilled, you understand."

"Willard."

"Well, it's true." He tried pouting but his nacho stuffed cheeks made it impossible. "You know damn well we both figured something was up."

Emma quickly gulped her drink, took a deep breath then blurted, "I need your help. I hate it, because I know you despise being asked personal questions, but I simply must. I have to find out about Richard's family."

"His first wife and child?" Maureen frowned, curious why after all these years they would suddenly be of interest to her sister-in-law.

"You've got to help me," Emma wailed desperately. " I don't know where else to turn."

"Of course I will, if I can." She'd never seen Emma so distraught. "However, I don't understand the importance, or why you're so upset. That was over years before you met."

"It's a long story."

"Oh, doll, we love stories. Let me get you girls another drinkie poo, and we'll chatter away."

"I hope you love ghost stories."

Maureen gasped. The glass she held slipped from her fingers. Willard leaped to his feet but both women ignored him. Maureen was staring hard at Emma, looking deep into her eyes. What she saw caused her to shudder, burying her head in her hands.

"Something ugly has happened," her voice was flat.

Emma nodded.

"I thought you'd chased it away."

"Me?" Emma was incredulous.

"You were such a no nonsense type person. When nothing was ever mentioned, or ever . . ."

Willard on hands and knees mopping up the spilled drink, demanded, "What never happened? Maureen, you cat, you've been keeping secrets. You know I hate that."

"Shut up, Willard, and quit wiping that carpet. You're rubbing a hole in the nap."

"What did you think I'd chased away?" Emma whispered.

"I'm not even sure," her sister-in-law whimpered, then turned lashing out. "Damn it, Willard, get me that drink."

"Yes, madam." He rose in a huff, nose in air, before peevishly snapping, "And you stop fooling around. Give Emma a straight answer. No wonder you have a reputation for being such a bitch."

His remark fell on deaf ears, both women totally involved in the other. "Why didn't you warn me about Lisbeth?"

"Lisbeth? Richard's daughter? What the hell are you talking about?" Maureen demanded.

"I'm talking about the monster that's haunting Shadow Lake."

"Have you lost your mind? Lisbeth was no monster. She was adorable. Everyone loved her."

"How did she die?"

"Why are you so fixated on Lisbeth?"

Emma leaped furiously to her feet. "Because the ghost of a child is haunting my home and turning it into sheer hell."

Maureen sank further back in her chair, almost seeming to wither and shrink before her visitor's eyes.

"Get me that drink, Willard." She sighed heavily. "Make it a double. Sit down, Emma. I don't know anything about a ghost. All I can tell you is what happened to me when we moved there. I've never told anyone before, and . . ." her voice broke, tears slipped unchecked down her cheeks.

Emma was aghast. She had never seen Maureen display any strong emotion, certainly never seen her weep. She felt terrible, but was nevertheless determined to discover the reason for the tears, no matter the cost.

"Here, my darling." Willard handed her the drink, before taking a crisply-folded handkerchief from his pocket and tenderly wiping her face. "You just stop this right now. I didn't mean it when I said you were a bitch." He kissed her wet cheek.

"I am though." She sniffed loudly. "A selfish bitch, or I would have warned Emma years ago. I'm so sorry."

"Warned me about what?"

"The house. It's evil."

"My house? The same house I've lived and loved in for years? Really, Maureen." She was scornful.

"It is," she wailed, "because if it isn't, then I'm some kind of filthy perverted horror."

"Bite your tongue." Willard threw his arms around her. "You are not a single one of those nasty words. You are a sweet angel; that is what you are."

"See why I really keep the old fool around?" Maureen's wet eyes peeped over his shoulder. "He's the best, dearest friend anyone could have."

"And don't you forget it." He pulled her into his arms rocking her like a child.

"Wait a minute. Did you say when you moved there?" Emma was frowning hard in concentration. "I thought the house had always been in the family. That you and Richard were born there."

"I can see him leaving that impression. He loved the idea of an ancestral home, and actually *it was* built by family. Just not our immediate family. It was my mother's great-uncle who built Shadow Lake. He left it to his brother, who left it to his son, and so on to Mother. We didn't move there until I was about eleven and Richard fourteen."

"Well, that's news to me. I wonder what else Richard omitted. Obviously something important the way events have been shaping up."

"The house had been vacant for years when Mama inherited. Mama didn't want to move because there was going to be so much restoration involved, but Dad and Richard fell in love with it and were determined."

"What about you?"

"I thought it was beautiful once it had been redone. I was especially happy about having my own room and getting to decorate it the way I wanted."

A cold chill swept her. She knew, but asked anyway. "Which was your room?"

"The small bedroom in the south wing. Richard was older so he got the large one, though I honestly think he preferred mine. He always said it was so cozy."

Emma shivered, remembering the way the house, particularly that room, seemed to warm and embrace every male.

I think that's why he made it Lisbeth's room. He thought she'd feel that way too."

"And now, it's Lucy's."

"You've opened the south wing?"

Emma nodded.

"But why? Richard told me he never wanted it opened again."

"It's a damn shame he never told me," Emma sharply retorted. "Why in the hell was it locked in the first place?"

"I don't know."

Emma couldn't believe her ears. "What do you mean, you don't know?"

"He never gave me a reason. I assumed it was the fact that losing his wife and child was so terrible he didn't want the memories brought back."

"For God's sakes. Ya'll are making me nuts," Willard burst out. "First, Emma talks about ghosts. You get hysterical over the house being evil. And now, you hint at some mysterious tragedy in your brother's life. I don't get any of it. Will somebody please start at the beginning and fill in the spaces for this ignorant ass?"

"Yes, Maureen, fill us in from the beginning. Why have you called my beautiful home evil, and why on earth, would you think of yourself as vile?"

Chapter Fifteen

"I'm about to tell you something I've never told a living soul. Something so shameful, I can scarcely speak the words. So Willard, if there's anything in the oven, turn it off. Once I begin, you won't want to leave."

"You are so right. Wild horses couldn't drag me away." His fingers fluttered weakly in the air. "It's only stew." His eyes opened wide as he whispered in awe, "I must have had a premonition."

"Emma, as dear to me as you and Richard are, and were, you must have noticed I'd do almost anything to get out of one of your invitations."

"Jessie commented on it, but honestly, I never paid much attention."

"You were totally absorbed in my brother." Maureen smiled sadly. "You were so good for him, especially after what he'd been through. I'll always love you for that."

Tears sprang to Emma's eyes. "Thank you."

"However, I still don't understand why you think his daughter is haunting Shadow Lake." She took a deep breath. "Anyway, I don't believe in ghosts. I doubt I can be of much help if you think the house is haunted."

"But . . ."

The other held up a silencing hand. "While I still have the

courage, let me tell you why I hate it. Although to be truthful," her voice broke as she shamefully lowered her eyes, "I could be using the house for a scapegoat. It could be the straw I'm grasping because I can't bear to think I'm such a foul human being."

"Maureen, believe me." Emma leaned over, lifting her friend's chin, forcing her to look directly at her. "It isn't you. Whatever you're about to reveal isn't of you, or the house, but some dreadful evil force lurking within. I swear this on Richard's grave."

"Oh, if I could believe that my whole life would be changed. I'd feel a weight lifted you can't begin to imagine."

"If you girls don't quit tippy toeing around and speaking in riddles I'm going to expire."

He puffed out his cheeks in a tremendous pout.

Maureen ignored the familiar moue. "You remember how different times were when we grew up? Sex wasn't mentioned, much less discussed, and certainly never in front of a child. Why, when I had my first period, I thought I was bleeding to death because no one had explained menstruation."

Emma turned away hiding the smile threatening to erupt at Willard's horrified expression from Maureen's frank disclosure.

"Anyway, the point I'm trying to make is that I was ignorant as a billy goat when it came to that particular subject."

"Not a very apt comparison, dearie." He snickered lewdly. "Billy goats are famous for being soooo randy."

"Either shut up, Willard, or go stir your stew."

Chastised, he sank back in his chair, a hand clasped over his mouth.

"But once we moved into Shadow Lake," her voice quavered. "Once we moved there, everything changed."

"What? What changed?"

"Me. My thoughts and feelings. Everything."

She rose and began pacing. "At first, I was happy. I loved my new room. Richard and Papa were thrilled out of their minds with the quote, unquote, ancestral home. Richard was nicer to me than he'd ever been. He took me fishing and included me in several of his pet projects. I was ecstatic."

"And then?" Willard asked.

"Then, my sweet innocent, it began. Dreams. No, not dreams, nightmares. Hideous, horrible, filthy, disgusting nightmares." She buried her face in her hands.

Emma felt terrible. She knew she was causing her sister-in-law excruciating pain but also knew it was necessary, as necessary as lancing a festering boil.

"They grew worse. More and more vivid. More explicit. I was sickened, disgusted, yet at the same time curiously fascinated. Soon they became so vile, even the fascination left. I'd try staying awake nights so I wouldn't dream." She turned her back unable to face them. "Then they turned into thoughts. Even awake I was flooded with them." She wrung her hands. "Oh, dear heaven. I was only a child. I didn't know what to do. I couldn't tell Mama. I certainly couldn't talk to Papa or Richard. I thought I'd go crazy."

In a blinding flash of insight Emma knew what the nightmares were, nevertheless, she had to ask, had to verify her suspicions. "Tell me, Maureen. You can talk to me. What were the dreams about?"

"Sex. Dirty, filthy, perverted acts of sex." She crossed to Emma's side kneeling at her feet. "Please, don't despise me. I already have enough for myself."

"You shouldn't. It's not your fault."

"It is. I hated the house because that's where it began, but houses don't make you feel and think nastiness. It was me. It started during puberty. I became some kind of sexual deviate."

"That's just not so." Willard leaped from his chair. "Why, I've never seen you act the tiniest bit interested in a man. I've often wondered why."

"How could I? I was afraid if I became attracted to someone all those repulsive thoughts would return. I was afraid to take the risk of what might happen. Hell, Emma, I'm no different from anyone. I wanted love, marriage and children like any normal woman." She shuddered. "Except I'm not normal."

"Yes, you are. Don't for a single minute think otherwise. It wasn't you." Emma sighed, wondering how many lives had been ruined by the spirit possessing her home.

"I've lived my entire life in mortal terror of those dreams returning," Maureen confessed. "That's why I was afraid to visit you."

"You don't have them any longer?"

"No. I discovered if I left home, spent a weekend at friends, or went on a family vacation, they disappeared. So naturally, I tried to stay away as much as possible, and to be even safer, I kept myself free of any emotional involvement. Oh, I longed to have a relationship like you and Richard. I never wanted to be some eccentric old maid, but I was scared if I began having feelings for someone they'd turn into something filthy. Everyone would learn what a monster I was."

"You are not a monster."

"No? What gives you the right to judge? You don't even know what the dreams were about."

"Tell me."

"I can't. I can't bear for anyone to know."

"Please, Maureen. You've kept this festering inside all your life. Release it. Let me help you."

"Help. How in the hell can anyone help a child who wants to perform unnatural sex with her father?"

Emma caught her breath. It was worse than she feared.

What in God's good name had invaded her house? How long had it lurked among the corridors, and worse, how many lives had it ruined?

"Oh, my dear, what did you do?"

"I left once I realized the dreams came only at Shadow Lake, when I was close to Father. I begged Mama to send me to boarding school. Then, I always managed to wrangle an invitation to someone's home for vacations, until, as I grew older, I found them lessening and eventually disappearing." She straightened her shoulders. "It was the best I could do. The only thing I knew to do, though I've lived my life in terror of them returning."

"What a burden for a child. And you carried it all those years by yourself? You never told anyone?"

"Would you have?"

"I suspect not." Emma took a long pull on her drink. "I'm sorry, but now you must tell me everything you know about Richard's family. After that, I promise I'll share my ghost story."

"Really, Emma." Willard's lip curled. "A ghost story?"

"Come back with me and see for yourself," Emma challenged.

His face whitened, teeth clattered against the rim of his cocktail glass. "You're serious."

"Damn right, I am."

"You mentioned a child." Maureen had ignored the byplay. "You seem to think a child is haunting Shadow Lake. Have you seen it?"

"Jessie has. Jessie believes it pushed Carol down the stairs. She's in the hospital now with a broken collarbone and concussion, among other injuries."

"Good Lord." Willard jumped to his feet, ignored the half-full decanter he'd been using, snatched a full bottle from the sideboard and topped their drinks to the upper rim of their glass.

"That's why I thought it was Lisbeth," Emma explained. "She's the only child I knew that died in the house. However, if you experienced something earlier, then the entity, or whatever, had to have already been there."

"But, I only had thoughts and dreams. I never saw a ghost."

No, but you did have an abnormal sensation of something evil. I think if I could get Lucy to admit it, she's having the same dreams."

"She seemed so normal."

"At the moment. If you'd watched her slithering all over Carol's boyfriend, or seen her total lack of emotion when her mother lay like death at the bottom of the stairs, you'd think different."

"Then you mean it's not me? I'm not something foul and crazy?"

"Foul? No. Crazy? Well, maybeee." Emma's eyes twinkled despite the pressure she felt under.

"We have to get her away."

"No, we have to get *it* away." Emma's expression was grim and determined. "We're going to destroy whatever it is that's causing these unholy desires in children."

"Well, count me in. I'm so damn mad I could probably oust it all by myself."

"I wish." Emma sighed. "But, it's not that simple. I know. I tried. Whatever, or whoever, this child is, the one thing I've learned is she's extremely evil and very, very cunning. I won't make the mistake of underestimating her twice. She's a fierce adversary, Maureen. The only way we'll remove her is by discovering her weakness, and that means finding out who, or what she is, and why she's haunting this particular house."

"You know." Maureen frowned, concentrating on the past, frantically searching her memory for any clue to the bizarre mystery. "That makes me wonder . . ."

"What?"

"If that . . . that creature could have had anything to do with what happened to Richard's family."

"It's a possibility, however, since no one's seen fit to give me any information, I really couldn't say," Emma complained.

"Darling, I wasn't trying to keep anything from you. Hell, I don't know many of the details myself. Richard wouldn't talk about it. He was devastated."

"Men have lost families before."

"Not like this."

"Like what?" Willard had sat quiet as long as possible. "How did they die?"

"Lettice killed their daughter. She poisoned the girl before blowing her own brains out in their bedroom."

"Oh, my God." Emma thought she might vomit. "Why?"

"She left a note, but Richard wouldn't let anyone read it. Later, he told me it accused Lisbeth of terrible things. That he couldn't believe a mother could think such disgusting thoughts about her own flesh and blood-" She stopped, the blood draining from her face as the realization of what she said dawned on her. "Lettice found out. Lisbeth must have been having my dreams.

"How old was she?"

"Ten. We'd just celebrated her birthday. I'd come for the party and was amused to see how crazy Lisbeth had gotten over Richard. She followed him everywhere, touching and stroking him . . ."

"Like in your dreams–you touched and stroked your father?"

"In the beginning, before they became stronger and more explicit."

"Lettice realized something was wrong."

"Good Lord. She must have thought the child a sexual deviate, like I thought I was."

"She didn't know what to do with the sick creature she'd birthed," Emma declared. "Rather than watch her grow older and more wanton, she felt she had no alternative but to destroy her, and then, no other recourse than to take her own life."

"My poor, poor brother."

"Yes, but even more pathetic, his poor, poor wife who knew no other way to save her child from a life of degradation, perversion, and God knows what else."

"That's why he locked the wing. He couldn't bear to be reminded his wife had killed their child and herself in those rooms."

"I'm amazed he could stay in the house."

"I wondered that too. I once mentioned it, but he said there had been years and years of good times. He refused to let Lettice, having lost her mind, destroy those memories." She paused thinking, her eyes lighting at another thought. "Emma, get this. I distinctly remember him saying, that besides, the house comforted him. He was certain at times he could feel his daughter's presence warming and loving him."

"Only now we know it wasn't Lisbeth. Damn it, Maureen. He never once mentioned any of this to me."

"He was ashamed of his wife's actions. After you married, the strength of your presence must have driven whatever it was away. It couldn't feed any longer on Richard's vulnerability because you'd filled his loneliness with your love."

If Willard hadn't known these two for years, known how realistic and down to earth they were, he would have felt like he had wandered into the local looney bin. He could sit still no longer. "So, why has it returned?"

"I have an idea." Emma clapped her hands together. "I don't know who, or why, it's haunting Shadow Lake, but I might have a clue as to why it's come back."

"Which is?"

"Carol. Lucy. And, my stupidity in unlocking the wing." She cocked her head thoughtfully. "No, it would have come whether or not that part of the house was opened. Although, I'm quite sure it's the main source of its power. Like a fool, I probably played right into its hands."

"That makes no sense. Carol stayed at Shadow Lake nearly a year. You didn't notice anything then."

"She was in high school when she came, practically grown. It seems to be young children it feeds on, and so far, at least as far as we know, females."

"Children," Willard's voice rose to a shriek.

"I'm almost positive. Listen . . ." she told her story beginning with Carol's letter and the strange howling of Jessie's dog. When she finished, it was to dead silence, each lost in their own thoughts.

Finally, Maureen spoke. "You're right. It's after young girls. They're the vessel it requires."

"Miss Maureen you were so clever to outsmart it like you did." He beamed at her with pride. "You were just to too brilliant."

She flashed a smile transforming her whole countenance. "I

was, wasn't I? Oh, Emma, I'm so sorry all this has happened, but I can't help but be glad too. This has changed my whole life. Can you forgive me for not being totally devastated?"

"Of course." Emma returned the blinding smile. "Especially since you and Willard are going to help me remove it."

"Not me, sweetie." His face whitened. "The only spirits I can handle are those in a bottle."

"And you don't handle those worth a damn. Count on us, Emma. I wouldn't miss this particular witch hunt for the world. When do we start?"

"We? Moi?" Willard began shaking his head in earnest. Then, seeing the women were both glaring, shrugged and gave up. "Oh piffle, if I *must* be a part of this insanity, then I'd suggest we start at the beginning." He leaped from his chair. "If I'm about to be scared out of my wits by some adolescent spook, then let's go about it the right way."

"Which is?"

"At the beginning. Like I said, beginnings are always best."

"He's terrific at solving puzzles," Maureen bragged. "So my darling little man, how do we go about finding the beginning?"

"Didn't you say some great-uncle built the house? And that his ancestors had left it vacant for years?"

She nodded.

"Why? I mean why would such a beautiful country estate be left empty?"

"I don't know. Perhaps," her face clouded, voice quivered, "perhaps, as long ago as that, something prowled the halls."

"Sounds like it to me." He preened. "Though it's a crying shame none of your relations left records warning their descendants something was fishy in Denmark."

"Maybe they did and over the years they were destroyed, or lost."

"It's a shame the house wasn't." Emma's heart sank. As much as she loved Shadow Lake, nothing could make up for all the heartbreak and suffering that had occurred there. "What about the original builder?"

"I don't know much about him," Maureen admitted.

"Did he have children?"

"Let me think." She pressed a hand to her forehead. "Seems to me, I remember Richard tracing Mother's family tree and mentioning something about her great-uncle and the fact he'd suffered a similar tragedy to Richard." Her eyes widened. "My Lord, Emma, how many people have been affected by this demon?"

"I can't imagine. Are you positive this great-uncle actually built the house?"

"Yes. I can't remember his full name but he must have been a Finley. That was Mama's maiden name."

"Well, it's a start."

"What is?" Willard had left the room, returning with a huge tray loaded with steaming bowls of stew and a basket of crusty rolls.

"We know a man named Finley built Shadow Lake. Evidently his family suffered at the hands of our ghost also."

"Which might mean he built over the site of a previous house. You know that wasn't unusual," he declared, as soon as he put down his cumbersome tray. "The first house could be the source of this evil, or I suppose, even the land."

"The land? How could that be?"

"A graveyard." Willard's excitement over the puzzle was overshadowing his fear. "I'll bet Shadow Lake is built on a cemetery."

"I've never seen any signs." Emma looked bewildered. "Wouldn't there be some evidence?"

"Maybe there's only a single grave. You know the single grave of a vampire was always set at a crossroads."

"Willard." Maureen clutched her heart.

"Or, an ax murderer . . ." He shuddered and looked over his shoulder.

"Or, a child molester," Emma said with distaste.

"We're starting to sound like a Stephen King novel. Still," Maureen tore off a piece of the fragrant bread popping it into her mouth before continuing, "that could account for it."

"A curse." Willard almost spilled his stew in his excitement. "What about Indians?"

"There were Indians on the island for more than four thousand years." Maureen was growing excited. "That's not a bad idea. Maybe an Indian cursed the land when it was taken from him by the white man."

"I don't know. This doesn't feel like a curse to me."

"Really, Emma, darling. How many curses are you familiar with?" Willard challenged.

"You're right." She giggled, feeling so much better now that someone else shared her secret. "How the hell would I know?"

"Records," Maureen announced. "Records. That's the first thing we need to do. Look up old records. They're bound to be some in the county courthouse. I bet if you look hard, Emma, you'll find diaries or bookkeeping ledgers stuck somewhere in the house."

"There's books all over the damn house." She scowled thinking of the monumental task before her.

"Oh, this is too-too exciting."

"I thought you didn't want any part of our little caper," Emma teased.

He was saved from a reply. The French doors burst open. Lucy exploded into the room.

"Auntie Em, I've had so much fun."

"Oh, you poor little darling." Willard threw his arms wide running to embrace the child. "You poor little innocent. Of course Uncle Willard will help save this precious babe."

Emma and Maureen would have laughed. Lucy's expression on finding herself engulfed by the pudgy little man, was a scream, but the ominous meaning behind his words stopped the laughter before it ever left their throats.

Chapter Sixteen

Emma had not sleep worth a hoot. Not that the bed felt strange, or was uncomfortable, but the evening's conversation certainly had been. Try as she might, she could not sleep with so many unanswered questions filling her mind like mud flooding a marsh. At first light she rose, tiptoed to the kitchen, jumping when a disembodied voice whispered, "Coffee's almost ready."

Willard peeped around the edge of the pantry. "Sweetie, I didn't mean to frighten you."

"Well, sweetie, you did."

"And aren't we just the most irritable little guest."

"Stuff it, Willard." Maureen stood in the doorway. "What do you expect after yesterday's bizarre disclosures. We're all as skittish as cats."

"I'm sorry, Willard, but Maureen's right. I am jumpy. In addition, you have to realize last night isn't the first night I've gone without sleep."

"Oh, my precious one," he crooned, filling a cup for her, "of course it isn't. What was I thinking. You just sit at the table and let ole Willard wait on you."

"Thank you." She sank wearily into the nearest chair.

"Stay a few more days. It would be good for you. Who knows, tonight you might even sleep, something I feel sure won't happen if you return to that house of horrors."

"Maureen, *it is not* Shadow Lake. I *know* the house isn't evil. It's whatever comes seeking children." She sighed with regret. "I can't stay. I have to get back and start ferreting out the reason for its existence. Carol will be home from the hospital in a few days. For some reason, she's in grave danger."

"Yes. I find that odd, don't you? I went over everything I could remember, and everything we'd discussed. It strikes me as strange Carol was attacked. It hasn't physically harmed anyone else."

"No one we know of," Emma said.

"What about poor Lettice and Lisbeth?" Willard's hands fluttered. "Aren't you forgetting them?"

"Lettice killed herself and her daughter. The ghost didn't."

"Are we positive?"

"Well, I don't think there was any doubt. After all, she did leave a note."

"Maybe that thing forced her to write it." He shuddered.

"Don't be an ass." She paused. "However, the ghost did put those ugly thoughts in Lisbeth's mind. I suppose you could consider it the instigator of their deaths. But I meant physical attacks, like the one on Carol."

"Actually." Emma lowered her eyes. "When I said Jessie saw the ghost push Carol, I wasn't being totally factual. The truth is, the ghost was standing beside Lucy. I believe she was the one who pushed her mother."

"Oh, sweet Jesus." Willard sat so abruptly his coffee slopped across the table.

"Why would she do that?" All at once Maureen's face whitened, she staggered back a step and clutched her chest. "Dear heaven. How could I have forgotten?"

"Forgotten what?" Emma rose in alarm, rushing to her sister-in-law's side. "What, Maureen? What?"

"Mother," she whispered. "The last time I was home from school, I found myself actively disliking my mother."

"Why didn't you tell me yesterday?"

"I'd forgotten. I think it must have been one of those terrible things you're so ashamed of, you just suppress it. I mean, the dreams were so awful. They went on for so long. This feeling about Mama didn't come until the last, right before a European trip. As soon as I left on it, so did the feelings."

"Why would you want to hurt your dear sweet mama?"

"I can't imagine, Willard. She *was* dear and sweet. I loved her very much, but for some reason, I remember thinking how nice it would be if she died." Her hand flew to her mouth. "Richard too."

"Richard?" Emma, knowing how fond Maureen was of her brother, couldn't believe her ears.

"I told you I was a dreadful person." Tears spilled down her cheeks. "I distinctly remember wanting them both dead. Even thinking of ways I could do it." She was sobbing now, crying in earnest. "I wanted them gone so there wouldn't be anything between Papa, me, and the house."

"Stop it, Maureen." Emma reached for the other woman's hands gripping them hard. "I told you before, it isn't you. It's whatever's in the house. However, you've just given me an idea. I believe you may have solved part of the puzzle."

"What part?"

"Think, Willard. She wanted nothing coming between her father, the house and herself."

"Right." His eyes widened. "Maureen, don't you see? This ghost wants it all. She's obsessed with Shadow Lake. If this thing could have induced you to murder Richard and your mother, then sweetie, there would have been nobody left but your father. One day, Shadow Lake and all the rest would have been yours." He gazed at her in awe. "I told you, you were just to too clever outwitting it like you did."

"Do you think Lisbeth tried to kill her mother?"

"I don't know, but if it were so, then between that danger and the sexual overtures, you can understand why Lettice acted as she did. She felt she had no other recourse."

"God help us." Maureen's hands shook as she lifted her coffee cup. "This is evil a great deal stronger, than we, as amateurs are prepared to face. We're going to need some outside assistance."

"Perhaps," Emma admitted, "but first, as Willard explained, we have to know who, or what, we're dealing with. I'm going to wake Lucy and get on the road. The sooner I find out Shadow Lake's past, the closer we'll be to its deliverance."

"When do you want us to come?"

"Give me a few days. See what else you can discover, or remember, and please, please find out all you can about ridding a house of evil spirits."

"Miss Maureen and I will be there the very instant you call," he promised before lowering his voice, eyes furtively sweeping the room, "but be careful, Emma. Much as I think that Lucy child is too precious, don't let her sneak up on your blind side."

***

Emma was bone tired. The burn on her hand itched furiously. She wished she could have rested a few days longer with Maureen, but didn't dare. She was terrified the longer that thing roamed the house, the stronger it might become, and the good Lord knew, it was strong enough already.

No wonder she was exhausted. Her mind was a whirling kaleidoscope of questions. How could someone become so evil? What could have transpired in the few short years of its life to make it so? Who, or what had originally destroyed it, leaving its spirit trapped at Shadow Lake? And why was it so fixated on becoming mistress of Emma's home?

At that particular thought, her heart flipped. She shot a hasty look in the rearview mirror. Lucy appeared to be sleeping soundly, curled tightly into a ball where she had crawled after bending poor Emma's ears senseless with her incessant babbling about ponies. Once Emma promised to brooch the subject to Carol, she quieted.

One mile passed, then two. Emma began to relax, when a

strange voice floated from the backseat. Emma jumped and her skin crawled. Swallowing hard, she gathered her nerve and looked in the rearview mirror. Lucy was sitting up, an odd smile on her face. With eyes gone dark and ancient, she softly lisped, "We might not have to ask her."

Not if Carol isn't around.

Emma was positive then, whatever had taken control of Lucy had not disappeared. Unlike Maureen, removing her from the source failed to work. The ugly thoughts were still in play. Emma knew Willard was right. She must remain on guard. Lucy's last statement had been too revealing. The glimpse of what lurked in her eyes was a dead give away.

And the thought that crossed her mind only a moment ago, the one causing her heart to lurch so painfully, alarmed her even more. She recalled the discussion that had taken place in the little girl's room. The uneasy feeling that had swamped her when Lucy asked who would inherit Shadow Lake and how adamant the child had become about not wanting to leave. The remembered conversation was making Emma more than uneasy. It was making her physically ill.

"Auntie Em?"

The steering wheel jerked. Emma fought to keep the car on the road.

"Did I scare you?" Lucy asked slyly.

Emma wanted to vomit. "No. There was a squirrel in the road. I swerved to keep from hitting it."

She knew she must not show fear, that if she did, it would sense her weakness and destroy her.

"That was nice. I know you wouldn't hurt anything on purpose, would you, Auntie Em?"

"Never, Lucy. I'd never, never hurt anything, or anyone, if I could help it. Jesus taught us we're to love all things He made, especially other human beings. You learned that in Sunday School, didn't you?"

The child emitted a strange giggle. The sound grated on

Emma's ears worse than fingernails on a chalkboard.

"Yes. But what if they hurt you first?"

"I don't believe anyone would hurt you."

"Cleo did."

"Only because she didn't know you well and was trying to protect her babies. She hasn't bothered you since."

"I don't try to pet her anymore. I don't like her."

"Well, that's a shame since you're planning on taking one of her kittens."

"That doesn't mean I have to like the mother. Mothers aren't always so great."

"I suppose not, but I think it would be nice if you tried. I'm sure Cleo's sorry about scratching you."

"I don't think so."

Emma almost ran off the road. The voice had been lower and deeper. A child's voice, but not the lilting treble of Lucy. Emma's palms were sweating. She again remembered Willard's caution not to let Lucy on her blind side. The child sitting behind her felt as menacing as someone holding a knife to her throat.

"I heard you talking to Mister Willard. He asked for a kitten too, didn't he?"

"He's been dying for one of Cleo and Anthony's babies. He could scarcely wait for them to marry."

"Cats don't marry. They mate."

Emma was shocked. She hadn't realized Lucy was that knowledgeable about sex. "What do you mean?"

"Oh, Auntie Em, you know. Even people have babies without getting married."

"Who told you that?"

"I don't remember. I just know. When is Mister Willard getting his kitten?"

"After Stanley and you pick yours."

"You mean *Mister* Tim's nephew? The boy that's so dumb?"

She seemed to have deliberately stressed the Mister, but perhaps Emma only imagined it. Dear Lord, she hoped she was imagining all the implications. But, deep in her gut knew better.

"Yes, dear. You remember I told you I promised him first pick, and Lucy don't ever let me hear you call him dumb again."

"All right, but I don't like him, and I don't want him getting first pick. Anyway, he is dumb. So dumb he won't know the difference if I pick first, or not."

That odd voice again. Was Emma losing her mind?

"It doesn't matter what you like. I made a promise. I don't go back on my word. Chances are, he won't want the one you do anyway."

"He'd better not."

"Lucy, you're beginning to make me angry. Keep this up, and not only won't you get a kitten, but I won't speak to your mother about a pony."

"But you promised, Auntie Em. Don't you remember? You just finished saying you don't break promises."

"Under certain circumstances; there could be a first time."

"Like there could be a first time you might hurt someone?"

This time the lilting voice belonged to Lucy, but Emma's heart sank, certain the threat had not.

Chapter Seventeen

"Will you jest look at this?" Jessie stopped so abruptly Emma plowed into her backside.

"I might," Emma retorted sharply, "if you'd remove your broad beam from the door."

Carol snorted loudly. The young man sitting beside the hospital bed was convulsed by a fit of coughing.

"I swears, Mr. Phillip, you 'pears to be in worse shape than Miss Carol. You sound somethin' awful. You'd best be takin' some of my special tonic fer that cold."

He was past replying.

"Shut up, Jessie. Leave Phillip alone, and for Pete's sake, move out of the doorway so I can see my niece."

"*My niece.*" Jessie sneered, advancing into the small room, enormous hips swinging freely, threatening to capsize the bed tray plus various other hospital paraphernalia. "Blood don't make her no more yourn, than it do mine. I loves her jest as much and that be what counts. She my niece too. Ain't that right, Miss Carol?"

Carol nodded, like Phillip, afraid if she opened her mouth, she would laugh so hard neither would ever forgive her.

"See there, ole' woman, she *our* niece and don't you forgets it. Now." She turned her head glaring behind her. "Why hasn't you moved on into this here room? I'se gotten outta the door."

"I'm waiting for you to settle and land. I have absolutely no desire to be slammed against a wall, or have *our* niece injured even worse, by being shoved atop her."

Jessie's eyes flashed but she held her tongue.

"Hello, Miss Emma. Miss Jessie." Phillip Randsome rose politely. "One of you ladies take my chair. I'll bring another from the hall."

"Thank you, dear, but I can perch on the edge of the bed. I'm sure Jessie will be comfortable in that very large oversized recliner by the wall."

Jessie failed to retort because her attention was totally absorbed in the lawyer's coarse coppery hair, vibrant green eyes, complexion as creamy and gold as a ripe apricot.

Lord, Lord, how that Miss Carol ever gwine chose between two sech good lookin' men. Ain't no way I coulds, and ain't no ways I would.

She giggled slyly at the naughty images sneaking into her imagination.

Now what's the matter?" Emma looked at Jessie like she had lost her mind. "Carol's been describing her pain and you're over there twittering to yourself like an idiot. Since when have you considered pain amusing?"

"Since I considered you the one in it."

"Ladies, please." Phillip either had to leave or stop their bickering. Raised a Southern gentleman, he knew how disrespectful it would be to laugh in the faces of two older women, but there was no way he could keep silent much longer. Already his throat was sore from all the artificial coughing, and Carol, damn her, wasn't helping. Every time she shot those gorgeous eyes brimming with mirth at him, he had to resort to another choking fit.

Taking pity on his plight, of which she was all too aware, Carol tried steering the conversation onto safer and smoother ground.

"When did you get home? How was Miss Maureen?"

"Last night, and just fine."

"She never changes, does she? You remember Uncle Richard's sister, don't you Phillip?"

"Indeed I do. She's a very memorable lady." His eyes twinkled. "And, if I remember rightly, so is that gentleman she employs."

Jessie snorted loudly. "I'd say that ain't half of what that gentleman is."

"Willard's a dear and you know it. You don't like him because he's always messing around in your kitchen."

"I says messin' 'round might be close to the right words."

"He and Maureen are coming for a visit." Emma interrupted before Jessie became more explicit about Willard's lifestyle.

"Here?" Carol's eyes widened. "That's surprising. For some reason I had this idea she didn't like Shadow Lake."

"You too?" Emma's eyebrows rose. "Lord, but I must be obtuse."

"What an odd remark. I don't understand."

"I'll explain later." Emma reached over patting Carol's hand. "What I want to know is how you're feeling and when we can expect you home. I want you staying as long as necessary. I don't want you home before the doctor says, or badgering him about it either."

"Sounds like I'm not much wanted."

"You know better than that, doesn't she, Phillip?"

"She should." He scowled. "I've told her the opposite often enough."

Carol giggled. "That's not exactly what I meant."

Jessie guffawed loudly.

"Have you spoken with the doctor today?" Emma blushed, unable to accept today's openness about sex.

"This morning. I hate to burst your bubble, but he told me I could leave tomorrow."

Silence greeted this pronouncement.

Carol immediately picked up on the somber look passing between Jessie and Emma.

"Aunt Emma, is something wrong? Have I done something? Is

Lucy turning out to be too much of a bother?" Her voice cracked. "Would you rather I found somewhere else to live?"

"Of course not." Emma leaned across the bed and kissed her cheek. "Don't be foolish. Lucy's no bother. Jessie and I love having you both."

"We surely does."

"It's just that . . ."

"That?"

"I'm upset over your accident. I don't understand how it happened." Emma peered at her. "Do you?"

Carol shivered. "You know that's the strangest thing. I can't figure it out myself."

"It was probably your shoes," Phillip chimed in. "Not that I'm complaining. No man's gonna fuss about a pair of high heels on a woman with legs like yours." This time he reddened, realizing he was a bit carried away.

"It wasn't my heels." She was adamant. "I mean, I didn't trip." She paused, reflecting. "At least, I don't think I did. It was more like someone pushed me, but no one was there except Lucy."

"Oh, Lawd." Jessie's eyes rolled.

"What is it?" Carol was becoming alarmed. "What's going on, Aunt Emma? What do you and Jessie think happened? Why don't you want me home?"

"We need to talk."

"Is it Lucy? Has it something to do with the strange way she's been acting? Good heavens. Surely you don't think Lucy pushed me." She grabbed the older woman's arm. "Please, please tell me the truth. What is the matter?"

Emma looked at Phillip, then seemed to make up her mind.

"I'd hoped you would stay in the hospital long enough I could solve our little problem, but I guess that's not going to happen." She gave a huge sigh. "I'd better explain everything so you'll be prepared."

"Prepared for what?" Carol could hardly breathe, her heart was pumping so fast. "Has anything happened to Lucy? Oh, Aunt

Emma, is my baby all right?"

"Shush child, of course she is. I wouldn't keep something like that from you."

"Miss Emma, would you like me to leave? If this is a private matter, I can come back later."

"It is rather a private matter, Phillip, but perhaps you can help. I imagine we're going to need the service of a strong young man before we're finished."

"I'm going to need the service of another doctor if you don't hurry up and tell me what's going on," Carol threatened.

And so, Emma did.

They left a much subdued couple in the hospital. Emma offered to call the doctor and get a tranquilizer for Carol, although she suspected it was Phillip who needed it, but both declined. They preferred having a clear head if they were to win back the soul of Carol's child.

"Funny, I never seed no freckles on Mr. Phillip's face 'fore, but when you was tellin' 'bout that ghostie, his face got so whites a whole bunch jest marched cross his nose."

"He was shook up, wasn't he?"

"He were worse than Miss Carol. She took it lots better than I thought she would."

"I understand why. She's been aware something was wrong with Lucy. It was probably a relief to learn the child was possessed by an evil spirit, rather than *was* becoming evil."

"Isn't no good choice either way," Jessie pronounced sadly.

"There's a big difference. All we have to do is get rid of this thing, then Lucy will be fine again."

"Yeah."

Emma removed her hand off the steering wheel and reached over squeezing her friend's. "We'll do it, Jessie. We're two tough old broads. We'll put our heads together, and with a little help, send this damn spook straight back to wherever."

Suddenly, Jessie laughed, a great booming blast. "I'm not too sure it won't be jest the two of us. The way Mr. Phillip looking when we left, I think he might not be much more help than Billy Bob."

"That reminds me. Did Ruby ever get him to tell her what happened when he was locked in Lucy's room?"

"Not very much, and that surprise me. She usually get everything he know plum outta him."

"What did she learn?"

"He say somethin' grabbed his arm in the dark pullin' him in there. He thought it were one of us cause he couldn't see nothin'. Then, he pretty sure it weren't, when the thing push him on the bed and lay down beside him."

"You're kidding."

"No, I ain't. Then he tole Ruby he were so scart he couldn't move. This thing were kissin' his face and rubbin' up against him like. Then he wouldn't tell her no more."

"Jessie, what in Sam Hill is in that house? Where on earth did it come from?"

"Don't know what, but I 'sects from hell."

"I don't have a clue where to begin, or how to exorcize it," she wailed.

"That priest sure weren't no help."

"No, bless his heart. He wasn't."

"I tole you I heerd of this white witch."

"We might have to use her."

"I don't blame Miss Carol fer wantin' to take Miss Lucy outta there."

"I know. That would be my first thought too, but I'm afraid it's too late. If you'd been with me coming home from Maureen's, you'd know that wouldn't do the trick. Whatever this is, it's either grown stronger through the years, or else Lucy is just younger and more vulnerable. It has control over her even when she's away from Shadow Lake. I could almost feel it, and once," she shuddered, "once, I'm positive I saw it peering out her eyes."

"Could it be cause she jest lost her daddy?"

"Jessie, what an acute observation. I'll bet you're right. They say children of divorced parents have all sorts of emotional problems."

"I knows. I seed it on my operas."

"You and those blasted soaps. I wish they'd show how to get rid of evil spirits."

"What if we can't?"

"Don't think such a thing. We have too. Otherwise . . ." she couldn't finish.

"Lucy lost if we don't, ain't she?"

"I'm afraid so. It's all my fault. I brought them here. Look at the danger I've placed them in."

"Shush, ole woman. You didn't know. We'll do it somehow. We'll jest pray to the good Lord and he'll bring us help. We'll get us our pretty baby, and our pretty house, back safe and sound."

"You know, I'm glad Maureen and Willard are coming."

"Never thoughts I'd say it, but I be glad too. Maybe that ole' Willard, being the way he is, that spook won't have no lovin' powers over him. Maybe it jest get so mad it go someplace else to haunt."

"You would think of that." Emma laughed out loud.

Chapter Eighteen

Ruby stood in the middle of the library staring aghast at shelves stacked floor to ceiling with books.

"Miss Emma. Don't you have any idea where to look?"

"Not a clue."

The younger woman heaved a gigantic sigh. "Then, I'd say we had our work cut out for us."

"If we weren't so pressed for time," Emma informed her, "it could be fun. Like a scavenger hunt."

"You're sure everyone's imagination isn't running overtime? Sort of a mass hysteria type thing? We studied cases of that phenomena in Psychology," she boasted, "and of course, everyone's familiar with the Salem Witch Trials."

"Believe me, child, this is no case of mass hysteria. Shadow Lake is haunted. Because you haven't seen anything doesn't mean it's not so."

"Well, it's hard to believe and even harder to visualize."

"Don't try, please."

"I would like to be here when something happens, Miss Emma. It would be easier to accept."

"Don't tempt the devil when you're in the same room with me, Ruby. I've seen and heard about all this old ticker can take." Emma's eyes darted fearfully into each dark corner. "I'll let you have Billy Bob's place next time we try an exorcism. I suspect you'll get an eyeful then."

"You certainly won't get him again, and that's gonna be a real problem when we do our spring cleaning."

"If this situation isn't resolved soon, there won't be a spring cleaning."

"Oh, Miss Emma."

"I'm serious. This is a terrible, dreadful force we're reckoning with. I don't know how many years it's lurked in these rooms." She grew thoughtful. "Perhaps that's why the house is called Shadow Lake, because of dark spirits. I never questioned the name, but that could be the reason." She faltered, taking a deep breath. "Anyway, Ruby, I do know it's old and evil. As evil as anything you'll come across in your lifetime. It must be destroyed. If we can't, I swear by the good Lord, I will, with my own hand, burn this place to the ground sowing it with salt like God had the Hebrews do when they conquered other tribes."

"Oh, Miss Emma, not this beautiful house."

"I swear to you, Ruby." Emma's features were set and grim. "It will not be given the satisfaction of ruining more lives."

"If that's the case, we'd better get busy. I don't want you setting fire to Shadow Lake. It's my home too." She straightened her shoulders moving resolutely to the shelves. "We need to do this in some sort of system. I'll start at the top, you, the bottom. We'll meet in the middle."

Emma chuckled, delighted she still could. "That reminds me of my grandmother. She used to tell me when I bathed, 'to always wash down as far as possible, up as far as possible and not to forget possible.'"

With that bit of sage advice, they begin systematically scouring for books dealing with family, former occupants, or history on house and land.

One hour, two hours, three. They were half-finished when Jessie and Lucy arrived laden with drinks and an enormous caramel cake.

"Time fer a break. Lucy and me been makin' this treat to spoil

Miss Carol with when she gets home from the hospital. But, we decide it won't hurt none to do a little samplin'."

"Sounds like a great idea to me." Ruby descended the ladder she'd been perched on for what seemed forever. "I've scanned enough books to make me a Rhode's scholar."

"Any lucks?"

Emma shook her head.

"What are you looking for, Auntie Em?"

"Just some old deeds and records I might need."

"Like for when you make your will?" The child's expression turned sly and greedy.

"Not exactly, dear," she answered, barely able to control the shudder she felt at the girl's question.

"What's a birthright?"

"Heavens, Lucy, where did you hear that word?"

"I don't know." But her eyes didn't meet her aunt's. "Maybe on one of Jessie's soaps. Anyway." She threw back her head, eyes blazing. "Does that mean the oldest one gets to have their papa's house?"

"Not always." Emma carefully cut and began passing cake, heart beating an erratic tattoo. "Although that was usually the case years ago. Now-a-days, parents tend to leave their possessions equally."

"How could you divide a house?" She was scornful.

"It's inherited by all the children. The lawyer handling the estate sells it, giving each an equal share of money."

"What if they don't want the money? What if they want the house?"

"In that case, the lawyer has someone qualified value its worth. The one wanting it buys the other's share."

"What if they all want it?"

"That would be very unusual. Most times none of them want their parent's home. They think them old-fashioned. Most young people want something new and modern, built to their own ideas and designs."

"They wouldn't feel that way if it was Shadow Lake."

Ruby and Jessie had been quietly watching the girl grow more and more agitated, sensing there was something important in Lucy's wanting to understand that particular word "birthright."

"Oh, I don't know," Emma began.

"They wouldn't." Lucy jumped to her feet. "Anyone would want Shadow Lake, and it wouldn't be fair for the oldest to get it. The oldest might not love it as much as the youngest." She stomped her foot. "It's not fair. It's not, I tell you."

They all stared, unable to comprehend what had set the child off.

"Lucy, dear," Ruby went to her side and knelt. Immediately, a numbing cold took possession of her. She had difficulty speaking. "Who-what are you get-getting so riled up a-about?"

"It's not right for someone to get something because they were born first. I want Shadow Lake for me," she screamed in a rage terrible to behold.

"Lucy." Emma rose so suddenly her plate fell to the floor breaking into a dozen pieces. She reached out without thinking and slapped the child hard. "Lucy!" She grabbed her by the shoulders, bent her head back and looked intently into her eyes. "Lucy. Are you there?"

The child glared back. Abruptly, something shifted deep in the black orbs, her expression softened.

"What do you mean, Auntie Em? I'm standing right here." Tears seeped from beneath long lashes. "Why did you slap me? I didn't do anything."

Emma clasped the child fiercely to her breast. "I'm so sorry. You were hysterical. I stopped you the only way I knew," she apologized, staring over the top of her head at Ruby, her face mirroring the horror Emma felt.

It was only Jessie, standing behind, that caught sight as Lucy's features shifted once again. Something cold and menacing flaunted its existence, openly defying Jessie with its presence.

***

Carol arrived, escorted in grand style. Tim on one side, Phillip the other, sandwiched between like so much filling in an Oreo cookie, and to them, just as delectable.

"They never gonna make it through that door all squashed up like that," Jessie warned, shrewdly measuring the width with her eye. "Gwine be something awful when they sticks there like corks in a bottle."

Emma solved the dilemma. Stepping forward she pulled her niece out of the men's grasp, neatly averting a testosterone battle. Hugging her hard, she declared, "Aren't you the lucky one. It might be worth a few broken bones if it meant getting the attention of two such handsome fellows."

Carol smiled wanly. "Maybe, if in the process you hadn't raised a rival from the grave."

Emma's eyes flew to Tim.

"It's all right, Auntie. Phillip and I told him everything. We're going to need all the help we can get." She shuddered. "Besides, from the way Lucy draped herself all over him, it seems he's already been selected as a potential victim."

"Can you believe this, Tim?" Emma's voice quavered.

"It's a lot easier believing something supernatural made my nephew go berserk than to believe he'd suddenly turn into a murderous monster. God's truth, Miss Emma, it was a relief."

"But, this is so bizarre."

"I know," he admitted. "But remember when you asked—and now I know the reason—about haunted houses? Remember I told you my dad believed in them? Well, I guess now I do, too. Anyway, I wish you'd told me then what you suspected. I hate thinking you've been carrying this burden all by yourself."

Without warning tears sprang from her eyes running down her cheeks as she stumbled forward sinking into a chair.

"Excuse me," she softly sobbed. "I'm so embarrassed. It's that none of you knows how good it feels not having to face this thing by myself. I honestly thought, at the time, I was losing my mind, or if I hadn't, soon would."

"She never even toles me," Jessie burst out indignant. "Not fer the longest time, and not till I done tole her I 'spects something were wrong."

"Mama. Mama."

Carol's face whitened. She instinctively stepped back into the protection of her escort's arms.

"Auntie Em, why didn't you call me?" Lucy's eyes flashed fire, then her features softened. She ran to her mother throwing her arms around her waist.

"Watch it, Lucy. Your mother's still in a lot of pain. She can't take being treated rough."

"I know that." The child turned, glaring at the older woman. "I know that. I'm not a baby. Why, I wouldn't hurt my sweet pretty mama for the world." She tightened her grasp on Carol who visibly winced.

"Please, Lucy," she cried. "Your Aunt Emma's right, darling. I'm black and blue from falling down those stairs. You're going to have to be extra careful around me." She managed a smile. "I guess our loving is gonna have to be at arms' length."

"Have you told that to Mr. Tim and Mr. Phillip?"

"Lucy."

This time, it was the cook who snatched the child from her mother shaking her hard. "What a little girl like you sayin' sech things to you mama. I'se a mind to swat your sassy bottom."

"Let go of me. You don't even know what you're talking about." Lucy's nostrils flared. "I've watched them hug and kiss on Mama when they bring her home. They both do it. I've seen them."

Carol let out the breath she'd been holding. Trying not to appear too embarrassed, she spoke softly, "You're right, dear. Everyone is going to have to hug me at fingertip length and blow me their goodbye kisses. And even more important, someone is going to have to learn it isn't good manners to spy on their mother."

Emma rose from the chair, anxious to end this unsettling scene. "We'd best get you to bed."

"You're right, Miss Emma. She's white as a sheet." Phillip put an arm around her.

Tim's hand shot out catching the child before she could follow. "Hey, wait a minute. I need a favor."

"What?" She clearly wanted to go with Phillip and her mother.

"Miss Emma told me the kittens are weaned. Stanley is driving me nuts wanting to pick his out. Do you think you could have them ready sometime tomorrow?"

"I don't . . ." she caught sight of her aunt's scowl and relented. "I don't see why not, Mister Tim. Course, we'll need to make sure Cleo and Anthony don't find out what's happening. I *always* make sure they're locked in another room before I pet the kittens. They get *real mean* if they think someone is going to bother their babies."

"Now, Lucy, that's not true. You play every day with those kittens."

"Well, we'll see." A strange smile crossed her lips. She pulled herself free of the man, racing through the front door and out into the yard.

Chapter Nineteen

"What's that for?" Lucy pointed to the red ribbon dangling from Stanley's fingers.

"Ma-mama give me," he shyly stuttered, "for my k-kitty."

"When I told him they looked a lot alike, he was afraid he'd forget which one he picked. His mother suggested tying a ribbon around its neck. That way he'll be sure to recognize it," Tim explained.

"How dumb." She disdainfully rolled her eyes. "Course, I forgot. Stanley is dumb."

"If-if you for-forgot that, then ma-maybe you need a ri-ribbon too," Stanley retorted, much to the surprise of the adults.

"Good answer." Emma beamed before turning to scowl at her niece. "Lucy, I believe you owe Stanley and his uncle an apology."

"I have to get the cats." She deliberately ignored the command and flounced away.

"I keep telling myself this isn't Lucy I'm dealing with, but Lord, Tim, it's hard. I mean, it's really, really hard."

"I can imagine." He sympathized. "How's Carol coping?"

"Better than me. The child is nothing but sweetness and light around her. Since she's laid up in bed, she's not getting the full obnoxious treatment the rest of us are."

"You didn't let her return to the same bedroom, did you?" he asked, alarmed.

"No. She's in one of the guest rooms in my wing. Lucy, much to her chagrin, in another. However, I suspect the child slipped into her old room as soon as she thought everyone was asleep."

"You didn't lock up that wing?"

Emma looked at him pityingly. "Doors have a way of opening here, locked or not."

"Yeah." Sheepish, he rubbed a hand over his face. "I'm like Stanley. I keep forgetting."

"I got up at dawn to sort through the rest of the books in the library. Ruby's still hard at it, but so far, not one has yielded a clue to our mystery. I swear, if Jessie and Billy Bob hadn't witnessed that damn ghost's shenanigans, I'd go straight to the nearest booby hatch and have myself committed."

"No need for that. Just seeing Stanley's reactions that day, and watching Lucy turn from a delightful young girl to some kind of midget femme fatale has been enough to convince me. I don't need to see things that go bump in the night."

"Well, believe me," Emma laughed shakily, "*bump* is the least of it."

"Lo-look Uncle Tim." The boy jumped up and down in his excitement. Lucy was rounding the corner of the house, a basket of white fluffy balls in her arms. A concerned Cleo and Anthony trailing in her wake.

"Here, then." She flung the basket at Stanley's feet, stepping back as Anthony jumped among his progeny, rearing up and spitting.

"Lucy." Emma admonished before turning to Stanley, anxious this display of cat temper, however justified, hadn't upset the boy after his recent experience.

She need not have worried. Stanley had sunk to his knees, face buried in the kitten's fur as they crawled up and over him. Anthony stood, his back to the young man as if including him in the protection of his family. Fur high, a menacing rumble issuing from his throat, eyes glazed and fixed on Lucy, he challenged whatever held her to do battle.

"I hate that darn cat." She was first to drop her gaze. "You better watch it, Stanley. He'll scratch you for sure."

"No, no, he won't." The young man ran a hand over the male cat's warm fur. Anthony dipped his head, the threatening rumble turning to a satisfied purr as he leaned back into Stanley's palm. "An-Anthony loves me. He-he knows I wo-won't ever hurt his ba-babies."

"So, what makes him think I would?"

"Not yo-you may-maybe, bu-but the other one would if-if she could."

A look passed between Emma and Tim. "What other one, Stanley?"

Quickly, Lucy stamped her foot. "Don't be silly, Auntie Em."

Anthony's head shot up. His ears flattened.

"Stanley doesn't know what he's talking about, as usual. I don't know why you pay attention to someone like him." She turned to the object of her derision. "Hurry up and pick out your dumb cat." She pointed, still keeping her distance. "How about that one? Billy Bob told me he was a boy cat and probably going to be as big as his daddy. You and Anthony are so crazy about each other. You ought to take him."

"I li-like this one." He smiled tenderly at the runt of the litter, busy trying to nurse his little finger. "Sh-she thinks I'm her ma-mama," he giggled.

"No."

"Lucy." Emma cried for about the fourth time. "Stanley can have whichever kitten he chooses."

"But that one's mine. I picked her from the beginning."

"And you were warned from the beginning," Emma reminded her. "I told you not to get attached to any certain kitten until after he'd made his selection."

"Oh, Miss Emma." Tim sought to make peace. "It's not important. I'm sure Stanley can find another he'd like just as well."

"No, I wouldn't," he cried, face falling.

"Nor will he have too." Emma was adamant. "I promised Stanley. I try very hard never to break a promise. There are five more kittens, all just as precious and just as special. I'm certain Lucy can find another that will suit."

Stanley had been trying to follow the adult's conversation, intent on learning if he was, in fact, going to be allowed the tiny creature sucking vigorously on his finger.

"I-I can have it?" His face lit up.

Emma nodded.

"Wow. Th-thank you, Miss Em-Emma." He turned to Lucy. "Did Bi-billy Bob say if this on-one was a girl or boy?"

"It's a girl." She spat like one of the cats, features contorted in fury.

"I-I thought so." He sighed in bliss. "I-I thought she was pre-pretty like her ma-mama. I wa-wanted a girl, so sh-she could have ba-babies when she go-got grown."

"Then you made a good choice." Emma smiled, delighted someone had been satisfied. "Of course, we'll have to find a proper husband when the time comes."

"I kn-know." He held the little animal close, kissing it over and over, crooning softly. "Will you please he-help me put my ri-ribbon on, Miss Emma?"

"Certainly." She knelt, and as he held the squirming creature, gently tied a large red bow around its neck.

"Oh, sh-she's so pre-pretty," he breathed in awe. Then, eyes shining exclaimed, "Yo-you know wh-what I'm go-going to name her?"

"What?" She was hard put not to cry, his delight was so intense. It made her ashamed of the actions of her niece, and of the greed permeating so many of her fellow beings.

"Pre-pretty Em-Emma." He ducked his head. "If-if it's al-all right with you."

"Why, Stanley." She pulled him to her hugging him hard. "I'd be honored."

"I'd already named her Mittens," Lucy announced firmly.

"Th-that's a nice name," Stanley agreed. "I bet any of the other k-kitties would like that j-just fine."

"How about some cookies and lemonade?" Emma spoke before Lucy could make a further retort. "Jessie made them specially for you to celebrate."

"Re-really?" His pleasure was contagious. "Ca-can I take Pre-pretty Emma and show her?"

"Of course." Emma led them toward the side terrace where Jessie had already set out glasses and plates.

"What a big to-do about nothing," Lucy muttered under her breath, stomping along after the others.

"It is a big to-do for Stanley," Tim dropped behind, speaking quietly to the girl. "Your aunt has made this a very special day for him, but you mustn't mind. She makes sure most of your days are special, so please Lucy, don't begrudge Stanley this one."

"He shouldn't have picked my kitten." She pouted.

"I'm sorry about that," Tim apologized. "But he didn't do it deliberately. Oh Lucy, can't you share in a little of his happiness?" he begged.

Stanley was holding the kitten out to Jessie, barely coherent he was stammering so hard in his excitement, trying to explain why he had picked that particular one, and what he had named her.

"Oh my," they heard her cry, "ain't that jest the prettiest one you picked outta that whole bundle of Cleo's babes. You jest went and gots yourself the very nicest one of all."

"I thought so, too." Lucy turned and ran inside the house.

***

The moon coming through the many-paned window cast a shimmering silver glow over the small bedroom, bleaching the bright yellow walls to pale grey, turning a cheerful daytime setting into a sinister night time tableau, made even more macabre by the sight of two children. Heads down, they whispered and giggled, one a creature of substance, the other a wraithlike vaporish mist slightly greyer than the grey walls.

Emma's heart thudded so loud she was terrified they would hear. Her fingernails pierced her palms. Mouth opened, she sucked air into lungs frozen in fear. She watched from her vantage point behind the partially open door to the south wing. Watched in fascination while this child, her niece's daughter she had brought here in perfect innocence, consorted with some creature from a different dimension. Whether hell or another plane, Emma neither knew, nor did she care. All she knew was that this thing was as evil as anything that ever roamed the earth and it was defiling her beloved home. It was stealing the soul of this child, and she, Emma, didn't have a clue as to why, or how to go about removing it.

Lucy stopped her conversation, tilting her head to peer out the open door of her bedroom into the darkened hall. Emma shrank back against the wall, certain they knew she was there, yet anxious to keep up the pretense, afraid she might be reduced to a state of gibberish should that vaporish thing in the shape of a human approach her.

She wondered if she had been set up, lured by Lucy to spy on them and see what a formidable foe she had been pitted against. It wouldn't surprise her. Nothing would surprise her again. For all she knew, she might have been decoyed for them to taunt and tease until the horror of what she faced stopped her heart. Until she slumped lifeless to the floor, an old woman scared to death, probably having peed in her pants to boot. At the thought of that further indignity, she straightened her back, stepped out of the shadows and with a surprisingly firm voice, spoke.

"Don't stay up too late, Lucy. You and your friend. I had a phone call from Maureen and Willard. They'll be arriving early tomorrow."

With that pronouncement, she turned on shaking legs and left, but not before witnessing the look of amazement on the girl's face and not before she had seen the other grow and swell. The mists thickened and swirled as a low rumble of rage filled the room, a stench of something putrid emanating from its depths.

Emma could scarcely believe she had been allowed to return to her room. Stepping inside, she closed the door and locked it.

Stupid. She threw the useless key on her dresser. But realizing what she had faced down and was still there to tell the tale, she began laughing and dancing around the room like some punch drunk fighter shadow boxing. With a triumphant cry she threw back her head shouting, "Got-cha."

At once the stench enveloped her. Eyes wide and watering, all thoughts of victory vanished. She fled to her bed grabbing her Bible from the night stand. Diving beneath the covers, she clutched the well-worn book to her bosom, as teeth chattering she prayed over and over the protection of the Twenty Third Psalm:

I will fear no evil
For thou are with me;
Thy rod and thy staff,
They comfort me.

Not until dawn did the fetid air dissipate. Emma, exhausted, fell into a restless sleep.

Chapter Twenty

Despite the fact she had gotten almost no sleep, Emma woke early. Hastily donning jeans and a sloppy sweat shirt, she slipped down the stairs. Jessie discovered her sitting on the terrace, coffee untouched, hair awry, eyes unfocused, staring across the tiny lake as the sun plunged golden shafts like flaming arrows into the depths of its placid surface.

"Pour that nasty mess out. Let me gives you some fresh," Jessie commanded, coffee pot in one hand, empty cup in the other. "Then you best tell me what you doin' outta bed this early with sech a strange look on you face."

For once, Emma broached no argument. After refilling her cup, hands and voice trembling, she proceeded to relate the evenings adventure.

"Whew." Jessie was horrified. "I'se telling you now, somethin' gotta be done 'bout this here spook. My heart not gonna be able to take much more, and I swear, Miss Emma, you not lookin' so hot neither."

"Not feeling so hot, neither."

"I can't believe you stood right there lookin' at that thing and then." She caught her breath. "And then, spokes to it. I gots to tell you. I always knowed you was a gutsy ole' lady, but I sure never figured you was that gutsy. Lawd, Lawd. I bet I'd of tinkled in my britches fer sure."

"You have no idea how close I came."

"It didn't say nothin' back?" She fearfully shot a glance at the upstairs windows.

"It didn't have too." Emma wrinkled her nose. "I knew exactly what it thought of me."

"What's we gonna do?"

"Beats me." She took a sip of coffee. "Damn, Jessie, this one is cold as kraut."

"Mine too. I best make another pot. We done throwed so much of this one out there won't be none to take to Miss Carol." She slowly rose. "Wonder what she gonna make of all this? I hates fer her to know how close that baby of hers has gotten to that ghostie." A shudder shook Jessie's massive frame. "Miss Emma, you think we be too late? You think that thing done stole the soul right outta our little girl?"

"No." Her heart thudded. "I refuse to believe we can't save Lucy. There has to be something we can do."

"What? You know I do most anythin' I can to hep, and so will Ruby." She frowned. "Can't say 'bout Billy Bob, but Ruby got ways a workin' on him."

"I know." Emma laid a hand over that of her best friend. "I wish you'd been with me last night."

"Well now, I has to admit I ain't too sorry to has missed it," she sheepishly confessed. "And, you might best 'member what I told you 'bout that white witch."

"I remember. I just hate bringing anyone in that might unleash more physic power. Seems we already have more than our share of hovering spirits."

"Maybe spirits meetin' spirits is what we do needs. I hear tell she is something powerful."

"I won't forget, but let's keep her for a last resort. Maureen and Willard will arrive sometime today. We'll see what they've turned up. Maybe they'll have some new ideas."

"Hope so, though what that Willard could come up with might be more than we can handle."

"Jessie, let's not tell Carol about last night until the others arrive. She's already worried sick. When she finds out Lucy is openly consorting with a demon, well, I think she needs the support of loving people around when that happens."

"Poor darlin', goin' throughs so much with that nasty divorce, now this on tops. What you think happen if you jest send she and Lucy away?"

"I'm afraid it's too late. Whatever Pandora's box I've opened has had the lid up long enough for all the filth to spew out. Whatever evil was in that room has Lucy securely in its clutches with no intention of releasing her."

"Well then, it jest gonna have to get itself some new 'tentions, cause it ain't havin' my little girl. Done lost one baby chile. I ain't losin' this one too."

***

Jessie, Emma, and Ruby were sitting at the kitchen table, heads close, voices whispering quietly when Lucy entered. Walking to the refrigerator, she removed the milk pouring a large glass before turning, a tiny smirk playing over her lips.

"Auntie Em, you almost scared me to death wandering the halls so late last night."

"Then you frighten easily." Emma could not believe the calm that settled over her at Lucy's words. Words thrown out like a challenge. "It takes a good deal more to scare me."

"Oh, now." She edged forward. Her eyes fastened on Emma's like iron files on a magnet. "I think you must have been a little bit frightened."

"A very little," Emma retorted. "Lucy, what were you doing up so late? Why were you in your old bedroom when your mother told you not to sleep there?"

"It wasn't all that late." Her eyes fell. "And, I like my own room best. I don't want to sleep where you've put me. It doesn't have all my dolls and things. I told you I wanted to stay in my own room, my very special room *you* fixed for me." She emphasized the words, peeking slyly out the corner of her eyes.

"I told you that wasn't going to happen. You cannot sleep by yourself in that wing of the house. It's too far away from your mother and me. If you'd get sick in the night, we couldn't hear you call."

"I won't get sick."

"You don't have any way of knowing that. We've had this discussion before. The matter is settled. You'll sleep in the wing with your mother, and I don't want to hear any more about it." Emma stood. "Now, perhaps you'd like to tell me about your friend."

"Friend?" The child's face was pure innocence. "What friend?"

"The one sitting on the floor with you."

For an instance, a flash of fear appeared, quickly replaced by one of cunning. "Those were my dolls. I told you I missed them. I was sitting on the floor chatting with them."

"That wasn't a doll I saw or smelled." Emma's voice was firm as a rock. "I demand the truth, Lucy."

Jessie and Ruby were holding their breath, aware of the clash of wills taking place.

"It was my doll. What else could it be? We both know there's no one else living in this house." She openly sneered, before adding, "Remember, Mama says when people spy on other people they see and hear things they wish they hadn't."

"That wasn't the case here, Lucy. I was very glad I saw what I did."

"You like seeing me play with my dolls? If I'd known, I'd have invited you for a tea party. I didn't know someone as old as you liked dolls."

"I would enjoy an invitation to have tea with your dolls, but that's not what I saw last night."

"Yes, it was."

"I don't think so."

"Then you must not be thinking so good, like Jessie says, cause that's who I was talking to." She walked forward, aggressively thrusting herself at Emma. "Who did you think was in there with me?"

Jessie's gasp was lost in Emma's answer.

"I don't know her name, but I intend finding out. Give me a little more time. I promise you I will. Her name and everything else there is to know."

"How could you possibly learn the name of someone that's not there?" Lucy taunted, then slammed the milk on the table, running from the room before Emma could think of another retort.

✳✳✳

"Have it your way." Emma threw up her hands. "I've already had one argument with Lucy and I'm not up to another. Sleep anywhere you want, but I'm warning you, I think you're being foolish. I don't believe you realize what manner of evil we're up against."

"Listen, Emma." Maureen stood her ground. "That damn spook has ruined my life, so don't be telling me I don't know how strong it is. I love what you've done to Carol's room and that's where I'm going to stay. I always wanted that room. Richard took it, but by gum, there's no reason I can't have it now. It's empty. The other wing is full. It would be stupid for us to double up when all this space is available."

"You aren't expecting Willard to sleep in Lucy's room."

"Of course not." She ignored Willard, white-faced, sinking with relief into the nearest chair. "He can sleep on the sofa in Carol's sitting room. It makes into a bed. He's done that before when we've been short on space."

"Well, that makes me feel some better. At least you won't be up there alone."

"What are you afraid of?" Willard's voice came out in a squeak. "Has something else happened?"

Emma put her finger to her lips. "Why don't you and Willard take your things upstairs and get settled? I'll send Billy Bob to help, I hope," she added the last under her breath, "and then meet me downstairs. We're going to have a family picnic by the lake. All of us, except Lucy. I arranged for Ruby to take her into town. She's been wanting to play miniature golf. I thought this might be a good time."

Maureen started to speak, but Emma shook her head from side to side.

"That sounds like fun." Willard rose. "Will Carol join us?"

"Yes. Her two young men, Tim and Phillip, are invited. Between them, they should have no difficulty getting her out there."

"Willard, you and Billy Bob bring up the bags. It won't take long to unpack," Maureen ordered, a thoughtful frown creasing her forehead as she begin carefully climbing the stairs holding tight to the bannister. "Yes, I can see how a picnic away from the house might be a marvelous idea. A wonderful place to have our little conversation."

Chapter Twenty-One

Once they settled round the picturesque lake, Jessie's lavish picnic spread out before them, Emma laid down the ground rules. First business of the day was enjoying lunch. She was determined nothing would detract from the scrumptious repast Jessie had labored over long and diligently. A quick look at Jessie's offerings and everyone was in total agreement.

Platters heaped with crispy fried chicken were placed next to an enormous basket of beer bread, each loaf baked with melted butter poured over at intervals to form a thick golden crust. It was so chewy and delicious, Emma declared it better than sex.

Jessie agreed it were "mighty fine," but not that fine. She just "'spected" it were so long since Emma had sampled any of that other treat she might not "'member" how very tasty it were.

At these words, Willard choked so hard everyone feared a trip to the hospital might be imminent. Fortunately, after a particularly hard thump, applied with much vigor and immense satisfaction by Jessie, he caught his breath and they continued filling their plates.

There was creamy white hominy, flecks of green chili peppers peeping through the cheeses, An enormous salad, scattered with almonds and noodles all tossed in a tangy sweet dressing, home-made pickles and trays of brightly deviled eggs. However, the real treat came when Jessie hauled out the old ice cream freezer.

Everyone fell on enormous bowls of peach ice cream, only moments after declaring they couldn't possibly eat another bite. Crisp buttery squares of shortbread went just as fast, and Emma grew alarmed at the amount of food hurtling down her guest's throats.

"Well." Jessie beamed observing the empty plates. "I sure 'nuff won't has to worry 'bout putting no leftovers in the fridge this day."

"Jessie, will you marry me?" Tim lay flat on his back, hand rubbing a much distended stomach. "How can I be so full and miserable, yet full and satisfied all at the same time?" He groaned.

"'Spects I has to say no, but a few years back I might has to a thought on it. Leastways, I might has to thought hard on allowin' you some of that treat Miss Emma ain't had fer awhile."

"Jessie." Emma cried shocked, though happy everyone had enjoyed their meal, and at least for the moment, forgotten the reason they were dining outside–dining far away from the menacing ears of whatever lurked in her beautiful home.

Jessie, Emma and Maureen cleared away the luncheon remains. The time had come to discuss what to do about their uninvited visitor, and it seemed no one was anxious to broach the subject. At last, cloth folded, lakeside tidy, Emma reluctantly related the previous evening's events. When she described watching Lucy in conversation with some ghostly apparition, Carol began sobbing so hard it almost broke her heart.

Emma felt such guilt for inviting her to Shadow Lake, but when she tried to apologize, Carol flung her arms around her, begging her not to blame herself. She assured her that whatever dwelt at the house had been there long before Emma. It was Lucy's presence, not hers, that had triggered its rebirth. By now, Carol, Emma and Jessie were all in tears.

Maureen stood apart watching. "Enough. I didn't come here to whimper like a baby. By damn, I came to kick butt!"

Willard applauded loudly. Tim stuck his fingers in his mouth whistling shrilly. In moments, they were all cheering and clapping like fans at a football rally.

"That's more like it." Maureen, the head cheerleader was pumping them up. "Now, are we going to sit here moaning and groaning, or are we going to show that pint-size spook whom this house really belongs too?"

"Me." Emma slowly rose and wiped her nose. "Shadow Lake belongs to me and I'll be jiggers if this thing is going to drive me away. Good *will* overcome evil. The Bible says so. If it weren't true, this planet would be inhabited by nothing but a bunch of self-seeking, two-legged animals run berserk. I don't know much about spirits," she admitted, "but I know there has to be a way to destroy them. We just haven't discovered it."

"We need a plan." Tim immediately commanded their attention. "You can't build anything without specs, nor can you safely tear anything down. We have to learn the basic foundation of this problem before we do more harm and worsen the situation."

"Emma was going to do that," Maureen informed him before turning to her hostess. "So, my dear, what have you discovered?"

She hung her head. "Nothing. Nada. Ruby and I tore the house apart without finding one blasted thing."

"Well, don't feel bad, sweetie," Willard twittered. "Maureen and I didn't do any better. There are simply tons of books written about haunted houses, particularly ones in the South, and they are soooo interesting. I mean you would not believe some of the nasty things our ancestors got up too." His eyes gleamed. "But alas, there's not much about what to do with them when they're unwanted. It appears they do the picking and choosing." He sighed, hands falling theatrically as he ignored the loud snort of disgust coming from Jessie.

"Especially if you don't know who, or what, is doing the haunting," Maureen added. "If we're to rid ourselves of this juvenile ghost, we're going to have to not only discover its identity, origin, and time period, but more important, why it's able to remain and what it's after."

"My child's body and soul," Carol cried, openly wringing her hands. "And how can we find that out? Aunt Emma's already looked everywhere. There isn't anything to be found."

"Maybe there is."

All eyes swivelled to Phillip.

"I told Dad what was happening. Once he'd recovered from his initial shock and disbelief, he had a great idea. We'd planned to visit Grandpa James in Atlanta this weekend. He's at one of those Baptist nursing homes. Dad says if we're lucky and catch him on a good day, he might recall any strange rumors about Shadow Lake. At any rate, there's a good chance he'll know something about the original owners."

"Oh, Phillip, do you think he might?" Carol's eyes shone.

"I'm making no promises, but I'll try."

"Bless you, Lord." Emma sighed. "At least, it's a start. Thank your father for us, Phillip. Anyone else?"

"I keep telling you 'bout that white witch," Jessie complained. "Don't know whys you won't listen."

"I have." Emma assured her. "It's just we're not to that stage."

"If you asks me, you getting to that stage pretty fast," she muttered darkly, popping the last piece of shortbread in her mouth before Willard could beat her to it.

"Did you remember anymore about the deaths of Richard's first wife and child?" Emma asked Maureen. "I've thought and thought about what you told me. It seems so bizarre. Do you actually think Lettice killed her daughter thinking she was some kind of sexual deviate?"

"I'm convinced of it," Maureen's voice dropped, her eyes darted toward the house. "After you made me recall the trauma of my childhood and the horrible desires that flooded my mind, I became certain that's what happened. Lettice had always been a cheerful, well-adjusted woman. There was no reason for her to go off the deep end doing what she did. She must have become aware of her daughter's aberrations. I think she murdered Lisbeth to keep her from being exposed to a life of degradation, or perhaps, from ending up placed in an asylum. Then of course, once she'd taken the child's life, she had no recourse except to take her own."

"Do you think Richard knew?"

"About Lisbeth? I hope not. However, from what he told me, I'm afraid Lettice might have written something in her suicide note to that effect. But, I believe he decided his wife had lost her mine and just dismissed those accusations as lunatic ravings."

"Think what she went through, and all alone," Emma's voice trembled. All at once, she felt a great load lift. She realized the jealousy she had felt for Richard's first wife had miraculously disappeared. In its place was a bond of affection and admiration. For an instant, her eyes lifted to the bedroom window in the south wing. She could have sworn the figure of a woman stood there.

Emma shivered. "She must have cared greatly for him."

"She wasn't the only one." Maureen smiled at her sister-in-law. "I don't know what Richard did to deserve the love of two such fine women, but he was certainly blessed."

"Why you suppose he locked that wing if he didn't know it were haunted?" Jessie had been mulling over this.

"The only answer I have, is that it probably did bring back painful memories. It was where the bodies of his family were found. Maybe he felt shutting it permanently might lessen his sorrow. And then, it's not like the extra rooms were needed."

"No," Carol said, "not until Lucy and I appeared on the scene. Oh, Aunt Maureen, do you really think it's wise for you and Willard to sleep there?"

"No," he exploded before his employer could answer.

"You 'fraid of that ghostie, little man?" Jessie taunted. "Well, if you worried, I wouldn't be. I 'spects you ain't got nothin' that gonna be attractin' that spook to you," she taunted, still irate over his earlier attempt to put pickle relish in her deviled eggs. "That spook be tryin' to get itself a *real* man, not one runnin' 'round stickin' he nose in strange women's pots and pans."

"Strange is soooo right," he lisped, "and I don't know which is stranger. The woman or the filling in her eggs."

"I noticed that filling weren't too strange fer you to keep from poppin' five in you mouth."

"Did not."

"Did too."

"Jessie. Willard. What in heaven's name is wrong with you?" Emma was aghast.

She knew the cook was territorial, but she'd never seen her act like this, nor had she ever seen Willard respond in such a manner. Usually he ignored the old woman, content to make faces behind her back.

"You ought to be ashamed. How can we drive this thing away if we're expending our energy fighting among ourselves? That only divides and weakens."

"Perhaps that's the plan." Tim's eyes narrowed. "I know you fed us out here to keep it from hearing our discussion, but Miss Emma, are you sure it didn't?"

She felt a chill cover her body. Shivering, she replied, "No, not really. I just assumed . . ." Her voice trailed away.

"Oh, Miss Emma." Jessie's eyes widened. "You 'members Rascal? It were here by the lake we heered him howling that first time."

They looked around fearfully. Carol reached out taking a hand of each of her suitors.

"And the window," Jessie continued, eyes dilated, whites shining, "'member you saw that bony hand scratching on your window. 'Member it were on the *outside* trying to get in?"

"You told me I was dreaming." Emma was fighting to breathe properly.

"That before I knowed we had us a ghost." Her voice broke. "That before I knowed our home done been haunted."

Instantly the waters began rippling across the lake. A cold wind swept its surface disturbing the peaceful scene, bending the cattails double, bringing with it an unbelievable stench.

"Something's dead." Tim started forward. "I'll see if I can

locate it. It needs to be buried. Wow. It's really bad."

"Don't bother. You won't find anything." Emma was no longer frightened. A firm resolve had overtaken her. "That's what I smelled last night. She's letting us know her boundaries *do* extend beyond the house."

"The little bitch is taunting us." Maureen was astounded. "She's literally rubbing her face in our noses. She wants us to realize she's heard every word we've said."

The blood drained from each face as the laughter began. Soft at first, it soon became shrill, much like what Emma heard the night she'd sat alone in her front hall waiting for whatever might appear. It grew in volume. No telling how long it might have lasted if Billy Bob hadn't run across the lawn calling their names, breaking the spell.

Emma could see he was upset and was further surprised by Anthony running at his side, pausing every step or two to leap in the air, trying to grab whatever he held in his hand.

"Miss Emma." He reached her side so breathless he couldn't speak. Silently, he thrust out his tiny bundle.

Gingerly, she took it from him. Carefully opening the young man's soiled handkerchief, she cried aloud at the sight of its contents.

"What is it, Miss Emma?" Tim stepped to her side. Wordlessly, she handed it over.

"Anthony dug it up." Billy Bob recovered his voice. "I were puttering in the flower bed and he commenced digging in the pansies. I thought he were jest," he ducked his head, embarrassed, "you knows, needin to 'cuse hisself, but then I saw he were pullin' on somethin'. I went to see what it were, and . . ." His eyes fell.

"What is it?" Maureen was growing agitated, as was everyone else. "What the hell did the cat dig up?"

Tim opened his palm. A tiny kitten lay crumpled. The ribbon knotted too tight around its neck, limp and soiled.

"Oh, sweet Jesus." Jessie threw her apron over her face.

"Don't tell me that's Stanley's kitten?" Carol was beside

herself. "Don't tell me my baby killed Stanley's kitten?"

"I 'spects she did," Billy Bob spoke softly. "I seen her playin' with them early this mornin'. Then I seed her diggin' in the flower bed before she and Ruby left."

"This can't be happening," Carol whimpered, catching hold of Tim's free hand. "What are we going to do? That was Stanley's kitten. What will we tell him?"

"Nothing," Emma was having difficulty speaking, the pain in her chest so great. "Undo the ribbon, Tim. Hand it to me. We'll laundry and tie it around the next smallest female. Thank goodness, Siamese kittens all look alike. Stanley won't know the difference."

"But what about my daughter?" Carol screamed. "We can't just bring in a substitute for Lucy. A nice, normal child instead of this murderous monster." She sank to her knees, crying wildly.

"Billy Bob, please bury the kitten where Anthony can't find and dig it up again, though I think he probably won't." She gazed thoughtfully at her pet standing quietly, staring so intently into her face his eyes had crossed. "I believe he wanted us to see what had happened." She knelt, gently lifting him. "Poor little father. You have good reason to hate our uninvited guest, don't you?" She grew more thoughtful. "And, for some reason she doesn't care for you either. In fact, she almost seems afraid of you."

"It seems to me, we don't have a lot of time left," Phillip's voice was grim. "I'd better not wait for the weekend. I'll leave for Atlanta, tomorrow."

"Good." Maureen agreed. "Events do seem to be escalating. Jessie, I don't care how Emma feels about your witch. I think you need to contact her."

"Done decided that myself." Jessie lowered her apron. "I gwine see 'bout it right aways."

"Tim, you wait until I get the other kitten ready. I don't want the chance of something else happening. I'd planned on keeping them for another few days, but they're weaned. It won't hurt to take them from their mother now."

"You promised me one of those precious darlings," Willard reminded her. "Do you think Lucy will kill it too?"

"No. It was just unfortunate Stanley selected the kitten Lucy wanted. We won't mention you getting one until you're ready to leave. By then." She stared over the lake in the direction the laughter had come from. "By then, the child will be back to normal."

"And if she's not?" Carol cried. "If she's still under the influence of this devil? What then, Auntie Em?"

"She *will* be back to normal and this spawn of Satan *will* be gone." Emma set her jaw. Raising a fist high in the air she issued her challenge. "You hear me? You *will* be gone!"

Chapter Twenty-Two

This was ridiculous. Emma was absolutely exhausted. So why in Sam Hill was she still awake? Surely it wasn't the pizza or Greek salad Ruby had brought home. Emma wanted to give Jessie a treat after preparing that huge picnic for lunch, and pizza was her favorite indulgence. It had been delicious and Jessie was delighted, besides which, spicy food had never bothered Emma before.

No, she grimaced in the dark, it was not the evening meal but the evening itself that was causing her insomnia. Truth be told, Emma was terrified something foul might come floating through her door at any minute. What had possessed her to hurl that challenge, "You *will* be gone," straight into the face of whatever hovered here? What on God's green earth was she thinking? A skinny old woman battling a force so strong, so evil, no telling how many souls or lives it had already destroyed. Fool. She probably only made matters worse. Now it had to prove itself. Had to do something drastic to put her in her place and assert its power and control. Damn. Damn. Damn!

She lifted a trembling hand and began stroking Anthony's fur. He was pressed hard against her side, head laying on her chest, eyes open and glittering. Indeed, that didn't do anything to lighten her frame of mind. Anthony had not dined on pizza and he was not sleeping either. In fact, she could feel him coiled tight, prepared to attack what threatened his home and loved ones.

"I'm sorry about your baby." She gently cupped his silky head in her hand. "You know, if I'd realized Lucy was a threat, I'd have sent the kittens home with Ruby." Tears spewed across her cheeks like a creek run amuck. All the pent up fears and horrors of the past months spilled out in her grief for the kitten. "I want them to have good homes. Want them loved and cared for like you and Cleo."

The cat lifted his paw placing it on her cheek, causing the tears to fall faster.

"Oh, Anthony, what are we going to do?"

Hearing her cries and sensing her distress, Cleo jumped out of the kitten's basket placed in Emma's room for safety. Springing onto the bed beside her mate, she mewled softly, pushing her head against Emma, butting and talking as she sought to comfort her mistress.

"What little darlings you are." Emma gathered both in her arms cradling them like babies. "Everyone should have an Anthony and Cleo to love and be loved. I think that's why God has given us such delightful creatures as you. To show what He means by unconditional love. A love Paul describes as patient, kind, never jealous, selfish, or proud. One that bears no grudges or seeks revenge. One asking only for faith, trust, and quite often sacrifice."

She kissed each between their ears. "And, my darlings, you most certainly fill all those requirements." She paused a moment, before continuing in a sadder vein. "You, and those like Stanley."

Emma had been relieved when the young man called thanking her profusely for the kitten. He promised he would love and care for it always. Then, her heart almost stopped. He asked her not to blame Lucy. That it wasn't her fault about Pretty Emma. It was the other one made her do it. He felt bad about his kitten, but would love this one just as much, and Emma should tell Lucy he was naming it after her. When she recovered her breath, she asked to speak with Tim. He swore he'd said nothing, but that Stanley had immediately known there had been a substitution. Tim was as spooked as she, though this only confirmed what Emma always suspected. Animals, and those gifted in other ways, commuted on a level most of us can never reach.

It had been Stanley's plea that helped Emma win the argument over what to do about Lucy. Maureen and her mother felt she should be punished, but the rest disagreed. They were afraid making an issue of the kitten's death might further antagonize the child. Might only strengthen the position of whatever was trying to possess her. Emma insisted they wait to see how the girl handled the situation. She was hoping if they ignored the incident, it might bring the creature's attention more on the adults and less on Lucy.

The thought of that *thing* made Emma shudder. She clasped the cats closer. She was afraid she might have squeezed too hard when she felt Anthony stiffen. A rumble began deep in his throat. Cleo leaped out of her arms and ran straight to her kittens. Emma knew what she feared had come to pass. The ghastly apparition was roaming the halls.

Heart thudding like a dozen tom toms, she slipped out of bed into her robe. Anthony close at her heels, she crossed to the door. She prayed for courage to touch the knob, remembering the pain from last time vividly. She hoped the wrappings covering her hand would serve as protection. But, dear God, what new horror waited on the other side? The bandages would only keep flesh from being burned. What other monstrous surprise did this thing have in mind?

Breath held, she reached out, twisted the handle and flung the door wide. Anthony shot like a space capsule down the hall to the south wing. She heard Carol call her name, but unheeding, ran after the cat. The fear of what might have happened to Maureen and Willard, or might happen to Anthony, moved legs, she was certain, would have otherwise remained frozen.

A loud crash sounded behind her. Something heavy and clumsy was chasing her. She was terrified to turn and face it.

Terrified of what she would see and what effect it would have. Now the damn thing was laughing. The same soft laughter she had heard earlier that evening, tiptoeing over the water, sneaking through the cat tails, taunting and teasing.

Any second she expected a hand—a bony hand—She remembered it well, fingers extended, clawing at her bedroom window. She was afraid it was about to fall on her shoulder, snatch her backwards and force her to look on its ghastly features.

"Auntie Em, where are you going? You look so funny with your hair sticking up and your gown puffed out like a balloon."

She wheeled around. Lucy stood, a sly grin twisting her face into such a horrifying grimace Emma was sure a ghostly apparition would have been no more chilling.

"Lucy. What are you doing up?"

Carol appeared in the hall leaning heavily against the wall. "I knocked over a lamp. I hope it didn't break."

So that was the racket coming from behind her, and Lucy, the source of those menacing giggles. Thank you, Lord. She thought she might faint from relief, but that was quickly dashed when a shrill shriek tore through the house, followed by shouting, cursing, and more loud crashes. Lucy darted past, but Emma was too quick for her, grabbing the child's arm bringing her up short.

"Carol, keep Lucy with you. I don't care what happens, or what you hear. Don't let her out of your sight."

The child's face turned even uglier. She balled her fists as if to strike.

"Don't even think it." Her mother's voice cut like a razor. "Get your butt in this room now, Lucy. I mean now."

Lucy threw Emma a look of pure hate, but surprisingly turned and followed her mother. Emma stood still until both were inside Carol's room and she heard the key turn in the lock. Then, heart hammering, she raced through the suddenly unfamiliar corridors of her home.

Chapter Twenty-Three

Emma burst through the door to the south wing straight into the arms of a creature more hideous than anything she could have imagined. Moonlight flooded the room outlining a being straight from hell. The face was a frozen white mask. The mouth an open maw yawning wide. A stream of shrill profanity poured through the gaping lips, as with a voracious appetite, it raised bat-like wings and reached for her. "Oh God," she cried out. It was Satan himself. She could even make out the horns atop his head.

"Yoweee!" She closed her eyes, threw her head back and totally lost it. Her screams were as loud, if not louder than her attacker.

"For Pete's sake. Both of you put a lid on it."

Emma's eyes snapped open. The room was ablaze with lights. Maureen stood to one side, Anthony draped over her shoulder, and the devil. She couldn't believe it. It couldn't possibly be, but heaven help her, it was. She slid to the floor in a heap.

"Don't just stand there, you ninny. Get her some water," Maureen ordered, "and pray she's fainted and not had a heart attack."

"I-I haven't." Emma began trying to rise, her body shaking as she fell back.

"She's having a fit. Quick, Willard, you idiot. Call 911."

"No. It's him." Emma pointed a trembling finger. "I've never seen anything funnier in my whole life." She collapsed giggling helplessly.

"Well, I never," he sputtered furious.

Maureen, aware for the first time of her friend's appearance, sank to the nearest chair and joined in Emma's laughter.

"Who-what in the name of hell happened here?" Emma attempted to rise again, but after another look at Willard's outraged expression, failed. "I thought the ghost was after you."

"It was." Willard drew himself up in an all-righteous indignation, bringing new bursts of merriment from the women. "And, damn you both, it wasn't one bit funny."

"No." She hiccuped. "I'm sure not." She bit her lip, using every ounce of self control to keep a straight face. "I'm sorry, Willard. I guess I'm so scared it's made me slightly crazy. I didn't intend to laugh. I mean, this isn't a laughing matter."

A loud snort from the other side of the room doomed her good intentions. She sank back to the floor, kicking her heels, hooting and bellowing. Even Anthony became alarmed, leaping out of Maureen's arms to investigate the strange antics of his mistress.

"Get a grip, Willard." Maureen fanned her face. "Wow, if anyone had told me I'd get such a charge from being scared half to death, I'd have said they were nuts." She grinned impishly. "I bet we weren't the only surprised ones, though. We probably frosted the fanny off whatever sailed in here tonight. Don't you think?"

The door across the hall slammed shut.

At once, the three sobered. Their eyes widened, searching every inch of Carol's sitting room.

"I think you better tell me what happened," Emma weakly demanded. "At least, after Willard cleans up." She felt another wave of laughter coming on, when with a loud crack, the mirror over the dressing table splintered.

"Damn. I hate it when she breaks things." Emma jumped to her feet. "Why don't you show yourself, you little twerp? Afraid you'll look as silly as Willard? Afraid all we'll do is laugh?"

"Shut up, Emma." Maureen's face whitened to match her companion's. "Don't push our luck. What happened earlier wasn't pleasant. I'm not anxious for a repeat performance."

"What did happen?" Emma, for the first time, noticed the cosmetic bottles scattered over the dressing table and the spilled make-up, most of which was splashed over Willard.

"When we left you, we got ready for bed," Maureen began to explain, "but weren't sleepy. I guess we were too keyed up after the combination of picnic events and pizza. Anyway, we decided to have a drink. It was probably much later than you when we called it a night."

"I couldn't sleep either. I was waiting for something to happen. I knew after I yelled that challenge, she'd do something ugly."

"You keep saying 'she.'" Maureen frowned. "Are you positive about the sex?"

"If she's not, I am," Willard spluttered, outraged. "And, you won't believe what *she* did."

"Painted you like an Indian on the warpath?" Emma couldn't resist.

"No, that was Maureen's doing." He glared at his old friend.

"Well, you don't need to get in such an uproar." She defended herself. "After all, I saved you."

"Saved me! You almost killed me."

"Stop it, both of you. This isn't going anywhere." Emma having risen from the floor spotted a small bar set up on the dresser. "Let's have a nightcap and each tell our tale."

"As soon as Willard washes." Maureen grinned. "Sorry, my dear, but as long as you look like a clown reject from some circus, I cannot concentrate."

Head high, shoulders back, he marched with mincing steps to the bathroom. The door closed. Seconds later they heard a loud exclamation and curse.

"I'd say he looked in the mirror." Maureen shook her head smiling. "What would I do without him, my comical little knight in not-so-shining armor."

"I'm fixing these straight up." Emma was admiring the cut glass tumblers she was pouring Blanton's bourbon into. "Wonder how long it'll be before the little bitch smashes these?"

"Don't give her any ideas. I bought those years ago and always take them with me. They're so beautiful they make the liquor taste better." Maureen drew a hand across her brow. "Emma, I think we're too old for this."

"Not a chance. Hell, Maureen, in spite of everything that's happened, I don't know when I've laughed as hard."

"Bless his tiny heart. He was a sight."

"So." She handed her guest a full glass. "What went on in here?" She waved a hand encompassing the room's disarray.

"We said our good nights and crawled into bed. Willard suggested leaving the door open between the rooms, in case I got scared." She snickered.

"Yeah, sure." Emma rolled her eyes.

"Anyway, I no sooner got comfortable when the temperature plummeted. I swear, it was so cold I could see my breath like vapor in the moonlight."

"That's a new trick."

"According to the books on haunted houses, it's a common occurrence," Maureen informed her. "Anyway, the room became a freezer. Needless to say, I was wide awake." Maureen took a big gulp of her drink. "However, I decided to act like I was sleeping and see what else would happen."

"And?" Emma prodded when she failed to continue. "What did?"

"It, she, whatever, slowly began pulling my covers off. I didn't know what to do. The thought of nothing being between me and that thing was more than I could stomach. I wanted to call Willard, but my tongue was glued to the roof of my mouth. I remember thinking if this creature puts it's hands on me I'll probably die." She downed the rest of her drink, quickly going to pour another.

"Did it? Did it touch you?"

She shook her head. "It was the damnest thing. The covers lifted. I was petrified. I remembered what you'd said about Billy Bob's experience. I thought it was going to crawl in bed with me, and for those few seconds, I came close to losing my mind."

"And then?"

"Just when I thought it was getting in, it stopped. I could sense it retreating." She reached for one of Emma's hands. "Just when I thought my sanity was going for good, I was awash in this scent."

"Isn't it foul?" Emma wrinkled her nose.

"Not this time." Maureen seemed wistful. "This time it was the scent of gardenias. Then, something brushed against my cheek. It wasn't frightening. It comforted me."

"That makes no sense. You can't experience fear and comfort from the same source."

"I didn't." She squeezed Emma's hand. "We're not alone anymore. Lettice, Richard's first wife, wore a perfume especially blended for her. It smelled like the most heavenly gardenias." She searched her sister-in-law's face. "Don't you see? She was here. We're not fighting whatever this is by ourselves. Lettice is helping us. I know it."

"Are you telling me there's more than one ghost walking around my halls?" Emma jerked her hand from Maureen, her voice shrill. "Just how many spooks are haunting this damn house anyway?"

"At least two." Maureen watched Willard enter, walk straight to the bar, down his drink and pour another. "Maybe we better ask Willard how many he sensed."

"There was more than one?" His voice rose.

"That's what Maureen thinks. She says Lettice drove the bad one away."

"What makes you so sure?" His eyes glittered, hands trembled.

"I smelled her perfume and she touched my cheek. It was warm and comforting."

"Well, whatever touched me, let me tell you, sisters, it was not warm nor comforting."

"Just exactly what did happen?" Emma asked.

"I was wiggling around trying to get comfortable. That sofa bed is sooo hard."

"I'm sorry," Emma apologized.

He ignored the interruption, anxious to tell his side of the story. "It got cold. Freezing. I was about to call Maureen but then." He scrubbed his lips furiously with one of his hands. "Something kissed me. It was unlike anything I've ever experienced." He ducked his head and in a whisper continued, "I don't know if you've ever suspected, Emma," his voice dropped lower, "but I'm not taken with women the way most men are. I mean, I love them, but I just don't . . ."

"You don't have to explain."

"Even so, I've kissed a lot in my time, but not like this. This creature was kissing me and it wouldn't stop. It was choking me. Smothering me to death. I couldn't breath, couldn't cry out, couldn't do anything. It was killing me. Sucking the life right out of my lungs."

"That's what I must have heard." Maureen took up the tale. "After Lettice came and the other left, seconds later I heard this awful gurgling coming from the sitting room. I ran in, hit the light switch but nothing happened. However, there was enough moonlight for me to see Willard struggling. I snatched the first handy weapon, which happened to be my make-up, and started pelting it at Willard's assailant."

"Now I know why he resembled a drunken geisha." Emma giggled.

"It didn't look like I was doing any good. I mean the jars just flew through empty air."

"Not all," he muttered under his breath.

"But then Anthony came screeching through the door leaping straight at Willard. Something pushed me aside, almost knocking me down. The next thing I knew, you were yelling louder than Willard and the cat combined. At that instant, the lights came on."

"You'd have yelled too, if you'd have run up against what I

did." Emma defended herself.

"Well," he retorted, "you were just as scary."

"No way. I didn't have a stark white face, Dracula-like bat arms, and horns on my head."

"You know." Maureen was delighted by her marksmanship. "I must have scored a direct hit to Willard's puss."

"Very funny, Annie Oakley." The two drinks were beginning to have a calming effect. "Emma, the bat wings are my dressing gown sleeves. It's pure silk, you know, and they're extremely full." He paused, batting his lashes. "An old admirer gave it to me. It was verrry expensive," he bragged.

"Why the hell did you wear it to bed?" Maureen demanded.

"In case I had to rise and come to your aid."

Maureen produced another unladylike snort.

"All right, we've explained the white mask and bat wing arms, but what about the horns?" Emma was still puzzled.

"I know," Maureen announced, pointing to the beauty mask sticking out of his robe pocket. "He's forever putting it atop his head then forgetting to pull it down over his eyes. It sticks up in two big humps when he pushes it onto his forehead."

"Well, I wish our other mystery were as easily solved."

"Oh, Emma, maybe Phillip will call with news tomorrow," Maureen said.

"Maybe." She slowly put down her glass. "I don't know about you guys, but I'm pooped. In fact, I'm so tired I don't think the dead could wake me." She clapped her hands over her mouth, realizing what she'd said as soon as the words were out.

"Dear God, Emma. What a stupid remark." Maureen snatched Anthony up and thrust him into her arms. "Here. Carry him on your way back to your room. The damn thing must be allergic to cats. It runs every time they show up."

"I hope you're right." Emma clasped him tightly against her as she fled past Lucy's closed door, down the hall to her room.

Chapter Twenty-Four

Jessie faced them, hands on hips, glowering as they slowly trailed into the breakfast room past the usual appointed time.

"Tellin' all of you right now. I don't run one of them fancy hotels. You gets up 'round here at a decent hour or you don't get no breakfast outta this ole' lady."

"We're sorry, Jessie. We'll make do with coffee if it's still available," Emma said.

"What's the matter with you?" Jessie stared, exhaustion clearly etched across her friend's face. "Why you lookin' so washed out, and why you ain't tellin' me you pays the salary and you eat when you damn well please? What went on here last night?" She threw up her hands. "Lawd, doan tell me. We done had us another hauntin'."

"Bingo," Maureen retorted, "and Jessie, could you please find some toast to serve with that coffee?"

"I find everythin'. I got us a good breakfast holdin' in the warmer oven. I jest mad cause I thought ya'll be sitting up all night partyin' and leavin' ole Jessie out."

"I wouldn't dream of it," Emma assured her, "and I'm real sorry you missed Maureen and Willard's welcome. I'd have been more than delighted if you'd taken my place."

"Willard?" Jessie's eyes gleamed.

"Don't even go there," Emma warned.

"Well, you just know she's going to," Willard spoke, still wearing the offending robe, nonthreatening in the daylight, "but not until after I've had coffee, or whatever." He raised a limp hand brushing back his tangled hair. "Oh Jessie, you will not believe." He played dramatically to his appreciative audience.

"I believes." She grabbed him by one of the dangling sleeves. "You jest get you fanny in my kitchen right now. Starts tellin' while I pour the coffee. They some hot cinnamon rolls in the oven. You can be eatin' one of them while I dishes up the rest of the meal. You can be talkin' while you chewin'." She pulled him after her. "We gonna jest call this here breakfast, brunch, Miss Emma, like they do in them fancy hotels. I ain't got no time to be thinkin' on no noon meal. Willard and me gonna get us that white witch and we ain't gonna have our mind worryin' on nothin' else."

"Well, that's a first. Jessie inviting Willard into her kitchen. Now I'm convinced something's weird at Shadow Lake," Maureen said.

Emma tried smiling, then gave up. "Maureen, I'm so tired I could . . ." she stopped, searching for another word, "could collapse," she finished weakly. "How much longer can we put up with this?"

"As long as it takes." Maureen's jaw set. "Until we drive the damn thing back where it came from."

"I can't. I simply can't go through another night like the last one."

"You don't have a choice." Maureen reached out turning Emma's face to hers, forcing her to look her in the eyes. "This isn't a house we're fighting for. It's a life. A child's life. Emma, it's not only Shadow Lake it wants, but Lucy too."

"You're right." She sat up straight. "I need my coffee, that's all." She frowned. "Where the hell is it? Jessie, where's our coffee?"

"Hold your horses, you skinny ole' woman. I has it jest as soon as I gets Mr. Willard's roll buttered. You know men needs a heap of feedin'."

"She's buttering his roll?" Emma failed to believe her ears.

"She called him a man?" Maureen was just as astonished.

"I wonder how much his story's grown in the telling." Emma giggled, Jessie's bossiness beginning to restore her to her old self. "And I wonder what role of hero and protector our little friend has assumed."

Maureen laughed. "Lay you odds, to hear him tell it, he's probably got Jessie convinced he's Georgia's answer to Rambo. I sure as hell wish he was." She winked. "Sylvester Stallone sleeping on my sofa would suit this ole gal just fine."

"Here's the coffee. Ya'll drink that and enjoy it slow like. I got a few things I gots to tend to in the kitchen 'fore I can bring out the rest."

"What? Buttering Willard's rolls?" Emma asked.

"Some peoples," she began, then abruptly halted. "Hey there, Miss Lucy, you comin' to join the ladies fer breakfast?"

The child stood in the doorway glaring at her aunt.

"One of Cleo's kittens is gone."

"I'd say more than one," Maureen retorted.

"Who asked you?"

"Lucy. What has gotten into you? You're speaking to an adult." Emma was aghast.

"Where is it? It was my second pick. You promised I had second pick after Stanley."

"I sent him the kitten, after Anthony dug up the one you killed—"

"I never," she screamed, fists balled.

"Oh, I think you did." Her head began pounding. She was too old for this.

"You're a liar. You don't know anything. If you did—" she caught herself.

"If I did, what, Lucy?"

"If you did, you'd leave. All of you."

"And you, my dear, what would you do?" Maureen asked.

"I'd stay." An intense look of cunning crossed her face.

"By yourself? A young girl. You know better than that." Maureen studied her. "You do realize that isn't possible, don't you, darling?"

"I've been by myself before." She turned blank eyes on them. "I've been by myself for a long, long time."

"How long, dear?" Again, Maureen questioned her.

"Longer than you've been around, old lady," she exploded.

"Lucy." Her mother, leaning against the door behind her, was appalled.

"So, you gave that stupid boy my cat. You're a liar after all, aren't you Emma?"

Carol, holding to the doorframe for support, reached back and slapped her daughter hard enough to lift her feet from the floor.

"Mama?" The child lay in a crumpled heap. A dazed look on her face.

Carol turned away sobbing loudly. Emma went to her.

"Shush, Carol, hush. It'll be alright. I promise Maureen and I will fix it."

"That wasn't my baby." Carol wept. "Oh, Auntie Em, tell me that wasn't my baby."

"No, dear. I don't believe it was."

"You damn well better know it wasn't." Maureen knelt by Lucy's side. "Are you all right, child?"

The girl's cheek flamed red. "What did I do? Why did Mama hit me?" She seemed more confused than injured. "Where's Jessie? I want breakfast."

"Here I is, honey. You comes on back in the kitchen with Willard and me. We got some hot buttery cinnamon buns jest waitin' fer a sweet baby's lips."

"I don't feel good."

They couldn't get over the amount of vomit spewing out of such a little thing, or the force with which it splashed them, the walls, table, cabinets and floor. The stench rising from it was unbelievable.

"Get her out of here," Jessie ordered. "Willard, you yell out the door at Billy Bob. Tell him we need him. The rest of you get upstairs and clean up. Lawd. I ain't never seed sech a mess."

"I'm sorry," Lucy whimpered, staring at the devastation she'd wrought.

A loud retching came from behind. Jessie whirled, screaming, "Not in my kitchen, you don't. Willard, you gets your fanny out the back door and into the yard before you brings even one crumb of those rolls back up on my clean floor."

"Carol, can you make it on your own?" Emma was concerned about her niece. The dreadful fall down the stairs and now this. "Can I help you to your room?"

"No, I'll be fine," she answered weakly. "Lucy . . ."

"I'll take Lucy and clean her up. Don't worry about anything. Maureen and I will manage."

"You can take that to the bank." The other woman smiled grimly, one hand covering her nose. "At least, Emma, nothing got broken this time."

"And that's supposed to comfort me?" She was carefully stepping through the nastiness. "How could one small child spill out so much, especially when she hasn't eaten since yesterday?"

"Use your head. Lucy didn't. This vomiting stunt is another charming trick I discovered in the books on haunted houses."

"There's more?" Emma didn't think she could take more.

"I'm not about to list them. We don't want to give it any ideas."

They were almost to the stairs when the phone rang.

"Take Lucy upstairs, please. Stick her in the shower, Maureen. I'll join you as soon as I answer this."

Minutes later, she joined her sister-in-law bathing Lucy.

Once the child was cleaned up and sent to Ruby, Emma took the opportunity to speak with Maureen.

"That was Phillip."

"Great. What'd he say?"

"His Grandad didn't have a good day."

"Oh no." Maureen's heart sank.

"Bless his heart, he swore he was staying until he did."

"Emma, we can't wait."

"What do you mean?"

"I mean this child is in mortal danger." Maureen took a deep breath. "That wasn't Lucy there for a while. You know it as well as I do."

"But, Maureen . . ."

"No, buts. We're going to replenish the holy water, stock up on more crosses and pray Jessie's white witch is as good as she thinks."

"What if we only make matters worse?" Emma was frightened, terrified of another confrontation.

"We don't have a choice. It's growing stronger every day. Soon Lucy won't be hearing voices, soon, like this morning, she'll be the voice."

Chapter Twenty-Five

"Carol. I want you to do exactly what you did last night." Emma sat on the side of the bed holding tight to her niece's hand. "I want you to keep Lucy with you, and under no circumstances are you to open the door. Not until I tell you, and not until you're positive it's me doing the telling."

"But, I feel so helpless. It's my child that's brought this creature here. I should be trying to destroy it."

"If you can keep Lucy away, you'll be doing more than your share. I suspect that might not be as easy as you think. Did she give you any problems last night?"

"No, though I almost wish she had. She simply sat on the foot of the bed, head cocked like she was listening to something I couldn't hear, with a funny little grin on her face." She shuddered. "Gave me the all out creeps."

"Tonight's probably going to be a different story. Jessie and Willard have gone for Jessie's witch. Maureen went for more holy water and to apprize Tim of the latest plans. Ruby will join us when she brings Lucy home."

"Maybe we should have her spend the night at Ruby's."

"I don't think so." Emma grew thoughtful. "I have the feeling Lucy needs to be close by. We want to be positive she and the house are both cleansed. Besides, this white witch might want her to be here."

"What about Billy Bob?"

Emma laughed loudly. "I've got as much chance getting Billy Bob back for another exorcism as I have getting Jessie to go on a diet."

"So, when does the action take place?" Carol was becoming nervous.

"Midnight, unless the witch changes the plan. That's when it seems to be most frisky." She reached in her pocket drawing out two gold crosses. "I want you and Lucy to wear these. I also want you to keep hold of your Bible and pray. It doesn't matter what you hear, see, or feel, just keep praying."

"Oh, Aunt Emma, I'm not sure I can. You're about to scare me to death."

"As Maureen hastened to inform me, you have no choice. Lucy is being absorbed by this demon. It's totally taking her over, and as you saw this morning, it's nobody we want in the family."

Carol managed a weak smile. "I'll do what you say. I promise."

"One more thing." She picked up a sack she had brought in with her. "Don't let Lucy know you have this, but Carol, for God's sake, use it if you must." She set a quart jar of water on the girl's bedside table.

"Is this?"

"Holy water. So far, it's worked better than anything else I've tried. I don't know how I'd have gotten to Billy Bob, if I hadn't poured it over that red hot knob."

Carol ducked her head, eyes filling. "I'm so sorry about this. If we hadn't come, none of it would be happening. You'd still be enjoying your beautiful home, and the worse thing you'd have to put up with would be Jessie's soaps."

"Well, I'm not." Emma took a deep breath before confessing. "I have to admit, at first that thought crossed my mind, but then I had another. What, if when I died and left you Shadow Lake, you'd decided to live here? What would have happened then, to Lucy or another child you might someday have? We already know about Lettice and Lisbeth. About Maureen and the battle of wills she fought." She lifted Carol's chin smiling encouragement. "Listen darling, I'm glad you and Lucy came. Glad Lucy brought it out now, while they're so many of us surrounding you with our love and support. It's going to take a strong united front to destroy this fiend. It's as evil as evil comes and it's been a long time gathering strength. But darling, we will be victorious. We will drive it from this house."

"Good luck, Auntie Em." She reached up kissing her relative's soft cheek. "Good luck and God be with you."

***

"I think I hear them in the kitchen." Emma had been pacing, almost driving Maureen nuts. "At least, I hear someone in the kitchen," she tossed over her shoulder, walking quickly in that direction. She stopped so suddenly, Maureen, following, ran into her at full tilt.

"Here we is." Jessie beamed proudly before pointing. "This here is Miss Aurora Stargaze."

Facing Emma, grinning like a banshee, was one of the oddest sights she had viewed in her eighty years. The woman was a good six feet tall and a beehive hairdo added another eight inches. Sticking throughout the coils and twists of curls were large hairpins. Stars, moons, and Zodiac signs dangled off the ends of them making musical sounds whenever she moved. A long caftan, rift with rainbow colors, covered her skinny figure and her feet were shod in the largest and brightest gold sandals imaginable. But what really took Emma's breath away, was how very pale she was. Her eyes and skin so colorless she was close to being an albino.

"As Jessie would so aptly put it, 'Sweet Jesus,'" Maureen whispered from behind her. "You know, I bet this works. She's enough to scare the damn spook right through the rafters."

Emma was struggling to regain her composure. Maureen's little asides weren't helping.

"I'm pleased to meet you." She graciously extended her hand.

"I'm delighted you've come to our aid."

"Well now, honey, that's my business."

Lord, she's chewing bubble gum.

"Jessie did explain this wasn't no free bee?" The woman said.

The cook ducked her head, scurrying over to the stove. "Could I be fixin' someone tea?" She kept her face hidden. "I can't offers nothin' to eats coz Miss Stargaze done say we has to be fastin' like. She don't want no food in our bellies."

"Part of the sacrifice you make when you're in this kind of work." She heaved a labored sigh. "Of course, liquid refreshment is acceptable." She batted enormous false lashes. "Though I must say, tea can sometimes be offsetting. Now a good slug of bourbon will open the sinuses and prepare you for receiving good vibrations."

"I think a slug of bourbon might go well all around," Emma announced, wondering what the hell Jessie had gotten them in for. "Willard, why don't you take Miss Stargap . . ."

"Stargaze, sweetie, like those guys looking through them scopes do."

"Yes, sorry. Take Miss Stargaze and Maureen into the library and fix us drinks. I need a little word with Jessie."

As soon as the door closed, Emma grabbed her by the shoulders shaking her hard.

"Are you out of your mind? I thought you said this woman was a white witch?"

"Ole' lady, your eyes done fell out? If that woman ain't white, then you be tellin' me what color she do be?"

"Oh, Jessie." Emma sank into one of the kitchen chairs, laughing and slightly hysterical. "A white witch means a harmless witch. One that only practices good spells and doesn't hurt a soul."

"Well, how I suppose to know that?" She was irate. "I ain't had none of that college learnin'. I jest a ignorant ole' woman that wanted you to know I weren't bringin' in no black voodoo woman. I were bringin' you a white woman, and she a witch."

"I very much doubt that." Emma wiped her face where the tears had streamed. "I think you've brought us a first class charlatan."

"A what?"

"Never mind. Who told you about this woman, anyway?"

"Vonda and Idella. They got their fortunes tole and she were right on both of them. She say they gonna meet a good-looking man within the week, and Lawdy, but they did."

"Both?"

"Shore 'nuff. He our new preacher and he is lip slappin' purty."

"And that was it? That they'd meet a good-looking man?"

"Ain't that 'nuff?"

"Jessie, you met him too."

"Yeah, and if I'd had Miss Stargaze tell my fortune, then they'd been three of us she'd been right about."

"If you say so." Emma's disappointment was fast overcoming her amusement. "But, Jessie, that's a fortune teller, not a witch."

"She a witch, too."

"What makes you think so?"

"She done drove a spirit right outta Reba's chickens. They wasn't layin' good and this white witch sez a few words over them. In three weeks they be layin' jest as purty as you pleases."

"I don't think that's an unusual occurrence in the chicken world," Emma informed her. "Well, let's give her a drink, some cash and send her on her way."

"You mean you not gonna use her?" Jessie was indignant. "Not after I has to set and listen to that Willard be tellin' how he drove away the ghostie? I thoughts we'd never find that lady and get back here. 'Bout drove me crazy, and to think I went through all that and now you ain't gonna even see what this witch can do?"

Emma didn't know whether to laugh, cry, or belt Jessie for being such an ass. Then, to satisfy her friend, and figuring she had nothing to lose, Emma promised to give the woman a chance.

***

It was there Tim discovered them–Willard, Maureen, Jessie, and Miss Stargaze, all several sheets to the wind. Ruby had just arrived but already sent Lucy to her mother. Now, eyes wide, she watched the drunken antics of the four, growing increasingly concerned over Emma, sitting quietly, gnawing nervously on a fingernail.

As soon as Ruby saw Tim, she leaped to her feet. "It's time."

"Ish it already middynight?" Maureen fixed the girl with a baleful eye.

"Near enough." Emma was disgusted. "Thank heavens you're here, Tim. Help me get this fiasco over so I can go to bed and quietly lose my mind."

"Miss Emma," he whispered, "what is going on and what," he pointed behind her back, "is that?"

All at once, she giggled. "Jessie's white witch. Ain't she a doozey?"

"Have we got the crosses and other suff," Maureen slurred, "and we mushn't forget the water." She winked at Tim. "Might need it for the bourbon."

"Everyone hold hands and hummmmmmmmm." Aurora gathered them in a circle, her voice making the whole room vibrate.

"I'll be damned." Emma snorted in disgust.

"You promised," Jessie reminded.

"Oh, what the hell."

"Sounds like a hive of bees." Tim was having trouble keeping a straight face. "Reckon if it shows we're suppose to sting it to death?"

"Will the sh-pirits speak?" The witch raised her arms and fluttered them weakly in the air over her head. "Will the poor dear dish-parted roaming this joint show itshelf?"

"I don't wants to see it, Miss Aurora. You don't need to be tellin' it that." Jessie's teeth chattered. "You jest tell it to go way."

"Will the sh-pirit–"

A blast of cold wind roared through the house slamming shut doors, hurtling chairs to the floor, spinning the crystal chandeliers, knocking off pictures, loosening its fury on every object in its path including the seven in the study who were buffeted backwards, clothes twisted askew, hair snarled and tangled, breath pounded out.

It stopped as quickly as it came, leaving the four tipplers as sober as their companions.

"What the hell was that?" Aurora suddenly seemed eight feet tall, and if you counted the inches she'd gained from her hair standing straight on end, she probably was. "What was that?" she repeated, dazed.

"Our resident ghost," Emma announced. "The one you're supposed to remove."

"Not me."

She was, by now, if possible, even whiter, making Emma wonder if Jessie might describe her this time, like rice–a white on white witch.

"I'm outta here. This place is haunted." She ran for the front door, caftan flying, hairpins scattering, leaving the others staring, mouths wide.

"How's she getting home?" Ruby was first to speak.

"She followed in her car," Willard replied.

"That's the last times I listens to Idella and Vonda," Jessie announced. "Some witch she . . ."

"Somebody help me." Carol stood in the hall swaying weakly, Bible in one hand, empty jar in the other.

Chapter Twenty-Six

They froze. All but Tim who leaped to catch her as she fell, swinging her up in his arms, cradling her close.

"Lucy." Emma whirled around looking everywhere. "Where is she? Does anybody see her?"

In mass, they rushed up the stairs to Carol's room. The door was slightly ajar. As they approached, Emma heard a sound that made her blood run cold.

Three blind mice,
Three blind mice,
See how they run . . .

Heart in throat, Emma pushed against the closed door. The others crowded after her.

"Jesus, sweet, sweet Jesus," Jessie's voice trembled.

She faced them. She was Lucy's height, had Lucy's features, Lucy's coloring, yet, was nobody anyone there knew. None of them recognized the little girl dressed in Lucy's jeans and Barbie tee shirt, and no one had the courage to cross the threshold and challenge her.

"Lucy?" Maureen could scarcely get the words out. "Is that you?"

The eyes glittered. The lips curled back from the teeth in a feral grimace.

"What do you think, Miss Maureen?"

"I think Lucy's there, but so is someone else." Maureen's fear was fast being displaced with anger. Anger at the creature that had stolen so much of her life. She suddenly threw caution to the wind. "I'd like to know the name of the little brat that plagued me for so many years. That is, sweetie, if you have a name."

"Of course I do. Isn't it a shame you don't, and won't, ever know it."

"*Missy.*"

It came from all around. The word, a soft sigh filling the room.

The head of the child jerked up. The eyes darkened.

"Who the hell was that?" Tim pulled Carol protectively against him.

"Lettice," Maureen cried in triumph. "Can't you smell her perfume?"

Empowered, she thrust Emma aside, boldly walking over to the child. "By now, you must realize you aren't the only spirit here." She taunted the demonic sprite with glee. "Lettice has arrived." She moved closer, threatening the stranger with her superior size. "She might have had to face you by herself, but we don't. You nasty little bitch. Your victims have turned into your worse nightmare. So, what do you think of them apples?"

She leaped at Maureen. A guttural snarl poured from her mouth. Hands raised, she grasped Maureen's hair pulling her face down, at the same time sinking her teeth into the older woman's throat. Blood and salvia mixed, splattering over the walls as the child mouthed and tore her.

Tim and Ruby leaped into the fray. The child seemed possessed of a hundred men's strength. Despite them, her hold on Maureen didn't slacken.

"She'll kill her," Carol screamed. "Aunt Emma, do something."

"What?" Emma was frantic.

A loud crash turned her attention from the dreadful carnage taking place before her. Something was clawing and shrieking behind Emma's bedroom door. She was in time to see it fly open. Anthony and Cleo propelled outwards like a pair of bullets in flight. Racing at breakneck speed, the cats hurled into the room attacking the thing feasting on Maureen.

Its hands flew up to cover its face. A shriek, far shriller than the cat's cries, issued from its mouth. It crumpled limp to the floor. They backed away. Cleo first. Anthony next, his eyes remaining fixed on the child. The deep snarls slowly faded, as step by step the pair retreated.

The scent of gardenias flooded the room.

"Maureen." Emma ran to her side.

She leaned heavy against the bedroom dresser, face ashen and a gaping wound in her throat.

"Ruby, call 911. Tell them what's happened. That we're putting her in a car and heading out to meet them. I don't want to waste a second."

"How's Lucy?" Maureen managed to get out.

"Don't know and don't give a fiddler's damn." Emma was beside herself, terrified she might lose her sister-in-law over this and it was not worth it. She would burn the hellish house down and salt it like she had threatened.

"She don't mean that, Miss Carol. She jest so upsets." Jessie tried to console the mother. "Here chile." She gingerly approached the girl laying on the floor, deep scratches covering her arms where the cats had attacked. "You feeling some better, honey?"

Lucy looked up, eyes slowly focusing.

Jessie breathed a gigantic sigh of relief. Whoever, or whatever it was, had disappeared.

"Lucy, darling, let your ole Jessie see 'bout those scratches. I need to wash them good and put on some iodine." She pulled her to her feet. Placing a gentle arm around her shoulder she walked the child into the adjoining bathroom. "Ole Jessie be real good at fixin' up younguns."

"Tim, did you leave your car out front?"

He nodded, busily examining Maureen's throat. "I think it looks worse than it is. The main thing is to keep her from going into shock." He yanked a spread off the bed. "Wrap her up." He turned to Ruby. "Do you think you and Willard can handle this end, while Miss Emma and I get Maureen to the hospital?"

"As long as you leave the cats," Ruby's voice quavered. "Oh, Miss Emma," she continued, "I promise I'll never again say I want to be part of something like this. Now I know why Billy Bob refused to come back." She stooped gathering Cleo in her arms, eyes straying fearfully to the bathroom door. "We'll manage. I hope," she ended timorously.

"Get my sweet baby out of here." Willard finally found his voice.

"We're on our way." Tim swept Maureen up, much as he had Carol. He and Emma rushed to his car.

The others stared anxious, uneasy, edging close for comfort.

"What happened in here, Miss Carol?" Ruby glanced fearfully around.

Carol sank onto the bed. She wanted to cry, to scream, to curse whatever force held her daughter in thrall, but she hadn't the strength. She was exhausted. Too much over the past year. The divorce, the move, and certainly worst of all, the haunting.

"I'm not sure," she began, voice trembling. "I was reading to Lucy out of the Bible. The story about David and Goliath. I had this eerie sensation we weren't alone. I looked around and didn't see anyone so I continued with the story. All at once . . ." she shuddered.

"Yes," Ruby prompted.

"Something clammy touched my arm." She brushed at the spot. "Out of thin air, the cross Aunt Emma gave me, that I'd put around Lucy's neck, fell into my lap. I looked up and there she was."

Lucy?" Willard cried out.

"No. *Her.* It!" For a second, Carol couldn't breathe her fear was so great.

"She stared right at me. Her eyes were filled with so much hate and loathing, I froze. She missed her chance," Carol's voice sank to a whisper. "If she'd chosen that moment to kill me, it would have been perfect. I couldn't move a muscle."

"And then?" Willard was pressed against Ruby. Without realizing it, both had clasped each other's hand.

"I called Lucy's name, but she didn't answer. She begin coming toward me from the foot of the bed where she'd been sitting. She was slithering like a snake. Sliding across the sheets, slow and menacing. Her eyes full of hate locked on mine. I knew if I didn't do something I was lost. Knew I wouldn't have another chance to escape. I remembered the holy water. I snatched it from the bedside table throwing it over her. She started brushing and clawing at herself, making these odd noises. Swearing and cursing horrible, horrible words. That's when I leaped from the bed and began crying for help." Her voice broke. Sobs shook her frame as she cried out her heart.

Chapter Twenty-Seven

Tim had been correct. The bite looked worse than it was, but the doctor was flabbergasted a child had been the culprit. The entire time he spent cleansing the wound, taking small sutures, giving a tetanus shot, he questioned them.

They had decided on the drive to the hospital, to limit their explanation, knowing if the true circumstances were revealed, the press would be on them like rabid dogs–Lucy turned into a side show freak, Emma's house into a tourist attraction. When they left, the doctor was glowering, aware there was more to the tale than he'd been told, yet unable to get at the truth.

Maureen, stressing she was fine, had insisted on returning, determined to be with Emma through whatever ordeal lay ahead. But minutes after they settled her in the back of the car, she slipped into a deep sleep. The sun was rising when Tim pulled into the driveway.

"What now?" He slowly turned to Emma.

"Only the good Lord knows." She was so tired she could barely crawl from the automobile.

"Maybe Phillip will call. I sure wish his old granddaddy would have a good day."

"Both of us."

Together, they managed to get Maureen inside where Ruby insisted on taking charge. The rest trailed dejectedly into the breakfast room. Jessie quickly poured coffee, all the while tearfully apologizing for bringing Miss Stargaze into Emma's house and stirring up the spook.

"Quit blaming yourself." Emma took one of her hands. "I don't want to hear another word. It's nothing to do with you, your white witch, or any of us. It's Lucy and Shadow Lake. What you did, didn't change a thing."

"You don't thinks?" Jessie was devastated by the evening's events, but her face brightened at Emma's words.

"I'm positive."

"Lawd, that do take a load off this ole' woman. Oh." Her hands flew up. "I most forgots. Mr. Phillip called. He home. He say we to meet at his office 'bout three. He apologize fer how late that be, but he were up most the night drivin' from Alanta. He say he spent the rest of it lookin' through his granddaddy's files."

"He must have found something." Willard sprang to his feet. "Maureen will be sooo happy. I can't wait to tell her." He was jumping up and down like frog legs frying in a pan of grease.

"I'm going upstairs right now. Jessie, pour her some coffee. She likes exactly two scoops of sugar, a dab of cream." He broke down. "Emma, I thought I'd lost her. I thought that creature was going to kill her and I didn't do one damn thing. Just stood there rooted to the spot like the cowardly lion of Oz." His plump shoulders shook. "Did she say anything? Did she ask why I didn't come to her rescue? Does she blame me?"

"Stop it, Willard." Emma rose putting her arms around the heartbroken little man. "None of us did anything. We were all frozen."

"No." He shook his head, miserable. "No. Tim and Ruby tried to help."

"And a fat lot of good it did." Tim felt helpless in the face of the other's unbearable grief. "Listen, Willard, if those cats hadn't jumped Lucy, I don't know what the heck would have happened."

"My sweet, precious friend would be gone," he wailed. "The best thing that ever happened to me, would have been torn asunder right before my very eyes and I'd have done nothing." He wailed louder.

"I said stop it." This time, Emma shook him. "It's over. Maureen's going to be fine. What you need to do is take her coffee and give her Phillip's news. She'll be delighted."

"She will be, won't she?" He peered through swollen eyes. "And I'll promise to take everything he says down in shorthand. There won't be a single word left out. She can read it all." He perked up, starting to preen. "She'll love that."

"Yes, she will," Emma agreed.

"Is that all Phillip said?" she questioned Jessie.

"That, and he were bringin' a surprise. Somebody we gonna be real pleased about."

"A surprise." Willard gleefully clapped his hands, his exuberance restored. "I just love surprises, and so does my precious sweetie."

***

They crowded into Phillip's office, nervously waiting to hear what he had discovered and curious about the lanky young man standing by his side. Both appeared tense. That, plus the dark walnut paneling, heavy velvet drapes, and wine oriental carpet, only heightened the air of sobriety. It gave them an uneasy feeling. A premonition of bad things to come. Emma was glad she had insisted Carol stay home with her daughter and Maureen. She was afraid the news Phillip had brought might not necessarily be what they wanted to hear.

"So," she said as soon as everyone was seated. Willard with pad and pen at the ready. "Who is this?" She smiled at the stranger. "And, what did you find in your grandfather's files?"

"This gentleman," Phillip spoke before nodding at the red haired individual, freckles sprinkled liberally over a large bony nose, which coupled with a wide generous mouth put one in mind of Howdy Doody, "is a specialist in the field of the paranormal.

He loves haunted houses. They're his meat and drink. He is absolutely foaming at the mouth to visit Shadow Lake. I'd like you to meet my new friend, Matt Chambers."

"Thank you, Lord Father, and you, Phillip, for finding and bringing him to us." Emma felt a burden lift, then lower at a sudden thought. "This is legitimate, isn't it?" Her heart sank recalling Aurora Stargaze. His appearance was almost as unusual. All that carroty hair sticking every which way from hands constantly pushing it about.

"He's associated with Georgia Tech and has more degrees than letters in his name." Phillip beamed. "Actually, he is Dr. Matt Chambers."

"Then may I say, I'm delighted to meet you." She rose extending her hand, introducing the rest in the room. "I pray you can help us. I imagine Phillip has given you all the details, although he doesn't know about our latest and far worse episode." She sank into a chair.

"Maybe you'd better fill me in," he said.

"It was horrible." In bits and pieces, she related Miss Stargaze's visit and the disastrous finale.

"I wondered why Miss Maureen wasn't here." Phillip was appalled. "I knew it wasn't like her to miss out on anything."

"May I speak?" Matt held up his hand.

"Please," Emma begged.

"I want you to realize there are few actual haunts–"

"Oh, but this is." She half rose in her seat.

"I agree, although when Phillip approached me, I was extremely skeptic. However, the more information I receive, plus last night's attack, leads me to the conclusion this is the genuine article."

"It is. It is." Jessie couldn't keep still. "If you lookin' fer real life ghosties, then you has come to the right place."

"I look, but seldom find." He sobered. "But this haunting has an unholy feel. Coupled with the information Phillip's uncovered, I'm prepared, even before visiting the site, to declare this a case of real physic manifestation."

"Man-i-whats?"

"Shhh, Jessie." Tim brought a finger to his lips. "I'll explain later."

"While we're on the subject of explanations," Phillip interrupted, "I assume you're anxious to hear what happened in Atlanta."

"You bet your sweet bootie." Willard jumped up and down, pencil poised.

"Well, day before yesterday, the visit to the nursing home was a total waste. Grandad James was in a world of his own, and I knew I'd get nothing. So I left and went to the University. I remembered reading an article written by Matt on ghost hunting, and thought, what the heck? He's an expert. If I couldn't convince him to come with me, he should at least be able to give us some helpful advice."

"And, thank you, Lawd, he were convinced." Jessie breathed fervently.

The young man grinned in that cockeyed manner he had, before admitting, "Don't give too much credit to Phillip's powers of persuasion. I'd had my eye on Amelia Island for quite awhile. It, as well as St. Augustine."

"Why?" Emma was puzzled.

"There are locations on this earth which appear to have a greater source of energy and magnetic field," he said, shrugging slightly, "or whatever you want to call it. We don't really know. Anyway, your little barrier island is one of them. Like St. Augustine, Florida, it definitely has more than its share of ghostly sightings. In addition, they have three more similarities."

He waited to see if anybody would try to guess them. When they sat silent and expectant, he continued, "Both were inhabited by native Americans, thousands of years before the white man came. Both are the oldest settlements in the state. And both have had extremely violent histories."

"You attribute that to the uneasy spirits roaming our homes?"

Emma asked.

"I wouldn't exactly put it like that. I only know the world is full of psychic 'hot spots,' and they fascinate me. In fact, your Fort Clinch is, to make a bad pun, probably what 'clinched' my desire to make this a career."

"What that ole fort have to do with ghosties?" Jessie was awed that hunting specters would appeal to anyone, for any reason.

"Actually, it has a wonderful case of haunting."

"What haunting?" Willard was bouncing in his chair again.

"Oh, that a fort ranger and other visitors have been privy to headless soldiers crossing the parade grounds at night. Some have seen three, others four. They walk no further than the flagpole and disappear. Truth of the matter is, I can hardly wait to tour the Fort. I understand it's been turned into a State Park with wonderful trails and camping grounds."

"Yes," Tim informed him. "And the locals put on a great enactment of garrison life as it was during the Civil War."

"This is amazing. I can't believe I've lived on the island all this time and never heard these things." Emma was almost indignant.

"I imagine you heard more than you realized. You probably dismissed them as 'old wive's tales,' like most people who don't believe in the supernatural."

"I'd heerd some of them tales," Jessie declared, casting a meaningful eye at her friend.

"Well anyway, that's why I was interested in Amelia. I've been meaning to investigate it for years. Been so darn busy I've never gotten around to it." His face darkened, his voice grew ominous. "Now, I don't have a choice. In fact, I think we need to let Phillip finish the story. Time is growing short and we have to set up my equipment before dark."

"I spent the rest of the day with Matt." Phillip took up his narrative where he'd left off. "Yesterday, I returned to the nursing home. I couldn't believe it. Grandad James was as lucid as me. We visited about family and old friends, until finally, I brought up the subject of Shadow Lake."

"What did you say?" Emma was curious.

"I told him some peculiar things had happened. I asked if he might have any ideas, or if he recalled any odd rumors about the house."

"Did he?" Emma found herself unable to sit still. She was anxious to learn the reason behind the visitations.

"He sat for a long while. I was scared I'd lost him again, when he suddenly heaved a huge sigh declaring his father had told him something strange about the family, but not about the house."

"Something strange?" Willard whispered in fear, the pencil still poised. He'd become so engrossed in the narrative he had forgotten to write a single word.

"Yes. However, he informed me, Grandad had no idea what he meant. The house had stood empty most of his lifetime. In fact, the only disaster he'd ever known personally, had been the death of Richard's wife and child. It had been one of those terrible tragedies that sometime occur."

"Oh, no." Emma groaned. "Then you learned nothing new?"

"Let me finish." He held up a hand. "I didn't say that. What I finally learned is that his father, my great-grandfather, had told him the bare bones of an odd tale. That a Steven Finley had built Shadow Lake for his wife and two daughters, and had been one of great-grandad's closest friends. Then, great-grandfather became privy to something shocking. Something so shocking it destroyed the entire family, leaving the house vacant for years."

"The ghost?" Jessie caught her breath.

Phillip shook his head. "Not then. Not yet."

"When?"

"Grandad James said his father had saved some documents and letters concerning the family in a sealed envelope. That Grandad probably should have burned them, but when he prepared to, something seemed to stay his hand. So, he placed them with his obsolete files. Grandad James thought he remembered where."

"I'm afraid to ask." Emma's lip quivered.

"Grandad wasn't too far off from where he recalled they were filed." Phillip breathed a sigh of relief. "Bless his heart. Anyway, Matt and I left Atlanta last evening and raced back. As soon as we hit town we came here. Whew. I had no idea there were so many old papers in the basement."

"And that particular file?"

"We found it. It took five hours, but by golly, here it is." He reached in his desk proudly waving aloft a sheaf of papers.

"Will this save Lucy? Save Shadow Lake?"

"It'll help. Without this information, I couldn't say," Matt answered honestly. "This is one of the most unusual tales of pure unadulterated evil I've ever come across. I thank you for allowing me to study it."

"I thank you for saving us."

"Don't thank me, yet." His brow furrowed, the freckles faded removing the look of light-hearted boyishness. "This isn't an ordinary supernatural manifestation. It's already established a strong source of power and energy from the child. This is not going to be easy exorcism."

"Oh, sweetie, you can say that again," Willard lisped.

"But surely you can do something?" Her heart was sinking. "I'm counting on it."

"When you told me about last night, you mentioned a new presence."

"Lettice. Maureen swears Richard's first wife is trying to help us. Is that possible?"

"Anything's possible, and certainly in this case. Are there any other sources aiding you?"

"Only the cats. Particularly Anthony, the male. It seems terrified of him."

"Remember, Phillip?" He pointed to the papers in the attorney's hand. "That's easy enough to figure out."

"What?" Emma demanded.

Ignoring her, he continued, "I need to know exactly what I'm dealing with. Therefore, I want each of you to tell me your story. I don't mind you repeating something somebody else has already said. You simply tell me exactly what you recall and what you felt at the time. It doesn't matter how trivial. Leave nothing out," he stressed.

"We can do that." Emma was anxious to begin, to drive the nasty entity from her house. "Then what?"

"After I record each of you, I'm going to let Phillip read something. Actually, one of the most distressing tales I've ever heard. One that explains why Shadow Lake is haunted, and excuse me ladies, but if it wasn't haunted, why it sure as hell should be."

Chapter Twenty-Eight

Each of the group was anxious to tell Matt the story of their ghostly encounter, and some, like Willard and Jessie, seemed unable to keep themselves from embellishing and rendering a slightly more colorful tale than the others remembered. But at last, when everyone had related everything they could think of, Phillip rose from behind his desk. Placing a sheaf of papers in front of him, he cleared his throat, opened the letters found in his great-grandfather's files and began reading.

June 6, 1905

Dear Mr. Randsome,

I beseech you to forgive me for making so bold as to address you in this manner, but being only fifteen years of age I have not obtained the wisdom to handle this problem and know of nowhere else to turn. I recall how often, when Mother was alive and well, you and your wife visited. How you always spoke kindly to me, never looking away in disgust as do many, and so, I presume upon your feelings for my mother, and humbly beg your help. Please, sir, for I have no one else.

I pray you will not think me some foolish young girl, early into womanhood, letting her imagining run afield, for truly, sir, I have not the wit nor experience to do this. In all my short life, I never dreamed such things, nor sweet Heavenly Father keep me safe, entertained such unhealthy thoughts. I cower in abject horror before the evil surrounding me. My hands perspire. I can scarcely grasp the pen so embarrassed I am over what I am about to write and the tale I am to tell. But Heavenly Father, I fear I have no choice. Please sir, I have no one.

Often you hunted with my father, and many times you dined at our table, but when Mother grew ill, it seemed the house sickened also. People ceased calling, leaving the four of us alone. My handsome father, who'd always sought beauty in everything, was suddenly left with a gradually wasting wife—myself—disfigured face, and Missy, a child of incredible beauty. It shouldn't have been surprising Father chose her to be his companion, shunning the sick room where his wife lay dying, avoiding the daughter he couldn't bear to look upon. That, I could understand and even perhaps, in time, forgive, but sir, he turned my little sister, and her not then seven, into something uglier than any disease, or physical disfigurement could ever be. Sir, he turned her into a monster.

Perhaps you think this the letter of a jealous girl, a daughter unloved and likely never to be. I swear to you, sir, it is not so. My mother gave me all the love anyone could ask for. I was happy, not minding in the least father preferring my sister. I often listened to him tell her of the house and grounds, how he had built it all for her, and how someday, they would be hers.

Once, when they failed to notice, I watched him place his hand upon her leg sliding it slowly up, all the while promising she would live there with him as his mistress.

That was three years ago. Although the scene made me uneasy, I didn't understand. I didn't comprehend what I watched, so innocent was I. But more and more, I came upon my father and sister touching in ways that made me uncomfortable. At last, I felt I must speak to my poor dear mother. If I had it to do over sir, I never would, for I fear I am the force which hastened her departure.

I shall never forget her face when in my ignorance, I related what I had seen. She cried out, clutching her heart. I had to hold her in my arms until the trembling stopped. That day I lost my innocence, for my mother told me things I was not ready to hear. And too, she confessed the fear she'd been carrying. The very fear of which I had brought proof. She asked me to bring Missy to her, and then leave them alone. I did as requested. Later my sister found me in the kitchen playing with a basket of kittens. There were five of them, tiny and newly born. Before my very eyes she snatched one up and with a strength I wouldn't think possible in a child so young, pulled its head off like cook does to the chickens she plans on preparing for dinner. I couldn't believe what I'd seen. She flung it aside reaching for another, but the male, who had been sunning on the window sill, leaped through the air onto her shoulder. His claws ripped down her cheek. She screamed and yelled as I pulled him off. Father heard and came running. He stopped, horrified when he saw Missy, and covered his eyes telling me to remove her from him. To keep her away. That his beautiful daughter was ruined. That now he had nothing. Missy ran to him, but he pushed her toward me, fleeing in disgust.

I washed and applied ointment to her damaged cheek. The scratch wasn't deep, but like all facial wounds bled profusely, appearing worse than it was. Missy never spoke a word until I finished ministering to her. Then, she vowed to make me sorry, glaring so viciously I felt my heart race in terror. She swore to punish me for taking tales to Mother, and for what my cat had done, no matter that she had killed his kit. And she promised to punish Mother for saying the love she and Father had for each other was evil. Before I could defend myself, she slapped me on my ugly side, telling me I was vile and grotesque. So grotesque, Father wanted me gone, just as he wished to be rid of his sick wife. So they, perfect creatures, could enjoy the beauty of each other, the house and gardens together.

I don't know what made me tell Missy. I very much regret giving her this knowledge, for now I fear daily for my life. But, in my anger I acted foolishly. It will never be yours, I boasted. It was Mother's money that built the house and she promised it was to be mine. I am, after all, the eldest, sir. It is my birthright.

She launched herself at me, but this time I was prepared. I held her off until her fury abated. That night my mother died. I have no proof, only the fact her pillow was not beneath her head when she was found, but tossed to one side, a drop of blood upon the linen case. That made me wonder, but I kept silent. I bore my grief alone, for I was the only one to miss her.

Since that day I have grown more and more afraid. Missy's face healed leaving no mark. Again, she and father have become close. I feel them watching me, my sister, in particular. I have recently suffered several accidents, none of my own making. Once she brushed against me going down the stairs. Had I not caught the banister, I believe my injury would have been severe. I have had to give up riding, although it has always afforded me much pleasure. Three times my horse has bolted. The saddle loosed and slipped. I do not intend to brag, but was I not such a good horse woman, I'm sure I would have suffered much. There have been other mishaps, till I dare not fail to look each step I take, nor leave my back uncovered. The only time I am secure is when, in my bed each night, I hear them in Missy's room. Soft sighs, moans and sometimes laughter, though not the laughter of an innocent child, drifts across the hall to me.

There, I have exposed the shameful secrets of this household. I have tried to keep silent, but I cannot any longer. I have tried to ignore the terrible sins my father and sister are committing, but I cannot any longer.

Oh, sir, as God is my witness, I do not know what to do. Please, sir, I have no one else.

> *Regretfully,*
> *Annie Finley*

"Sweet Jesus." The whites of Jessie's eyes shone brightly. "That poor chile. See there." She whipped around accusing Emma. "I told you those soaps was true life. I knowed you didn't know what you was talkin' 'bout."

Emma bent her head. "Jessie, I bow to your expertise. I'll

never question your judgment, nor deride your soaps again."

"There she go with those big words. She know I don't know what she sayin'. Jest usin' them to get even."

Matt took the letter from Phillip. "This explains a lot, don't you think?"

"An awful lot," Ruby agreed. "For certain why, I suppose it's Missy, hates Anthony and Cleo. She's afraid of being scratched like before. I didn't know spirits could feel."

"I doubt they can, but think. It's not the pain this ghost child fears. It's becoming unattractive. She's terrified of having her beauty marred." He pointed a finger. "If that happened, her father, and if he, why not everyone, would reject her. She'd become an object of pity like her sister. Losing her beauty, she'd also lose her power."

"That the gospel trufe. You a right smart young fella, Mr. Matt."

"So." Tim rubbed his hands in glee. "We've discovered our ghost's identity."

"Now we gots to un-discover it," Jessie declared.

"You know," he continued, "it's hard to imagine a child, dead for so many years, could wreak such havoc."

"This isn't a normal child," Matt explained. "This particular little girl was raised in unusual and destructive circumstances. Circumstances beyond her control, but which she seems to have embraced with open arms."

"Along with her father." Emma was disgusted.

"Yes, along with him," Matt agreed, before finishing his explanation. "She must have been extraordinarily beautiful. The apple of her father's eye, in direct contrast to her sister, who undoubtedly had some terrible disfigurement. I suspect she'd always been pampered and made over, then when her mother grew ill, there was no one to thwart her. Her every desire was fulfilled. Of course, we realize why. The father was interested in her for sexual pleasure, and in order to gain a willing partner, filled her full of grandiose promises. Promises it turns out, he wasn't in a position to make since the property he made so alluring, actually belonged to his wife. Something highly unusual in those days." He grew thoughtful. "And which, was slated to be passed to the eldest as her natural birthright."

"Ruby." Emma's head shot up. "Remember in the library when Lucy asked me what that word meant?"

"We couldn't figure out where she'd heard it. She got all upset when you told her Miss Carol would inherit Shadow Lake."

"Another piece of the puzzle." Matt was growing more and more excited at the thought of what awaited him.

"But why is she haunting now?" Willard clutched the pencil high above the pad, the point yet to touch the paper. "And what happened to that pitiful child, Annie? And what, for heaven's sake did Phillip's great-grandfather do to that horrid, foul man who was their father?"

Phillip lifted another sheet of stationery off his desk. "And now, as Paul Harvey would say, 'for the rest of the story . . .'"

Chapter Twenty-Nine

June 13, 1905

Never in my many years practicing law have I encountered a more sordid, or outlandish story of depravity than was unfolded in this letter which crossed my desk scarcely a week past. A week I've spent agonizing over how best to approach a man, once a close and cherished friend. Whether to accuse him of an act both unspeakable and unforgivable, or to inform him the mind of his eldest child has snapped and has become filled with bizarre imaginings so disgusting, I shrink to write them down.

Each day I've wrestled, and each evening, prayed for guidance. I fear I am not giving my other clients full service, for my heart and mind are totally consumed by this noxious tale. I cannot believe I could have ridden by the side, supped with, shared any of the many occasions good friends do, and not been aware of such a bestial nature; yet, the girl's plea rings true, her cry for help appears real. Dare I, in good conscience ignore the child? A child who's sought me in such desperate plight, whether real or imagined?

I must cease being a craven coward. Tomorrow, I will ride to Shadow Lake and speak with Steven. Still, I find I can not face him with such monumental accusations. It is too much to expect from a friend. I will hand him Annie's letter and this my scribbling. I will leave the room allowing him time to collect himself before giving me his explanation. Surely, he will realize the act Annie describes is too unpardonable to discuss, and if it be true, then there is but one course left for him. Still, I find it impossible to believe that he should be so foul, or that his youngest daughter, one so exquisite, so young, could be so vile; but then, I read and reread Annie's letter. My tears drop on each page, for God help us, I sense the truth and fear pouring from her pen.

I shall spend the night in prayer. Prayer that I will not falter from my mission. Prayer for the children. Prayer for Steven, and certainly, prayer if this is real, that he has courage to take the action he must. Surely he will, in order to keep the truth from being known and shame from falling upon his family's honorable name.

Dear Father, I pray for all of us, for I fear there will be no easy solution to these ills. As Annie writes, "Help me sir, for I have no one else."

The silence was total. It was like they were collectively holding their breath. Phillip searched each face. Seeing only hushed expectancy, he put the sheet of paper down on his desk. With a heavy sigh, he picked up another.

June 17, 1905

*May God forgive me. While I yet wrestled with my
coward's heart, Satan was busy wrestling with souls,
and I find, was the victor. I shall bear the guilt, the
burden until I die. Dear Father, why did Annie pick
such a weak man as myself? Why not someone worthy?
Someone strong who would have acted immediately? I
see her pale still face each time I close my eyes. I take
away each blemish, carrying her scars upon my heart
each and every day. I have failed her as miserably as
her own father. Why did I wait? Why didn't I run
immediately to her side? Surely, I should have realized
no young girl could impart a tale so disgusting. It had
to be the truth. Annie, sweet innocent child, can you
forgive me?*

*I rose early today, full of dread, but determined to
carry out my mission. I canceled my office
appointments and with heavy heart rode out to
Shadow Lake. It is such a beautiful home. The tiny lake
and lovely gardens surrounding it make it a setting
worthy of some artist's brush. Normally, it would lift
my senses just to gaze upon such beauty, but today,
today the sight made me quite nauseous.*

*As I approached, I noted an unusual amount of
activity. Reining up my horse, I heard someone call my
name. Steven was shouting, screaming like a man
demented. I watched in horror as he ran to the lake's
edge where he fell on his knees, gathered something into
his arms and covered it with kisses.*

*My heart almost failed. Dear Father, what had I
stumbled upon? Remus, the gardener for years, ran to*

me. He was wet and trembling. Grasping my hand, he began frantically dragging me towards the grief-stricken man. I stopped, demanding an explanation. In a quavering voice he told a story which shouldn't have surprised me.

Annie, as was often her habit, had been preparing to take a boat out on the lake. As she pushed it away from the bank, Missy suddenly appeared, jumping in and snatching the oar from her sister's hands. Remus watched her paddle into deep water where, he blanched and stammered, she'd stood, raised the oar over her head and struck her older sister. He described poor Annie as she struggled to maintain her balance, but dazed and wavering from the blow, she slipped slowly toward the boat's edge. In a flash, he related how Missy had pushed the other, sending her into the water. At the last instant, Annie reached up tangling her fingers in the younger child's long curls. Together, they toppled into the lily-filled depths.

Both drowned. He'd not been able to reach them in time. When he brought them up, they were still joined, with Annie's fingers grasping the golden tresses of her sister.

This time the nausea was so great I couldn't fight it. I turned, spewing the anger and disgust I felt for Steven upon his cobblestones. Annie was no child rife with jealousy. She was a child living in a situation so dire I cannot think how she'd managed to keep her sanity, or life, as long as she had.

Anger, a vast, fierce, roaring anger, swept me to the girls' father's side. In disgust, I watched him mouth and slobber over the demon child, while the good and innocent lay neglected and alone. Trembling, I knelt, closing the eyes so pitifully puckered and scarred. I softly kissed the cold brow, determined she'd not leave this world without some small gesture of love. I silently begged her forgiveness, before turning to Steven demanding an immediate audience.

"My child," he sobbed, crushing her body to him.

"Your child be damned!" I cried.

His eyes flew wide. I think he knew then, that I was privy to his secret.

I reached in my pocket drawing out the letters. He gently lay the girl down before taking them from me. He walked to the water's edge and I followed minutes later.

"Tomorrow." He handed them back. "I would appreciate, for those times past, before I became the man you read of. Come tomorrow and it would be best if you brought the sheriff with you."

I couldn't trust myself to speak. Afraid if I opened my mouth a dam in my brain would break, and losing all control, I would fling myself upon him seeking vengeance for his eldest daughter. Silently I nodded, then turned to leave.

"Phillip." He reached out to touch me. Seeing the look of revulsion on my face, he dropped his hand. "I have no excuse," he faltered, "but it is important that you understand. I wasn't always like this. It was after my

wife became so ill, and even then." He suddenly seemed bewildered. "Do you believe in evil?"

I only stared.

"Do you think a child can be born evil?"

I gave him no reply.

"Some are born without arms or legs. Why not, without a soul?"

He waited for an answer but I had none to give. He appeared to be trying to blame Missy for his actions, to say she had been the temptress, not he the tempter. I find that impossible. Still, it gives one pause when you remember it was she who did the killing.

We rode out at daybreak. None of the servants were present. The front door stood open. He lay stretched across the bed of the child he'd taken such perverse pleasure in, his shotgun fallen to the floor.

I often wondered why the sheriff never questioned the reason I'd ask him to ride with me that morning. I have since wondered if he suspected something of the truth.

My wife and I arranged the services. I made certain Annie lay next to her mother. Missy and her father slightly apart. No one seemed to notice the unusual placement and I offered no explanation.

Dear Father, I pray in the great hereafter you will lead me to Annie. I would wish the chance to fall on my face and plead her forgiveness. And I swear to you, that I shall never again turn a deaf ear to someone's cry for help. Never again, will I turn away when someone brings me their wounded heart. Never again, will I let my craven nature keep me from providing comfort, as your Son comforted us.

I put these words down in case there is ever a need for them to be exposed. I hope it will not be the case, but feel loathe to destroy the last of Annie. I will secret them in my files and if the need for them should come about, I will feel somewhat vindicated for having ignored the poor girl's plea.

> *Phillip Randsome*
> *Attorney at Law*

Even the men had tears in their eyes. Ruby and Jessie wept openly.

"That poor sweet child," Emma's voice broke, "so all alone. Every single day of her life had to have been a living hell."

"And what a dreadful little bitch her sister was." Willard snapped the idle pencil. "Wait till I tell Maureen."

"I hate to end this discussion." Matt was solemn. "I know you're anxious to rehash this information, but we don't have much time," he announced.

"Why not?" Tim questioned.

"The date." Emma's hand flew to her mouth. "Read that last date again. Please, Phillip."

"June 17, 1905."

"Today. Isn't today the seventeenth of June?"

"Yes." Matt's eyes narrowed. "I wondered if any of you would make the connection. Today is exactly one hundred years to the day Missy and Annie drowned."

"And that means . . ."

"She will probably be at her strongest. We have to remove her before midnight tonight. It's why, as the anniversary has approached, she's gotten so daring. Why she's been able to control Lucy so easily," Matt explained.

"Let's get moving." Tim leaped to his feet.

"I think we'd better. It's going to be a real battle for the child. As you saw last night, she's not far from taking complete possession. If you'll lead the way, I'll follow in my van. It's loaded with equipment."

"Ghost hunting equipment?" Jessie's voice shook.

"You bet your sweet booty," Willard shouted, jumping up and down, ready for action. "And you can sure as heck bet this is one little ghost that's gonna get blasted straight to hell!"

Chapter Thirty

Emma was first through the door. She had been a nervous wreck since leaving Phillip's office, worried sick about Carol and Maureen, and about what Missy might manipulate Lucy into doing. She heaved a sigh of relief when she heard normal sounding voices coming from the library.

"Maureen." She crossed to her side. "Are you strong enough to be out of bed?"

"Don't coddle me." She was irritable. "And don't waste your time playing nurse. I want to know? Did Phillip discover the answer?"

"Yes." She beamed, then stood there smiling like a jackass.

"Well?"

"First, where's Lucy?" Emma looked around.

"In the garden with Billy Bob. He's weeding. I made her go help. She's not happy."

"Good. You won't-"

A loud commotion from the hall interrupted her, noises and voices growing in volume.

"You knocks a hole in that woodwork and I gonna pound your backside all the way to Atlanta, little man."

"Sounds like everyone's arrived safe and sound." Maureen managed a smile as she listened to Jessie threatening Willard with increasing bodily harm. "At least, for the moment."

The door was flung wide. Tim and Phillip staggered past carrying a piece of heavy equipment. Matt followed, pointing to where it was to be placed.

"Maureen, Carol, I want you to . . ."

Bells clanged! Rockets soared! Fireworks exploded! Sirens screamed!

Emma had read about such things. If she remembered rightly, in Puzo's novel, *The Godfather*, the son experienced it upon catching sight of a young woman walking through a field in Sicily. The natives called it 'the thunderbolt'. An actual case of love at first sight, so powerful, that not only the two involved, but everyone in the room seemed hit by a charge of electricity. Sort of what, to some degree, she felt, had happened when she met Richard.

Tim and Phillip stared aghast.

Tim, finding his voice, muttered, "Thanks a lot, pal."

Phillip seemed bewildered. "How could I know?"

"Well, you do now." Tim's countenance fell. "I hope he has as great an effect on the ghost."

"Will you looks at that?" Jessie pulled Emma's arm. "I swear, if that ain't gonna put Mr. Tim and Mr. Phillip plum outta joint."

"Oh." Ruby breathed rapturously. "This is so romantic."

No, this was unbelievable. Even Maureen was standing mouth wide, and Willard was squirming so, Emma didn't know if his emotions had the best of him, or if he needed to go to the bathroom.

"Carol. Carol!" Emma shouted to get her attention. "I'd like you and Maureen to meet the young man who's going to give us back our beautiful home."

The house shook slightly but everyone seemed oblivious, caught up in the unfolding act of courtship.

"Hel-hello." Carol blushed, stammered and giggled.

Emma would have thought Carol looked such a fool she would have turned Matt off, but he blushed, stammered and giggled too.

"Pleased to me-meet you. I'm Ma-matt Chambers."

"Dr. Matt Chambers," Jessie piped up proudly, "and he gonna send that Missy chile straight back to you know where."

This time they felt the house tremble. It would have registered at least six points on a Ritcher scale. They clutched each other, scrambling to keep on their feet.

"Well, Matt," Phillip challenged, "you believe this one's genuine?"

"Wow." He threw his head back, eyes swiveling around the room. "That was some trick."

"Trick?" Maureen was indignant.

"Just an expression, ma'am." He flashed his Howdy Doody grin. "I meant this is the sure enough thing and she is one powerful little spirit."

"So, what are you going to do about it?"

"As soon as I unload the van, I'll tell you." He put a finger to his lips. "We don't want to give away our plans."

"I guess not." She seemed miffed, but sat quietly on the sofa, motioning for Willard to join her. "Will it be giving away any secrets if Willard clues me in on what he learned?"

"No. I think she already knows that."

"Carol, you can sit here by me." Maureen moved to one side.

"Oh." Matt cleared his throat. "I was hoping, maybe . . ." He paused, embarrassed.

"Yes," Carol prodded.

"That maybe *you* might show me around."

"I can do that." Phillip jumped up. "Carol's recovering from an accident."

"I'm fine." She gingerly hobbled over to Matt's side. "In fact," she beamed at him before adding, "I've never felt better."

Behind the moonstruck couple's back, Tim stuck his finger down his throat mimicking someone gagging.

Maureen, amused by all the goings on, extended a hand to Willard. "I'll read about it, just in case. Let me have your notes, dear. I can hardly wait to see what you've written."

Jessie hooted. Emma and Ruby took one look at Willard's

stricken face and collapsed into their respective chairs.

It was dusk by the time they finished running all the cables, setting up recorders, positioning trip wires and adjusting cameras. It hadn't been an easy task, particularly in the vicinity of Lucy's room. It seemed as fast as they completed one job, another came undone. It was especially noticeable after Lucy returned. Wherever she walked, something of Matt's went awry. Carol had nervously introduced them, but the child only glared, turned her back and refused to acknowledge his presence.

When it became evident they were not having any luck with Matt's equipment, he shrugged and gave up. None of the devices were an actual part of the exorcism, he informed them. They were machines he used to authenticate the hauntings.

Matt tried in vain to engage Lucy in conversation but she repeatedly ignored him. As the evening wore on, she grew more and more agitated.

By now, Carol had heard the full story. As the shadows deepened she became frantic, terrified Matt could not save her daughter. When the clock struck ten, she grabbed his arm, demanding he do something.

Sensing her intense fear, he capitulated.

Everyone followed him into the library like an army seeking guidance from its general.

Ignoring their unasked questions, he cocked his ear at the last peal of the grandfather clock.

"Should be here any minute now," Matt announced.

Emma was perplexed. *Who should?*

Chapter Thirty-One

The door bell pealed. Emma's eyes widened. She couldn't imagine who'd come calling at this late hour.

"Sorry, folks." Matt rose to answer the summons. "Father Ben had another appointment and couldn't make an earlier flight."

"Father Ben?" Maureen asked the question everyone wanted answered. "Who the hell is that?"

Matt returned, a young Catholic priest by his side.

"Meet the other half of my team." He acknowledged the man's presence to the group. "Emma, you had the right idea, but not enough knowledge. Evil spirits recognize only one authority. Like it says in the Bible when Jesus met the man with an unclean spirit. The demon cried out, 'I know thee. Thou art the Holy One of God.'"

"That be in Mark," Jessie informed them.

"In Matthew, Luke, Acts, and James as well, who tells us 'the demons believe and tremble.'" The priest smiled sweetly. "It's a shame we don't pay more attention to the most informative book in the world."

"Then you mean the holy water, crosses, and wafers were . . ."

"Everything you needed, Miss Emma, but the knowledge and authority," Matt finished speaking.

Busy talking, they failed to notice the child slip quietly from the room.

"Father Ben will drive Missy from Shadow Lake, and Carol, he will recover Lucy," Matt promised.

"But, Matt." Carol spun around. "Where is Lucy?"

"WHERE DO YOU THINK?" The voice roared through the house followed by the stench they'd come to associate as part of her.

"Whew. She's a ripe little thing." The priest wrinkled his nose. Walking to a nearby table he set down a small bag and began removing the instruments of his trade. He handed each of them a cross, after first blessing it, along with a small vial of holy water.

"Keep these with you and please stay close together," he instructed. "There's strength in numbers."

"How 'bouts I stick rights next to you then?" Jessie's teeth chattered.

"You're welcome." The man of God smiled, but sadly this time. "However, I don't think you'll really want too."

"I 'spects you knows best." She hastily wedged herself between Tim and Phillip.

"Matt, I need the child and the strongest room the evil emanates from." He picked up his bag. "If I recall, when you phoned, you mentioned a bedroom."

"KEEP OUT OF MY BEDROOM!"

Lucy's voice had deepened. She stood at the foot of the stairs, barring the way, eyes blazing.

"Ah, yes." Father Ben slowly approached. A cross in one hand, the Bible in the other. "You must be Missy."

He didn't flinch when she opened her mouth spraying him with putrid slime.

"Lucy." Her mother's legs folded. Ruby caught and helped her to a chair.

"Be still, Carol," her aunt demanded. "You mustn't break his concentration."

The priest continued walking toward the possessed girl. Little by little she backed up, hands covering her ears, as he called upon his God to drive the tormentor away, and remove Missy from the body of the living child.

"She's mine!" Missy began spinning, faster and faster, yet beneath the screams of rage one could hear a childish whimper of despair.

"My baby," Carol sobbed.

"Now."

Matt raced up the stairs dousing the child in holy water.

She spit and clawed but the spinning stopped. A string of profanity poured from her lips. The things she suggested the priest do had Emma's ears blazing.

"Take me to your room, Missy." The man of God ignored the curses and suggestions, slowly closing the gap between them.

"You want in my bedroom? *My bed?*" She sneered. "You, and this man my mother wants for herself?" She smiled seductively. "Both of you together?" She batted her lashes, threw back her head and spat. "It would *take* you both, a puny man of God and a bony red-haired boy."

"You must prepare to leave, Missy. You know your time has past."

"No! I'll never leave Shadow Lake."

Emma's heart sank at the creature's words.

"It's mine. He promised."

"Your papa was a liar, Missy. Like the devil, the father of lies."

Her screams assaulted their eardrums loud enough to break them. They prayed for relief covering their ears.

It stopped. They lowered their arms and watched in amazement as her feet left the floor. She floated effortlessly to the top of the stairs.

A quick nod from the priest and he and Matt ducked beneath the hovering form, dashing into her bedroom and slamming the door.

The others ran the rest of the way out of the library, awed by the rage coming from the girl as she shrieked and sobbed, pounded the door, hissed and spit, spewing vomit and worse, but the door remained closed.

Between her cries of fury they could hear the priest chanting in Latin, hear him shouting instructions to Matt. Each stared, horrified, as she attacked the panels, clawing and scratching, leaving great gouges in the wooden door.

Emma wondered if the others were as frightened as she. It seemed impossible mere men could take on such a formidable force and destroy it. She held her breath, then realized she too had a weapon–the *only weapon* she could use.

She closed her eyes. "Please, God, release the soul of this tormented child that walks the halls of my house. Send her to You and forgive her for the pain and suffering she's brought others. She's only a child, Father. An innocent one used as a pawn by a vile and evil man. Please, Father, take her and give us back Carol's little girl. Please, please, Father. I beg of you."

Emma opened her eyes on a sight she would never forget.

The demon child had calmed and quieted. Placing her hands against the bedroom door, she slowly pushed. As she strained, eyes bulged, veins popping, the door groaned and buckled inward. Just when those watching were positive it would break and spill her into the room with the men, she ceased.

Jessie screamed.

The child swivelled her head around, seemingly aware, for the first time, of those standing at the foot of the stairs. Lips pulled back, Missy snarled like a rabid animal before throwing herself off the top step onto them. Tim and Phillip broke rank, each holding up a cross and vial of holy water.

"Get out of my way!" She tossed them aside like feathers, murderous eyes fastened on Carol.

"Missy."

She whirled around. The priest stood in the doorway of her room, beckoning. "I believe you wanted in."

With a loud cry she leaped on him wrapping her legs around his waist. Her hands curled around his throat. He reached for his cross but she didn't retreat. With a shriek, she fastened her thumbs onto his neck in a death-like grip.

"She's killing him!" Tim ran up the steps, Phillip racing after, joining Matt, as they struggled to free the priest.

"I can't get her off him!" Matt shouted. "Where's the holy water?"

They emptied their vials over her.

It didn't work. She seemed to grow stronger each second. It was mere minutes from midnight. Emma watching, knew they were doomed. Knew if the hour finished striking, they would lose not only Lucy, but Shadow Lake forever.

"*No!*" The voice came on a gust of wind as the scent of gardenias overpowered them.

A mist gathered in the doorway of the opposite bedroom, Carol's bedroom. It quickly gathered into a thick mass, crossing the hall and enveloping those struggling in a heavy vapor.

The noise coming from the possessed child was unbelievable. Carol was sobbing hysterically. Emma felt she was losing her mind. The fog-like substance had become so dense it was impenetrable. She could hear Matt shouting encouragement to the priest as he helplessly tried prying the creature's fingers off the man's neck.

"I can't break her grip!" Tim cried in horror.

Seconds later, he was thrown through the air. Phillip was tossed close behind.

Once more they sprang to their feet launching themselves into the swirling melee.

The clock began to chime. Emma's heart thudded painfully. They were lost. She had made the deadline. Missy had won.

No. Emma refused to accept that. Disregarding her age and the monster hanging like a leech off the holy man, Emma began to ascend the stairs, eyes fastened on the child, determined to join those in their last desperate attempt to separate the combatants. She had taken no more than three steps when, it wasn't possible, but another shape had formed. This one poured down the hall swift as a thunder bolt! The shock of its impact sent the men flying in every direction as it joined Lettice in her battle for Lucy's life.

And underneath it all, a small voice called out.

"Help me. Please, Mama."

The sounds were pitiful. Without thinking, Emma began mounting the stairs again. It was no wonder, Carol, with a loud cry, tore herself away, trying to reach her child.

"Stop her!" Matt and Tim shouted in unison.

"For God's sake, don't let her get to Lucy." Matt desperately pushed against the vapors surrounding the screaming, possessed child, but failed to penetrate them.

Ruby and Willard caught Carol, holding her tight, although her struggles were almost as great as whatever battled for Lucy's soul.

"Leave me, you bitches!" The creature twisted from side to side, fighting to get away, away from the suffocating vapor.

"*No more.*" The voice was soft and melodious. It came from a young girl. Emma immediately knew who it had to be, who the second vapor enclosed. It settled like a sigh throughout the house, seeping through the halls, enclosing the mist surrounding the priest and the attacking child. "*Missy. You know the house belongs to me. Mother promised.*"

The screams that echoed through the rooms were like nothing any of them had ever heard, and beneath the cries, the scent of gardenias grew stronger and stronger.

Ten, eleven, Emma's heart plummeted. All was lost. Twelve.

The mists dissolved. Lucy slipped limply to the floor.

"My baby." Carol fought on. "Oh, Ruby, they've killed my baby."

Matt, sweat pouring off his face, gingerly stepped around the child's still form. "It's all right, Carol. She'll be fine." He reached out, removing her from Ruby's arms. "Hush, my dearest. Lucy's going to be just Lucy."

"Really?" Tears streamed down her cheeks.

"Really," the priest affirmed hoarsely before kneeling at the child's side.

Chapter Thirty-Two

They were crowded onto the terrace laughing and chattering happily, thrilled at sight of Lucy, a milk mustache, her cheeks like chipmunks stuffed full of rolls, and Anthony, contentedly stretched across her lap.

"Hush, old friend. It's past." Maureen's eyes were suspiciously bright. "You can't imagine how good I feel. I can't describe what it's like, knowing the weight I've carried all my life is gone. Course," her features darkened as she continued, "it shouldn't have been there in the first place. Never was anything wrong with me, other than being ornery. Damn little bitch."

"And so." Emma patted her hand. "What are you going to do with your newfound freedom?"

"Something naughty, I promise you that." She grinned. "Hasn't Phillip's mother been dead for several years?" Her eyes gleamed with acquisition. "Last time I saw his dad, he was a fine figure of a man."

"Why, Maureen, you old rascal."

"Speaking of which. Isn't that Jessie's dog sunning on the terrace steps? First time I've seen him around."

"First time he's been," Emma acknowledged. "And last time I'll ever complain about his muddy paws."

"Look, Auntie Em."

Cleo strolled out, four kittens tumbling awkwardly after her.

"Aren't they darling? Which have you picked, Mr. Willard?"

"I do have an eye on one," he admitted. "But, I'm waiting till you make your choice, Lucy."

"Oh, I love all of them so it doesn't really matter. You take which you like best. Any are fine with me." She burrowed her face in the male cat's warm fur. "I already have Anthony and Cleo."

Carol's heart soared. Her daughter was back to normal and she owed it all to, as Missy scornfully stated, this bony red-haired man she couldn't seem to keep her hands off. Her breathing quickened as she recalled what else the demon child had said. The thought of him in her bed made her pulse race.

"Are you all right?" He leaned close. "I promise you. It's over."

"I know." She hoped the naked desire she was feeling didn't show. "It's only the excitement and relief. Seeing everyone so happy and relaxed. Oh, Matt, how can I thank you?"

His eyes caught, holding hers. A single rocket soared before bursting.

"I can think of a million ways." His lips brushed the top of her hair and she almost swooned. "Let's take a walk."

Tim and Phillip watched in disgust.

"You really blew that one, man," Tim complained.

"Don't know why you're so grumpy," Phillip snapped. "You weren't going to get her anyway."

"Oh, yeah?"

"Oh, yeah."

"Boys, are you bickering?" Emma was laughing. She had overheard the conversation, and though sympathetic, could not help being amused. Besides, she liked Matt and sensed he would make Lucy a wonderful father.

Ruby and Billy Bob crossed the lawn. Emma waved them over.

"Bring some chairs. Have coffee and rolls with us. Jessie's gone to take another batch from the oven."

"I'll go help." Ruby was so happy Shadow Lake was saved, and so excited about the new romance, she fairly danced into the house. She was scarcely out of sight before her clear soprano rang out, a love song filling the air.

Tim and Phillip scowled at her retreating back.

"Maureen, do you know how much I adore this place?" Emma was wistful. "What would I have done if Matt and Father Ben hadn't saved it?"

"I feel I owe you an apology." The priest was sitting, enjoying the gorgeous day, delighting in his new friend's joy and relief, and most of all, thrilled with Matt's blossoming romance.

"An apology?"

"Yes. I never should have attempted an exorcism as exhausted as I was. One needs complete rest and fasting for three days before. I had done those things," he explained, "but I'd also just finished wrestling an unclean spirit from a young man. It was exceedingly strong, as well as wicked. I'm afraid I was totally worn out."

"Father, you don't know how much I appreciate you pushing yourself."

"It wasn't me I was concerned about. I was worried I wouldn't have the strength to battle another of Satan's minions in such a short period of time. If I'd had a choice, I'd have made you poor things suffer Missy for another few days," he admitted. "However, when Matt called and explained, he mentioned the time element. I knew there wasn't an option."

"I'm eternally grateful and I'm going to be sure your parish gets a nice gift. Matt told me you purposely picked one of the poorest in the city. However, I wish there were more I could do. Something personal, for you."

"His eyes twinkled. "Perhaps, there is."

"Really? Please, Father. Anything."

"I was admiring your Siamese cats."

"That's right. You didn't see them last night. Matt had us take them to Jessie's. He was concerned they might disturb his equipment, or throw off the exorcism. Anthony had taken an enormous dislike to our visitor."

"I can imagine. Animals are very sensitive. Despite that old myth about being a witch's familiar, cats don't take kindly to evil spirits."

"Did you notice the kittens?" She frowned. "Cleo had six. We gave one away . . ."

"Matt told me what happened to the other. You mustn't let it disturb you. Lucy didn't kill the kitten."

"That's what Stanley said."

"Ah, yes, Tim's nephew."

She nodded.

"Well," he hesitated, "if all of them aren't spoken for, I'd love one." He reached down scooping up a tiny ball of fluff. "I haven't had a cat since childhood and I've always enjoyed them."

"I'd love for you to have one." She clapped her hands. "Or two, if you'd like."

He chuckled. "We do have lots of mice at the parsonage."

"This is wonderful. I can't think of anything better than sharing my pet's children with people I love. Stanley, Lucy, Willard, and now, the last to you. Oh, Father Ben, you've given me such pleasure."

"Ain't nothin' compared to the pleasure I gonna give him. Tonight we gonna break out the checkbook and eats one of those chatty brions with nice fresh mushrooms." Jessie smacked her lips loudly.

"If you're going to fix that," Willard informed her. "I'm going to make my delicious baked spinach." He kissed the tips of his fingers. "And an English Rum trifle."

"Don't make no mind to me what you fix, little man. Won't be as good as my fix'uns, and that the gospel trufe."

"How many are coming?" He was excited, anxious to best Jessie at her culinary arts.

"You best be askin' Miss Emma. I don't do the 'vitin, jest the feedin'."

"Everyone." Emma threw her arms wide. "Every single soul here, plus." Her eyes flashing on Maureen, twinkled. "Phillip's father. After all, his suggestion was the key to our deliverance."

"You are so right." Maureen shot her a conspirator's look. "Phillip, you run along home and make certain your papa doesn't have other plans for this evening."

Emma was so happy she thought her heart might burst. As in the past, she looked across the lawn to the little lake nestled in its beautiful setting, once more tranquil and at peace. She sighed blissfully as her eye fell on the young couple, heads close, walking along the edge. She knew before long she and Jessie would be alone again. Well, she would not have it any other way, though it had been nice having someone besides a bossy old cook to share space with.

"Was that the first time Annie, or Lettice, ever materialized?" The priest startled her out of her reverie.

"You recognized them?"

He nodded, before opening his hand. "This was on the child's bed. I found it after everyone left." A withered water lily lay crumpled on his palm.

She took it carefully before gently pressing it to her cheek. She knew it was meant for her, as had been the soft kiss on her cheek and the softer sigh of "thank you," that followed when she had retired for the night.

So what if she and Jessie were no longer alone. Emma had always adored the scent of gardenias, and if she ever had a daughter, she would have wished for one as brave as Annie. Her eyes lifted to the south wing. The curtains in Carol's bedroom swayed gracefully. Emma smiled. There was more than enough room for four.

JESSIE'S DINNER PARTY

There's only one thing Jessie enjoys more than preparing, and that's sharing recipes. She hopes you enjoy these but does have one request. Please, NO substitutes, especially where butter is called for. Nothing else matches the flavor, particularly in baked goods. Jessie believes if you put this much time and expense into a dish, then go all the way.

COCONUT ICEBOX CAKE

- Prepare a yellow cake mix per directions on box. After mixing, stir in 1 cup chopped pecans. Bake in a 9x12 pan as specified.

- When cake is done baking and while still hot, punch holes throughout with a toothpick. Pour over the following mixture:

- 1 can of condensed milk mixed with an 8 oz. can of cream of coconut milk. Let this sit until cool.

- Ice cooled cake with a large container of Cool Whip. Sprinkle a can of flaked coconut, along with a few more chopped pecans over that. Keep refrigerated.

(Normally Jessie frowns on using mixes as she is a cook of the old school, but after tasting this, she vowed not to be so judgmental.

MILKY WAY CAKE

- (Don't eat anything else for a week. There are that many calories in this, but what can a girl say? It's died and gone to heaven for!)

- Melt (8) 1/4 ounce Milky Way bars with 1 stick butter, cool.
- Cream well, 2 sticks softened butter with 2 cups sugar.
- Gently beat in 4 eggs. Then, the Milky Way mixture, with 1 tsp. baking soda.
- Alternate into the mixture: 2 ½ cups flour, with 1 1/4 cups buttermilk and continue mixing.
- Add 1 tsp. vanilla and 1 cup chopped pecans.

- Grease and line three 9-inch cake pans with waxed paper. Divide batter evenly between the three, baking at 325, for 30-45 minutes. Cool and remove layers.

- Ice with Fudge Icing.

FUDGE ICING

- Combine 2 ½ cups of sugar with 1 cup of evaporated milk. Put in heavy saucepan and cook this to a soft ball stage.(234 degrees) If you don't have a candy thermometer, go out and buy one. Don't waste your time and money otherwise.
- When it reaches 234 degrees, remove from heat. Immediately add 1 stick butter, 1 cup of marshmallow cream, and 1 (6 oz.) pkg. of semi-sweet chocolate chips.
- Stir until everything melts. Add 1 cup of chopped pecans.
- Ice, spreading between layers of cake to make a large three-layered cake. So rich, I sometimes slice layers in half and make 2 smaller three layer cakes. It freezes beautifully.

BEER BREAD

- Mix very lightly:

- 3 cups self-rising flour
- 3 TBS. granulated sugar
- 1 can of room temperature beer.
- Batter will be slightly lumpy.

- Melt 1 stick of butter.

- Pour into a greased 4x8 loaf pan. Pour 1/3 of the melted butter over the top. Put into a preheated 375 degree oven and bake 40 minutes.
- Pour over another 1/3 of the butter and bake 10 minutes more.
- Repeat with last 1/3 of butter for another 10 minutes.
- Remove and pig out!

JESSIE'S CHINESE SALAD

Enough for 12 people.
Jessie keeps dressing and noodles in the refrigerator using only the amount she needs. This is also delicious served as a main dish if you add fried chicken tenders, chopped and tossed with the rest of the ingredients.

Dressing:
>   1/3 cup red wine vinegar (make sure it's red wine)
>   2/3 cup sugar
>   1 cup vegetable oil
>   garlic salt, salt and pepper to taste (set aside)

Noodle mixture:
>   2 pkg. of Ramen chicken noodle dried soup mix. Break noodles into small pieces. Jessie bangs them with a mallet while they're still in the pkg.
>   2 tsp. sesame seeds
>   1 small pkg. silvered almonds

Saute all of above in 3 TBS. butter, including the seasoning packets from soup, until lightly brown. Watch carefully, or it will burn. Just takes a few minutes.

Greens for salad:
>   1 head napa cabbage, sliced very thin
>   1 bunch green onions, chopped
>   1 head leaf lettuce, torn into small pieces. Toss.

BEEF TENDERLOIN

Buy a whole beef tenderloin. Have the butcher remove as much of the ligament as possible. No matter the size, if you do just as Jessie says, it will work. Slice off the amount you want to prepare.

Rub your tenderloin with a mixture of soy sauce, Worcestershire sauce, a little lemon juice, garlic salt, olive oil and cracked black pepper. Let it set in this overnight warming to room temperature before cooking.
Put uncovered in a <u>preheated</u> oven of 450. Bake for 15 minutes exactly.
DO NOT EVER OPEN DOOR!!!

Turn oven down to 350. Bake for another 15 minutes.
NOT ONE SECOND LONGER ON THESE TIMES!!!

Remove meat. Cover tightly with foil and let sit for another 15 minutes. Save pan juice. It can be thickened with a little flour and used as gravy, or, as Jessie prefers mixed in with her mushrooms. She usually serves wild rice with this meal as it is delicious with the mushroom gravy on the side.

TENDERLOIN MUSHROOMS

Sorry, but Jessie just does this by touch and taste.

- Buy your fresh mushrooms and slice. Use at least 1 pound.
- Melt a stick of butter in a large skillet.
- Saute about 1 clove thinly sliced garlic and then add mushrooms.
- Add cracked black pepper, parsley and a small amount of powdered beef bouillon to taste. NO SALT!

Now, add some juice from the tenderloin. When it tastes out of this world, thicken with a little cornstarch you've dissolved in a tiny bit of cold water.

You'll vie any New Orleans restaurant in the city with this menu.

WILLARD'S SPINACH BAKE

Jessie hated admitting her arch rival in the kitchen was up to her standards. But being a good sport, felt she had to include his scrumptious recipe.

- Take a 10 oz. pkg. of frozen spinach and cook as directed.
- Squeeze well, until dry.

Add to above:
- 1 can artichoke hearts, quartered and drained.
- 1 stick butter melted and mixed with 4 oz. pkg. of cream cheese
- 8 oz. sour cream
- salt and pepper to taste
- 1 cup of grated Parmesan cheese.

Put in buttered casserole, fairly flat one, and sprinkle freshly grated Parmesan cheese over top.

Bake 350 for about 30 minutes, or till slightly brown and bubbly.
ENJOY!

ACKNOWLEDGMENTS

I want to thank the people of Amelia for letting me share the beauty of their lovely island.

The town of Fernandina Beach has some of the most unique and delightful Bed & Breakfast accommodations one could ever hope to find, as well as shops, excursions and marvelous tours hosted by the museum. If you'd like more information on the numerous historical B.& B.'s; the many Victorian homes and other historic sites on tour; and the different and exciting events scheduled each month, I'd suggest you contact the Fernandina Chamber of Commerce. They will be more than happy to answer each and every question you might have. Call 800-2 Amelia, or use the web site, www.ameliaisland.org.

I'd also like to thank my readers for allowing Emma and me to spend a little of their time with us, as well as encourage them to visit our special island. I think they'll find we haven't exaggerated a single one of its charms.